Judy Astley has been writing novels since 1990, following several years as a dressmaker, illustrator, painter and parent. She has two grown-up daughters and lives happily with her husband in London and Cornwall.

For more information on Judy Astley and her books, see her website at www.judyastley.com

D0434665

www.**rbooks**.co.uk

Also by Judy Astley

JUST FOR THE SUMMER

PLEASANT VICES

SEVEN FOR A SECRET

MUDDY WATERS

EVERY GOOD GIRL

THE RIGHT THING

EXCESS BAGGAGE

NO PLACE FOR A MAN

UNCHAINED MELANIE

AWAY FROM IT ALL

SIZE MATTERS

ALL INCLUSIVE

BLOWING IT

LAYING THE GHOST

and published by Black Swan

Other People's Husbands

Judy Astley

BLACK SWAN

TRANSWORLD PUBLISHERS
61–63 Uxbridge Road, London W5 5SA
A Random House Group Company
www.rbooks.co.uk

OTHER PEOPLE'S HUSBANDS
A BLACK SWAN BOOK: 9780552774642

First published in Great Britain
in 2008 by Bantam Press
an imprint of Transworld Publishers
Black Swan edition published 2009

Copyright © Judy Astley 2008

Judy Astley has asserted her right under the Copyright, Designs and
Patents Act 1988 to be identified as the author of this work.

This book is a work of fiction and, except in the case of historical fact, any
resemblance to actual persons, living or dead, is purely coincidental.

A CIP catalogue record for this book
is available from the British Library.

This book is sold subject to the condition that it shall not,
by way of trade or otherwise, be lent, resold, hired out,
or otherwise circulated without the publisher's prior
consent in any form of binding or cover other than that
in which it is published and without a similar condition,
including this condition, being imposed on the
subsequent purchaser.

Addresses for Random House Group Ltd companies outside the UK
can be found at: www.randomhouse.co.uk
The Random House Group Ltd Reg. No. 954009

The Random House Group Limited supports The Forest Stewardship Council
(FSC), the leading international forest certification organisation. All our titles that are
printed on Greenpeace approved FSC certified paper carry the FSC logo. Our paper
procurement policy can be found at www.rbooks.co.uk/environment

Typeset in 12/15 pt Bembo by Falcon Oast Graphic Art Ltd.
Printed in the UK by CPI Cox & Wyman, Reading, RG1 8EX.

2 4 6 8 10 9 7 5 3

With much love to my favourite OPH.

A vast thank you to Katie Fforde and also to Chrissie and Peter Blake, Linda Evans, Alison Barrow and the brilliant Transworld team.

This book is for all you Good Women who think, no, this would never happen to me. You're probably right . . . And yet . . . Who knows?

One should either be a work of art, or wear a work of art.
(Oscar Wilde)

Underwear. Everywhere. Mood lighting, musky scent and the brisk swish-rasp of a satin ribbon bow unfastening . . .

'Sara, Sara! What about this one? Don't you *love* it? *I* love it!'

Sara looked at the pink lacy basque that Marie was holding in front of her, taken from the saucy-corsetry rail in the Agent Provocateur display. It was the colour of a lightly boiled prawn and in all honesty Marie's skin tone wasn't the best match for this crustacean shade. She was freshly spray-tanned courtesy of Tiffany at Spoils Spa and her skin had a strange greenish tinge, a little too literally 'olive'. Sara hoped for her sake either the colour would settle over the weekend or that this was an unfortunate quirk of the Selfridges lighting. No one, after all, goes to a

1

tanning salon and chooses the shade closest to cowpat on the colour chart.

Sara tried to picture the basque as Marie's lover would be viewing it. (Well, lover . . . he wasn't quite yet but by the end of next week, according to Marie, he certainly would be – as many times over as she could get him primed.) It was an uncomfortably pornographic image and best erased from the brain, but in the interests of being helpful – which was what she was here for – Sara had a go at being objective.

'Um . . . it's definitely gorgeous, no question. I love the lace and the frilly edge bits but I'm not sure about the colour; isn't it maybe a bit . . . girly?'

'*Girly?* Well of course it's *girly*!' Marie squealed. 'It's take-no-prisoners seductive *underwear*, full-on shag-me kit! Which bit of "girly" isn't appropriate here?'

Sara hesitated, wondering if replying, 'The fact that you're a good many years past girlhood?' would be cattily unkind, if true. She managed not to. Why burst Marie's jolly bubble? And where had this negative moment whizzed in from? You didn't have those about your closest friends . . . did you?

'Sorry – I just meant, well, you know, *pink*. Pink is a great look if you're under seven but after that, really, never again unless you're out with a hen party and doing irony. What's wrong with good old black? I know it's a bit clichéd for a seduction scenario but don't you think it would suit your skin tone better?'

Marie pouted and looked at her reflection in the mirror. The basque covered about a third of her body width, even allowing for her being fully dressed. 'If I could just squeeze into it and see . . .' she murmured, narrowing her eyes and smiling dreamily.

Sara had a closer look at the pink satin and lace item. 'And also . . .' She took it from Marie and felt the structure that would make a brave attempt to haul in Marie's pillowy midlife body. 'Isn't it maybe a tad . . . rigid?' Still running with the prawn motif, she imagined Angus (the putative lover) unpeeling Marie from the boned and shaped corsetry. It wouldn't be easy. In spite of the near-permanent low-carb diet, Marie was no lightweight. It would take a fair effort to roll her around to get the thing undone.

'Plus, just a suggestion, on a boringly practical level,' Sara went on, feeling that although she was several years younger than Marie she was putting more and more of a matronly downer on things. 'But seeing as it's the first time you'll be having sex with him, might it not be an idea to wear something a bit easier to slide out of? You don't want him to get flustered by having to fumble with fastenings.'

'Lot of "f" words there, sweetie.' Marie giggled wickedly. 'And maybe it doesn't actually have to come off . . .'

Sara winced, trying to delete another onslaught of mental images, and switched off the lights on the quasi-porn scene in her head. Marie looked young, suddenly, she realized; almost teenage. It must be to do with how geed-up she was feeling inside – perhaps there was such a thing as pre- as well as post-orgasmic glow. All those pheromones and the extra adrenaline had to be swishing about and stirring up Marie's remaining sludge of oestrogen. What a cocktail! If this was a side effect of anticipated illicit passion, why wasn't everybody at it? Why wasn't she? In fact she wasn't at *anything* in that department since Conrad had gone funny and moved into the studio at the end of the garden. Over the years he'd spent many a night in there; she'd got used to him not coming back into the house after a day's painting then finding him halfway through the next morning, crashed out on the bed on the upper level, still dressed, having worked till the early hours. But over the past couple of months he'd gradually taken more and more personal possessions in there, slept there almost nightly but turned up as usual in the house every morning as soon as the scent of toast wafted down the garden, as if occupying separate premises was a perfectly normal next stage for a long-haul couple. She hoped this wasn't an age thing. Perhaps it really was kicking in, this massive difference of twenty-five years between them. She felt discontented and dull. It was a new feeling. During this shopping-for-shagwear trip it was quietly gatecrashing her psyche and slyly making itself at home, like the kind of headache you get when it's an hour on from the moment you first realized you were hungry but still hadn't got round to eating more than an unwise piece of cheap chocolate.

Sara gave the basque back to Marie and from the next rail picked out a hanger on which swung a tiny pair of apple-green silk knickers, edged with a delicate frill of softest tulle. Oh, the bliss and promise of such brief slivers of fabric, she thought with a new deep longing. Oh, to still have a young lithe body on which this would look so right. Wouldn't it be wonderful to buy this without your first sensibly dull consideration being that ribbons that tied at the sides would just look lumpy under your skirt and add inches to the hips; or thinking that with fabric this slippery you'd have to knot them pretty firmly to avoid accidental unfastening and the sudden appearance of your pants at your feet, possibly on the Tube or in the street? For these ribbons you needed youth and grace and an eager, excited man who would unfasten them with his teeth.

You needed a man *with* teeth. That was something else. Conrad had developed a terror that all his were about to drop out. 'One will go; the others will follow it. Teeth are like sheep,' he'd stated (rather madly) when a bit of walnut had got jammed between two molars. He'd given up muesli after that, closely followed by crusty bread, apples and his favourite ginger biscuits.

Lucky Marie, Sara thought, surprising herself. Where had that come from? She was supposed to be the staid friend, the (fairly) sensible foil to the mad folly of Marie's secret love tryst, not heading in the direction of enviously thinking, if only . . .

'You know, Sara, he'll *adore* this!' Marie insisted, still brandishing the basque. 'Men *never* get this kind of thing at home – it's the stuff of all their fantasies! And if I team it with these French knickers . . .' She reached for another hanger and put the matched items together. 'Perfect!' she purred.

'But Marie, how does this thing do up? Oh wow, look at all this . . . !' Marie had turned the corset round. Sara tweaked at the complicated zigzag of lacing at the back.

'This lot could terrify him!' she laughed. 'Poor Angus. I hope he's not one of those all-thumbs men; he could be playing cat's cradle with this for hours!'

'Would you like some help with anything today?' A willowy, pretty girl, no more than twenty and dressed in a short black overall, gave the two women her best professional smile although her eyes had a chill professional glint, as if her true vocation was colonic irrigation rather than corsetry.

Why do they always say *today*? Sara wondered. Which *other* day would be an option?

'I shall try it on,' Marie said. 'Maybe with a few others.'

'Oh! Is it for *you*?' the assistant said, her eyes widening. Sara could see the poor girl was finding it impossible to cover an incredulous jaw-drop moment.

'Well of course it's for me! Who else?' Marie snapped. She shook her newly honey-streaked hair back and glared. The girl took a step back, alarmed.

Sara giggled. What must they look like, these two up-from-the-suburbs women (respectable teachers in the Adult Education sector), collecting heaps of frothy underwear and discussing the practicalities of undressing for illicit sex? Only the day before, Marie had been sitting in Sara's kitchen asking her if she could spare some foxgloves for the church flowers, and now look: any minute she'd be asking about nipple tassels and technique tips for the successful twirling thereof. Sara could imagine her at the college a week from now, setting a homework project for her Writing for Pleasure class on the subject of 'Next to the Skin', to be interpreted as and how.

The assistant's smile returned, though warily. 'Sorry – I just . . . um . . . wondered . . . about sizes. This one's a Small . . .' She had a speculative glance up and down Marie's body. 'I'll see what I can find . . .' And she raced off to check her stock.

'You see? This is what he'll love,' Marie hissed. 'The contrast between the outside nice-lady Jaeger-classics me, and my inner Madame Fifi.'

'But he won't know about your inner Fifi till half your clothes are off,' Sara pointed out. She was being a party-pooper here and she knew it. She felt bad-tempered and envious, and all the more cross because this feeling had ambushed her from nowhere. She didn't *do* cheating. It hadn't crossed her mind, she'd never given it a thought – other than a mild fancy for Keith Richards – which suddenly seemed to show a lamentable lack of imagination for a woman still in her mid-forties. She had male friends, separate from the ones that were 'joint' with Conrad, but only ones that were unquestionably hands-off. They included gay Will who she went to see films with, during which he'd moan about the latest appalling domestic habit of his partner. She sometimes had a lunchtime drink at the pub on the Green with Stuart who taught car maintenance at the Adult College and who dropped off vegetables from his allotment at the house on a weekly basis. He had drunkenly sworn at the college Christmas party that he'd die happy if she'd let him spank her with whippy willow twigs over a fallen tree in the park. Her sex life had been virtuously in-marriage with Conrad for over a quarter of a century, and had resulted in two daughters and a recent grandson.

The word 'matriarch' slid into her mind as she flicked through the fishnet-stockings display, and she pictured herself years down the line as an old lady with a cloud of white hair, presiding over a large family lunch, surrounded by grandchildren, great-grandchildren, sundry partners and in-laws. She gave herself the deep black outfit of a Mediterranean widow (accessorized with a few diamonds), for Conrad would surely be long dead, being so very many years older than her. Would she be the treasured Queen Mother type of dowager, or a dour battleaxe? Battleaxe would be fun for her, less for the rest of her progeny. Her natural inclination was to be generous and friendly, so she hadn't clocked up the requisite half a lifetime of forthright outspokenness for old troutdom. It would also be hard to be a grumpy trout without Conrad around to back her up.

'You might think it's all right now while you're young but it'll tell, one day, that twenty-five-year age gap. You mark my words,' her mother had doomily cursed, like the bad fairy at the Sleeping Beauty's christening, when Sara had announced she would be moving in with her college's visiting-celebrity lecturer. As it happened, Conrad's energy level had, until recently, shown few signs of flagging. He'd claimed Sara kept him young, and in all but the years-lived sense he was, being one of those active and beautiful older men. He was not the average golf-and-gardening pensioner, more the Leonard Cohen, Willie Nelson and Robert Redford type. Here and now in this dark and sultry shop-within-a-shop, Sara had her first-ever rebellious suspicion that in spite of everything, perhaps he was somehow making *her* old.

The assistant came back clutching an armful of complicated underwear and looked nervous as Marie bounced excitedly away with her into the curtained fitting room, trailing a selection of frills, lace and ribbons. Sara sat on a purple velvet chair and waited, flicking through a catalogue in which too-skinny, long-legged women pouted and smouldered, looking sulky and a trifle bored, posed with leather paddles, jewel-handled whips and, for reasons possibly only fathomable to the photo shoot's stylist, a lot of tiny fluffy dogs. Sexy it really wasn't, though the clothes were undeniably gorgeous. How would it feel, she idly wondered, to wander round Sainsbury's knowing that under some very unremarkable day-to-day clothes you wore knickers that this brochure coyly described as '*ouverte*'? Would the check-out girl think you were loopy for standing there with a dopey look of amused knowingness on your face? Probably. As you pushed your trolleyload away, she'd catch the eye of her companion on the adjacent till, tap her head with a finger and comment, 'Hormones, Maureen,' in a whisper just loud enough for you to catch.

'Owwwwwww!' came from behind the padded-silk curtain, followed by 'Ooomph!' After a few silent moments, Marie's face emerged and she hissed, 'Sara! Over here! Come and tell me what you think!'

'Do I have to?' Sara laughed, changing places with the assistant, who scuttled out of the lilac-satin-lined cubicle with grateful haste.

'Well?' Marie stood with her hands on her hips, peering curiously at her own reflection as if there was something she couldn't quite understand about it. The corset had done its job – Marie's loose, well-spread middle was hauled in and tamed and the laces at the back were firmly knotted. Her breasts threatened to spill over the top and her cleavage was a mighty canyon. The effect was, Sara thought, pretty magnificent. The lighting was better in here, too – the hint of olive had softened and Marie's skin glowed a sun-smoothed pinky-brown.

'I look ridiculous, don't I?' Marie sniffed, her eyes filling. 'What the fuck do I think I'm playing at?'

'Actually, I think you look completely amazing,' Sara told her truthfully, giving her an affectionate squeeze.

'That salesgirl thinks I'm a total idiot. I bet she thinks sex should be illegal for anyone over thirty. I half want to say to her, "You wait, girl, it doesn't just go away, you know,"' Marie said, casually using a pair of black satin knickers to wipe a spilled tear from her face. She realized what she'd done, met Sara's eye in the mirror and the two of them broke into laughter, which immediately turned into the kind of full-scale schoolgirl hysteria that threatened to be completely unstoppable.

'Oh quick, Sara! Loosen this damn thing!' Marie gasped through the hilarity. 'I can't breathe!'

'I can't – she's knotted it!' Sara said, fumbling with the ties. 'Heavens, do you think Scarlett O'Hara had this trouble?'

'All right for her, wasn't it?' Marie puffed. 'She had a well-practised servant to lace her in and out of her stays . . .'

'Yep. That's the answer – you need the faithful Mamie, squeezing you down to a sixteen-inch waist.' Sara tugged at the cords, at last finding a tiny bit of give in a knot.

Marie shrieked, 'Sixteen! My waist was *born* bigger than that!'

'Well, this sort of settles it, surely?' Sara said, as at last Marie's flesh tumbled free, already livid-lined and pinched from its confinement. 'I mean, how would you get the thing on to go and meet Angus if you don't have someone to do your laces up? You can hardly ask Mike. That would go beyond a husband's marital duty, wouldn't it? To help his wife dress in porn-star underwear to meet her lover . . . ?'

'He'd be very good at it, though,' Marie mused as she put her own comfy black bra on again. 'But it would take him hours, because he'd want to get each bit of the lacing perfectly even. He'd probably use a spirit level. No, I'm buying this. It's got hooks as well. Maybe I can put it on backwards, do them up then swivel it round and get in properly. But even if I can't, even if I just look at it now and then in the drawer, I'm having it. It'll remind me. Whatever goes right or wrong with Angus on Tuesday, I'll want something to make me smile.'

Marie piled up the underwear, picked out the basque and the French knickers and took them to the counter where the girl, restored to professional poise and hiding any surprise she might be feeling, dealt efficiently with the credit card, wrapped the goods and packaged them in a shiny, ribbon-bound box and bag, then handed it all over to Marie as if it was a personal gift from her.

'Enjoy,' she commanded, smiling. She even looked as if she meant it.

'OK – what now? Anything you need to look at? Shall we go for a drink?' Marie asked Sara as they headed out of the shop into the noisy bustle of Oxford Street.

'Actually, I'd quite like to get home,' Sara said, looking at her watch. 'Panda and Cassandra are coming for supper so we can talk about what Conrad wants to do for his birthday, and I told Cass I'd take Charlie down to the river to feed the ducks for a while. I'd like to give her a bit of peace, an hour or so to herself even if she just wants to slob out on the sofa and watch telly.'

'Aha! You see, you have men in your life too,' Marie teased. 'It's not just me.'

'Yes, but in my case one's my baby grandson and the other one's . . . well, *Conrad.*'

'Hmm. Conrad. Still nesting in his studio, is he?'

'Yes . . . I don't really get what the deal is there. When I try to talk to him about it he just *looks* at me as if he doesn't know what I'm talking about. Is it normal, do you think? Is it like those couples from way back who end up in separate bedrooms just because they think *well, at our age* . . . and talk about how it's now about *companionship*? Everything else is much the same . . .'

'The same?' Marie gave her a disbelieving look, which Sara ignored. There was a fine line between sharing concerns with your girlfriends and full-on disloyalty to your life partner. Conrad, in spite of or possibly because of having for so long been a public figure, guarded personal privacy very carefully and wouldn't at all understand that sharing intimate concerns over a kitchen table and a bottle of Sauvignon Blanc was pretty much a normal woman-thing.

'You're too generous with other people, that's your trouble. You should sit Conrad down and demand an explanation as to why you've now got the whole bed to yourself. *And* you do too much for your lot. I bet you had tonight's supper sorted by the end of yesterday afternoon,' Marie told her as they dodged a pair of skateboarders hurtling through the shoppers.

Sara said nothing – it was a bit much, coming from the person who had dragged her out to Selfridges to help her choose slutwear, but it was also true, actually. Because she knew she was coming out with Marie today, the lamb tagine had slowly cooked most of the previous afternoon while she'd been teaching the rudiments of colour theory to Beginners Art, and it only needed heating. Salad was all washed and ready for assembling. There was a lemon tart in the fridge. Superwoman eat your heart out (lightly grilled, with a chilled pear sauce).

'What about some *you*-time for a change?' Marie continued. 'If you don't stop putting other people first, Sara, you'll end up making the cakes for your own funeral tea.'

Sara at twenty was a student of fine art and liked her colours clear and bright and her world to be nuclear-free. She came from Devon, an afterthought child, ten years younger than her sister Lizzie and the product of an unusual mix of a progressive education and a TV-free home. She had lost her virginity at seventeen to the Sean Bean lookalike guitar teacher in her village, with Ry

Cooder playing something ethereal in the background, and by the time the relationship came to a natural but friendly end, she was well grounded in 1960s guitar heroes. Popular culture hadn't really got near her – she was not a fan of Duran Duran or Spandau Ballet, but liked Puccini, Bob Dylan and early Rolling Stones. She didn't wear Katharine Hamnett slogan T-shirts or jackets with oversize shoulder pads or have her hair in a Bananarama fright-fuzz. She was small and slim with long light brown hair that curled at the ends all by itself, especially in the rain. She tended to scoop it all up out of the way and shove a pencil through to keep it in place when she was drawing, and Conrad told her, some time after they'd got together, that it was the slender, vulnerable back of her neck that he'd fallen in love with as he was passing her chair while she sat concentrating on drawing the sulky life model who was draped across a green velvet couch. Sara liked clothes from a previous age – any previous age – silks and velvets and 1950s polka dots. Full skirts, tulle petti-coats. 1930s skimpy knits. She wore lacy Victorian nightdresses over jeans, old Biba watered silk under PVC. An ancient Chanel jacket, treasured Ossie Clark printed chiffon, suede boots, berets, lavender kid gloves.

Conrad at forty-five was about to quit teaching and was seeing out the last months of a college contract, calling in a couple of times a week to deal with the life class and to annoy the rest of the teaching staff by turning up in the kind of drop-head Mercedes that they would never be able to afford. Over a fast few years he had suddenly become the kind of fashionable artist that painters who weren't so lucky pretended to despise. His bizarrely abstract portraits were very much in demand by those who'd recently become celebrities. Cabinet ministers, musicians, models, bankers, bonkbuster novelists: a full-size Conrad Blythe-Hamilton was just the thing to hang on that big, empty stairwell wall in a pretty, newly acquired Cotswold pile. His work was ever more expensive, eye-catching and recognizable as a sign that the commissioning arriviste had made it. Thanks to the PR skills of Conrad's agent, Gerry, his subjects were under the impression that they had been selected and summoned to be painted. To drop into a conversation that you were on his waiting list was an irresistible piece of trump-*that* showing off.

In his private life Conrad was bored and rootless. He was one of those who even other men described as 'beautiful'; he moved with careless grace, had long brown rock-star hair, smile lines at the edges of his eyes and a slightly asymmetric mouth that had women longing to kiss it. Like a child in a toyshop he had spent many years dating one beautiful nineteen-year-old after another, simply because these were what he came across in his working life at the college. The relationships would last for months or weeks or even mere days. But recently, watching his date yawn while he was telling her about seeing Jimi Hendrix live, he'd had a 'what's the point?' moment and suddenly seen himself heading for a long life as a grumpy loner who other men thought terminally immature.

When Conrad reported to Gerry that for the seventh time he'd been asked to be godfather to one of his friend's infants, Gerry told him, 'It's a sign they see you as a permanent bachelor.'

'No it's not,' Conrad had growled, full of that life-passing-by feeling, 'they just want me to leave them money or give them a painting.' This was probably true but all the same, Gerry's comment had hit home. It was like forever being a bridesmaid, never the bride. Too often recently he had been out with friends and actually been interested when they'd discussed the latest goings-on of their children. Some of these had now reached teenage years, getting rebellious, making trouble, fighting their way out of home and security. One evening he was in Langan's Brasserie while those at the table around him described the horrors of a thirteen-year-old's birthday party where the dress-up theme was Hippy – parents aghast to see their own youth sent up as a joke. He'd felt left out, as if they were all talking over him. His own youth had coincided with the beatnik era and he'd been into the peace movement long ago by way of anti-nuclear Aldermaston marches, not by wearing flowers in his hair and a bell round his neck. A terrible realization hit him that not only was he too old to identify with the younger of his companions, but that in a perverse way they were also somehow older, more in tune with the world than he was. They were grounded, settled with their families and dogs and disorganized, untidy homes full of random *stuff*.

He poured another glass of wine and tried to puzzle out what this new and uncomfortable feeling was that he was experiencing. To his surprise, he could only identify it as envy. In a flashed-up moment of honesty, he concluded that he should, if he wanted his loner life to change, find himself someone closer to his own age. She would probably be a divorcee, he reckoned, as the others talked of O-level panic and violin-practice hell. Possibly she would come complete with children. The realization that he would very much like some (though preferably biologically his own) almost made him cry. Sadly, and with huge reluctance, this also meant he shouldn't pursue the girl whose slim neck he had longed to stroke in the life class the week before. So, not you then, Sara McKinley, he thought, already feeling bereft for what wasn't going to happen. It was time to grow up.

Sara didn't much enjoy weekends in London. She went

to clubs with her college friends because she didn't want to be unsociable, but the music wasn't the sort she'd have chosen; she wasn't much of a drinker and her drug days had added up to a brief summer sharing her sister Lizzie's home-grown cannabis supply and wondering what the fuss was about. During the empty weekend days she'd go to a gallery or to junk shops looking for clothing treasures, or if it was warm she'd lie in the park reading. London boys who were her contemporaries seemed silly and young and too much into how they looked and how much money they needed. They were forever telling her what they were going to be, in the great future One Day. It annoyed her, this lack of *now*: she preferred people who were already grown-up – people like . . . well, she quite fancied Conrad Blythe-Hamilton, but then didn't everybody?

It seemed an extra-unfair example of 'wrong' to have your bag stolen at a CND rally. It was October and Sara was in Hyde Park, where the 200,000-strong anti-nuclear march ended. No one else from the flat had wanted to go so she was there alone, trying (and failing) to catch the words of Neil Kinnock on the stage. She'd only put the bag down for a second while she searched her pockets for some chewing gum. The police would tell her, with seen-it-all resignation, that a second was all it took. Realizing it had vanished in that moment almost made her give up on humanity. Who would do that, here, where everyone was linked in support of a cause for peace and justice? Furious and feeling decidedly let down, she pushed through the crowd to the Hyde Park Corner gate and wondered how she was supposed to get back to Earls Court with no money and no Tube ticket.

That was when she collided with Conrad. The police were right: some things do only take a moment. Robbery was one; falling in love came a close second.

An artist is his own fault.
(John O'Hara)

Conrad sat on a storm-blown tree trunk that lay alongside the path through the bracken and brambles and waited for his dog to catch up. If he still smoked, this would be the perfect moment for a cigarette. He could relax and puff away contentedly, while gazing into the split and shredded oak bark at the metropolis of insect life and the oozing fungus growing on the sodden, crumbling wood fissures. Idly, he wondered if he was now old enough to have got to the point where he might as well take up the horrible smoking habit again. Even after twenty smoke-free years he missed it now and then. Was there an age where you were allowed to think, oh bugger it, drink/eat/smoke/be what you want because it really won't make a difference any more? Had he done enough by now with the good diet, the moderation of drink and the general health awareness to allow himself some sin-time? In a couple of months he would have hit the biblical three-score-and-ten. He murmured it out loud. Seventy. Not good. Sara wanted him to have a big party: friends and family from all over. Caterers. A marquee. The house all tricked out with flowers like a bloody wedding. Sara would do it beautifully – she was good at organizing. She was good at everything. That was one of the first things that had struck him about her, how efficient she was, even at only twenty. Right from the off she'd been such a grown-up for someone so young. She'd never played the girly card and expected him to make the reservations, fix up the minicab. When she'd had her bag stolen at the rally she'd been perfectly prepared to hitch-hike back to Earls Court rather than sit on a bench and cry till some rescuer took pity. And in the years since, not once had he set out for an airport wondering if the travel arrangements were properly sorted or if the girls' passports were up to date.

Back at the start, it had taken a while to work out that she really, *really* liked him, so cool and un-needy as she was. This was something he wasn't used to – the usual exchange rate for enjoying the bodies and beauty of youthful women was that they had immature minds to match. Sooner or later he'd find they would squeal over a broken fingernail or sulk for hours because he hadn't noticed their shoes. *Shoes*, for heaven's sake. Sara simply didn't do this. She was serene and sweet and instead of being some accessory to his life, as other girlfriends had been, she seemed to complete it. The anxiety that she might calmly vanish from his existence had given him worrying palpitations, enough to send him for a medical check-up.

Gerry, his agent, currently had various magazines lined up to do 'celebration pieces', whatever they were, but the thought made him feel moody, like a stroppy toddler. How to tell Sara NO to a party without hurting her feelings? How to turn down publicity that would get his name profitably more prominent in the public eye? The current art aristos were a hell of a lot younger than him, but all the same, was there anyone left in this nation who *couldn't* say, 'Oh, that's a Blythe-Hamilton' when they looked at one of his paintings? When did he (and Hockney, and Allen Jones, Peter Blake et al.) become almost brands rather than painterly individuals? Not that he was quite up there with that lot. He never would be now – well, not till he was dead, anyway, and even then only if some arts wallah in the media made a big enough song and dance.

Still, whichever way you dressed up seventy, it was quite *old*. Not *venerable* yet – that started at least ten years further on, surely – but you couldn't go round any longer pretending it was late middle age. In the mirror he could see exactly what was meant by 'long in the tooth'. He had to get up in the night to pee (occasionally twice, depending on wine intake), his left hip was iffy and it was a long time since he'd even considered doing anything more physically demanding than a few idle lengths of the pool. He had become mildly afraid to have sex lately too, ludicrously superstitious that you were only allowed so much of it over a lifetime and that he had to eke out what was left. Shame, because he didn't fancy it any less frequently, it was just another illogical fear, like the dreams where all his teeth fell out or his hair vanished overnight. He didn't feel particularly unfit – but you became content with that, rather than testing if you were right to feel that way in case you weren't. Being mildly vain and stylish (long and plentiful white hair, firm body, good posture, one-time Gap old-celebrity denim model of choice) helped too. But he couldn't pretend the Reaper wasn't out there now, pacing the floor not too far away and looking at his watch. Now and then, especially in the pre-dawn hours when he woke and contemplated the lack of time ahead, Conrad thought he caught the distant sound of apocalyptic hoofbeats. When he'd mentioned it to Sara she'd been dismissive, told him it was trains going over the Thames bridge.

Floss was, in dog years, even older than Conrad, and deserved patient consideration. She was slowing. This familiar circuit (field–towpath–field) now took at least twenty minutes longer than it had done the year before, and Conrad knew he wasn't the one needing the extra time. Floss surely couldn't carry on much longer, being fourteen and having gone well beyond a spaniel's normal lifespan. Did she also see a doggy Reaper in the corner of her eye? How lucky they were if they didn't have that apprehension of their own demise. Who could think that being an animal, and not knowing the things that humans know, could be an inferior deal? Floss would be his last dog. This decision came from out of the blue to Conrad as he waited for her to finish snuffling round the base of a hawthorn tree. He added it to the secret Last Things list that he'd recently started mentally compiling. It had begun with New Year's Eve, when he'd realized he absolutely didn't want to kiss everyone at the party just because it was suddenly January 1st. Any woman who wasn't Sara, however stunning she was, seemed to taste of old cheese. So that was it for New Year's Eve – an early night from now on, in bed and asleep and let the year turn itself round without him.

He'd also decided he'd had his last trip to America. If Americans wanted to buy his paintings he would plead age and infirmity, and they could come over here for them. He wasn't going to exhibit there again – he hated the travel, the food, the 'have a good day', the overwhelming niceness (and *so* nice. It made him long for British surliness), the smiley, smiley teeth. They could do a retrospective after he'd gone and someone else could deal with it.

In all honesty he didn't much want to paint again, either. That was another thing, one that had crept up recently. He'd done his stint. Those youthful idealistic days when he'd imagined he actually had something to say in paint were long over. He'd run out of art conversation. He couldn't talk about 'exploring' and 'discovering' any more, not without thinking surely someone would find him out, catch on that if he painted a stripe of blue down one side of a canvas, it was exactly that – a stripe of blue in a pretty shade. It didn't have any more meaning than that it was the colour and shape that the whim of the moment suggested. How naive were people that it never occurred to them to call his bluff? Hadn't they noticed the emperor had slowly stripped off his clothes and was now naked?

So, four things now on a list that could only grow: kissing strangers, America, work and pets. Even if Sara *did* get another dog he wouldn't really get to know it, not the way he knew Floss. He no longer had the energy or time to train up a puppy. A rescue dog was a possibility, but they took a long while to settle and get to know you. They were wary and lost-looking, like eleven-year-olds having their first frightened days at secondary school. You saw the dog-thing all the time out here on the fields by the riverbank – he could tell a newly homed Battersea mutt a hundred yards off.

Floss shuffled closer, sniffing at the path, telling him it was time to move. Conrad got up to follow her and the two of them ambled along, turning left on to the Thames towpath where the view was of riverfront gardens on Eel Pie Island. Occasional cyclists whizzed past but it was the jogger who caused the trouble. Conrad idly threw a long, fat stick for Floss and she lolloped after it, giving him a backward glance as she ran. 'It's OK, girl,' he called to her. 'If it's demeaning to chase it, don't bother.' Floss took no notice but picked up the stick and started bringing it back to him. The collision was initially between dog and runner, who, overtaking man and dog, sidestepped the long stick that protruded from Floss's mouth and managed, at the same time, to crash into Conrad. As he tripped and slid uncomfortably down the steep riverbank, he heard a muffled 'Sorry!' as the jogger hurtled onwards, iPod blasting, pedometer clocking up, no thought of looking back.

'Fuck and bugger.' Conrad swore in the direction of Floss, who stood above him as if wondering what she should do. She gave a couple of uncertain barks. He tried to shift himself towards a handhold but the nearest shrub was just out of reach. Instead, alarmingly, he felt himself slip closer to the water. There had been a lot of rain lately and the river was running fast and high. He could let himself slither down to a cold watery death or he could sit like a helpless baby and wait for rescue. What a choice. An old man's choice – and not really one at all.

'You all right love?' There was a cackle of witchy laughter from above him and Conrad warily risked looking up, to see a pair of women of similar age to himself. One of them he'd seen a few times before – a cheerful egg-shaped sort in a lilac beret and the inevitable beige mac, who always addressed the good-morning greeting to Floss rather than to him. Fine by him – he appreciated peace and privacy. Dog-walking didn't *have* to be the social event that so many liked to make it. You had to decide on the why and if, when it came to mid-walk conversation

He couldn't move. Conrad was stuck and felt strangely remote in his realization that he wasn't physically capable of getting himself out of this position. A younger, fitter man would have no trouble scrambling up the bank. A younger, fitter man would have power in his limbs, flexibility, strength. He'd had those, rather assumed they were still there in some kind of emergency pack – where were they? Somewhere along the years they'd been used up without him really noticing. What was it he'd just been thinking, only minutes ago, about feeling much the same as usual (apart from the hip, the night peeing, the sex expiry, the longer-teeth thing)? Now he didn't feel remotely youth-strong. When he needed it, the vitality bag proved to be empty. This was vile. Demeaning.

'You don't want to be sitting down there, dear,' Lilac Beret's companion called, 'you'll catch a chill. Here, have a hand.'

The two women, holding on to branches of elder, reached down and gratefully he allowed them to haul him up the bank. They were surprisingly powerful.

'At our age we have to look out for each other. No one else will,' Lilac Beret told him. 'Bloody runners, that girl never even looked back.'

'You could sue,' her friend ventured, looking eager at the idea.

Conrad thanked them, brushed mud from his jeans, called to Floss and slowly, heavily, conscious of his fast-thudding heart, retraced his steps to the path through the bracken towards where he'd left his car. At our age, he thought miserably. These could be the people he would one day be sitting alongside, parked in a care home to endure an incontinent future of wipe-clean chairs and endless blaring daytime TV. They were kind, friendly, cheerful and sweet, but he wouldn't want to share the rest of his life with them. Would they think him a miserable git because he didn't want to join in the sing-songs of 'White Cliffs Of Dover' and 'Roll Out The Barrel', or might they too prefer to listen to Bob Dylan and John Lee Hooker? No, he didn't think they would. Something about the lilac beret on one and the turquoise satin jacket on the other said Cliff Richard to him – back in the late fifties they'd have thought Cliff racy but a Nice Boy, safer than Elvis. Before him they'd have been keen on Frank Sinatra.

He added another item to his list of things he wasn't going to do any more. Life. It was time to leave life's party. The girls were grown-up now and more or less sorted. Sara would have time to find someone else, someone with a racing chance of outliving her, someone who wasn't going to sap the last of her vitality by falling apart at a fair old pace, as he surely would. Leaving her a widow in only her mid-forties was the kindest, most generous thing he could do for her, to save her from having to live for years with a decaying husk of a man. It would be his final gift. It was time to go.

To his surprise, the decision quite cheered him up. For one thing, it meant he could get back to having sex. He liked sleeping in the studio; watching old movies or cricket on TV at four in the morning was a guilt-free delight, but he did miss Sara's warm soft body. He would somehow keep his own premises but visit her bed, the way the nation imagined royalty managed these things. With his personal expiry date sorted for the near future, he could surely count on having enough sexual gas left in the tank for the duration. Good – a cheering upside to imminent death. Now all he needed was to work out how to die.

Conrad drove over Richmond Bridge, turned off the main street and parked under the chestnut trees on the far side of the Green. 'Two minutes,' he said to Floss, who was now lying in the passenger seat's footwell, half asleep. He climbed out of the car, shoved 50p into the parking meter and hoped he could still walk fast enough to Tesco Metro and back for the time not to expire. Inside the store he went straight to the front till. 'Twenty Gitanes please,' he said. 'Oh, and a cheap lighter.'

It wasn't supposed to be like this. Why hadn't anyone told her? Cassandra chucked *Pride and Prejudice* on to the floor, got up from the sofa and went into the bedroom to look at her six-month-old son as he slept and snuffled in his cot. She stood beside him, corkscrewing a slightly greasy strand of her hair in her fingers and watching the baby's uneven breathing. Why couldn't she just cut off from this mother-thing, relax and get on with something useful instead of counting the minutes to when Charlie woke up again? When would real life come back? Would it ever? When he was awake he needed all her attention. When he was asleep she was permanently tense, forever on the alert for that first stir, the involuntary upward jerk of the tiny arms, that little bleat before the baby worked out what waking up meant and started howling for food. Cassandra was guiltily aware she was supposed to use these precious few hours to catch up on her work. She had an essay on Hardy and the Industrial Revolution to write and should be working her way through Jane Austen in any spare time. Spare time? What was that?

'You should have quite an easy time of it in the early months,' the midwife had told her in that breezy manner of the childless. 'It's a simple matter of feeding and sleeping and the odd bath.'

For the baby, that was supposed to be. So, right – that was a joke, was it?

Cassandra, several months into motherhood, could still barely fit those things in for herself. The health visitor down at the clinic had given her that look, the one that said, 'If you approach things in an organized way it'll all be fine.' She was keen on the magic word 'routine', as if babies, mothers and their useless bloody partners ran on some infallible form of autopilot. The woman had been *so* wrong. That was a *total* joke, a cruel one; not only had Cassandra completely lost track of what 'spare' was in terms of time, but her ability to absorb any serious literature seemed to have gone the same way as her once-tight stomach muscles. Body and brain, she was reduced to a formless jelly. Twenty-one years old and nothing but a blubbery, exhausted lump. What would she be like at *thirty*? How did people ever have more than one child? Presumably by having two of them in the active-parent mix. That would help.

Cass lay on the bed, pulled up her top and pinched a thick wodge of her midriff flesh between her fingers. It looked mottled and felt doughy, and she was sure she could see individual clods of fat beneath the skin. It reminded her of the clayey lumps of earth on her mother's spade last year, when she was digging the hole in the garden to bury the last of the pet rabbits. There'd been so many, one after another since Cass's fifth birthday, and their names, and the order of their being, were fading from her memory. What were once loved pets with individual characters were now morphed into one giant, multi-shaded bunny.

· Sometimes in the stew-hot hours of the night during the last weeks of her pregnancy, while Paul was beside her deep in the sleep of the blissfully untroubled and she was lying awake with one foot out from the duvet trying to get cool, she'd gone through the rabbit names, trying to get back to sleep by remembering them in order. She could always start off OK with Blossom, then Flopsy and Moll and Steven (where had that one come from? Pandora probably – she could just see Panda's big-sister sneer, hear her haughtily insisting, '*My* rabbit's having a *proper* name'), but from then it was a blur. Her mad aunt Lizzie had confided that she did the same getting-to-sleep trick but with old lovers, starting from the schoolboy who'd dealt with her inconvenient virginity and moving on through the one-night stands of the hippy late sixties right through to what she called the 'amusements' that she'd indulged in during her three marriages. Would that be it for ever now for Cass, she wondered? No lovers, just half-forgotten pet rabbits to count when lying awake and weepily sleepless in this tiny, tatty flat?

Paul. She could guess where he was now. He'd be in the Union bar playing pool and eyeing up the Sports Science students. He liked a firm, tight bum on a girl and where better to find one than on a sleek, springy athlete? He'd liked Cass's; swore (though mostly when he was pissed) that he still liked it, but then the other night he'd asked her (and there had been, as he'd asked, an element of heading for a staircase in the pitch dark), did it always take this long to get back into shape after a baby?

'How the hell should I know?' Cass had shrieked, out-raged by the question, screaming out insecurity of which he should have been more aware. She didn't feel like a girl any more. She'd crossed over into woman-land, mother-land, and would never come back. Paul, on the other hand, didn't seem to be in any way different since fatherhood. He was just the same silly what's-the-hassle *lad*.

She looked at the clock beside the bed. Charlie wouldn't sleep much longer – it was hardly worth starting the essay now, and she'd only made half a page of scrappy notes anyway. If she started, it would either all be rushed rubbish or she'd have to break off and would lose the thread when she went back to it. She was taking Charlie over to her parents' place for dinner too, which took out the whole evening and meant that yet again the work wouldn't get done. Not that she minded, really – the thought of home food and home comfort and even sharing table space with her prickly know-it-all older sister was almost enough to make her sob with longing.

This wasn't working. Paul should have been home an hour ago. He'd promised that today he'd come back early and deal with all the surplus junk in the tiny space she could hardly call a hallway: the surfboards still sandy from his previous weekend's trip to Croyde, the skis that had been there since February, the heap of smelly trainers. He'd turn up eventually, all dopey grin and 'sorry' in that annoying public-school drawl that became ever more incomprehensible and devoid of consonants the drunker he got. The sink was full of dishes (his), the bedroom was a junk shop of abandoned clothes (his) and cheap rubbish furniture (the landlord's). Drawer fronts were coming apart and the wardrobe door was off, leaning against the wall.

Cassandra and the baby were a tiny, tidy island in the middle of the chaos.

'Sod it,' Cass murmured, looking at the debris. She didn't want this disorder around her perfect new-minted child. Paul had promised he'd change, be more organized, keep things clean, respect the baby's newness and fragility and make at least some effort to try and hit the standards aimed for, surely, by any parent. But the reality was that nothing had changed for him, unless you counted the way all the girls, many of whom would never previously have given him a second look, thought him 'so sweet' for the way he was with Charlie. How little it took – he only had to push the buggy into the college and they were all round him like flies on meat, going 'aaaah, cute' and not just at the baby. Other than that, well, life ticked on just the same for him – bar/football/getting wrecked/daytime telly/Monster Munch.

Cass reached under the bed and hauled out a couple of big bags. She packed quickly – there wasn't much here that was hers, really. So many of her clothes still didn't fit her that she'd left them at home in her old room, hardly able to bear to see them, let alone bring them back to this scuzzy little flat and have them taunting her from inside the doorless wardrobe. She didn't want this any more. She was heading home. And not just for dinner.

Art must take reality by surprise.
(Françoise Sagan)

'Goodness – I know babies need a lot of kit but . . .' Sara commented, as Cass made her third trip from her car into the house with bags. What she'd brought was lined up in the hallway, starting with Charlie in his car seat at the bottom of the stairs and stretching back to Cass's laptop and a pair of black bin bags by the door. These looked suspiciously like laundry, which was no surprise – both girls had left home yet still seemed to think the washing machine was for their casual use – but Sara hoped it wasn't Paul's washing as well as Cass's and Charlie's. Cass was only twenty-one – she shouldn't be drudging around for her idle boyfriend. Moreover, Sara's inner feminist reminded her, what did age have to do with it?

'There. I think that's it,' Cass said, sitting on the bottom stair and reaching down to tweak Charlie's sock, which was dangling off his foot. 'Just about everything. You don't mind do you, Mum?'

She looked despondent and slightly sheepish, not meeting Sara's eye. Sara also noted that her hair looked straggly and matted and needed washing, and that the skin around her nails was bitten and flaking. Poor girl, this independent-motherhood bit was taking its toll. She'd been so determined that it would be all right, that she and Paul could manage, pointing out that there were solitary teenagers, years younger than her, coping fine by themselves in tower-block bedsits. She, on the other hand, was a privileged and relatively affluent student, flat-sharing with her equally privileged and *definitely* affluent trust-fund boyfriend. The three of them were, she'd insisted proudly, A Family.

'I'm not sure. It depends what's to mind. What's wrong, Cassie?' Sara could guess what was coming. It didn't take a genius to recognize that a stricken-looking daughter unloading all her worldly possessions was going to be on the premises for more than an evening. Was this post-natal depression kicking in late or something else?

Cass's eyes filled with tears and she covered her face with her hands. The cuffs of her pink linen sweater were bitten and holed. She hadn't done cuff-chewing since she was fifteen and was picked on by the school nasty girls who gave her a hard time when Conrad, in a *Sunday Times* piece on the gardens of contemporary painters, had been photographed naked lying face up on the diving board, surrounded by pots of priapic agapanthus at their most suggestive about-to-flower stage.

Sara sat on the stairs beside her daughter and put her arm round her. 'Come on, tell me. It'll be all right.'

There was a long intake of breath, then out it all came. 'I can't *do* this! I'm so *tired* and I thought it would be so easy!' She shook and sobbed. 'And *why* can't I do it? Other women can!' Sara winced at the word 'women', recognizing, as Cassandra herself had earlier, that this represented one of life's big moving-on moments. She'd become a grown-up along with becoming a mother. Barely beyond her teens, she seemed years older, right now, than her single, child-free sister of twenty-four.

'No one can do it all by themselves, Cass. It's the same for all new mothers.' Sara knew this wasn't necessarily the most reassuring thing to say, but she could only go with the truth as she knew it. 'And you've got all your university work too – that's as much as having a demanding full-time job as well as a baby. What about Paul? Doesn't he help you?' Sara felt the inner feminist prodding her again for using the word 'help'. It made the childcare sound as if it was really entirely Cassie's role, as if when he joined in he was bestowing a generous favour, not taking an automatic fair and equal share of the responsibility –

but then in the early months, if the feeding doesn't involve bottles, it was hard to prevent it being mostly a mother's role.

'He's got rugby training all the time,' Cass muttered. 'And his dissertation to do. And . . . I *hate* the flat . . . it's a minging filthy pit. It never feels clean, whatever I do, and . . .' The tears began rolling again.

Sara picked up the nearest of the bags and started to take them upstairs. 'It's all right – you don't have to explain. I can guess,' she said. 'Your old room's big enough for you and Charlie for now. We can sort something else out later, depending on what you decide about staying.'

'It's only for a little while, Mum. I'll be OK soon.' Cassandra picked up some bags of books and hauled them up the stairs. On the wall at the top was the familiar strange, gold-dappled painting Conrad had done of her and Pandora as children, playing in the garden. His signature spare yet bold brushstrokes looked so casually placed and random to the passing glance, but there was that depth, that magic capturing of the easy animal grace of children running. You could almost hear them laughing, smell the soft, lush grass beneath their flying feet. Cass touched the painting with her finger as she passed, feeling love and warmth and the safety of being back home.

Charlie was too young to care about the ducks or admire the view across to Petersham Meadows, but walking by the river was what you did with babies and Sara liked the continuation of tradition. She'd wheeled her own daughters along this path, thrown bread to the ancestors of these same mallards. Any hour of any weather-bearable day, parents and grandparents were out here with infants, enjoying this time-honoured way of entertaining them. Sara, leaving Cass at the house to do whatever she wanted in precious, uninterrupted peace – whether it was unpacking and sorting her room, washing her limp hair or simply lying on her old bed staring at the glow stars on the ceiling – pushed the buggy along the towpath and talked to Charlie as he waved his hands excitedly whenever the patterns of shadows from overhanging trees fell across his face. They seemed to delight him, these swift-changing moments of light and dark. He smiled, sometimes breaking into a giggle, startling himself with new noises and reactions. How wonderful, she thought, this constant discovery that babies had. How innocent and delightful to be thrilled by the pattern of shadows, the fall of a twig.

She thought of Marie, whose discovery of new love was giving her that giggly all-is-bliss look that Charlie had in his sweet baby way. She too was like someone who was looking at everything around her as if for the first time. Where, Sara wondered, did that leave her husband? Relegated to the unwanted pile like so much jumble?

Marie said the Angus thing was 'separate' – but how could that work? She felt curious about it, really trying hard to think inside Marie's head. Mike was almost as much her friend as Marie was. She often met up with him in the park, dog-walking. How was she ever going to face him, knowing what she knew? And what a mad waste of time it all seemed. Sara knew she was lucky: how, she thought as she watched the swans chasing the mallards across the Thames, could sex with someone who wasn't Conrad be better than what she already got (if a tad rarely, just now)? It had always been top of the range with him. No wonder she had trouble imagining casual adultery – what, exactly, would be to gain?

At the slipway outside the White Swan pub, she pushed the buggy a little way down the slope so Charlie could get close to the ducks and geese that had already sensed the presence of a bag of stale bread and were whizzing across the water towards them.

'Hey, look at the ducks, Charlie!' Sara knelt beside him and threw a handful of bread into the water. Charlie was solemn, staring eye to eye at a bold Canada goose that had come out of the river and was fast approaching, too close for comfort in Sara's opinion. On land it was a huge thing, way bigger than Charlie, standing almost to her own waist and in too-easy pecking range of the baby's fuzzy-haired oversized head. She shooed it away, throwing bread for it to chase, and it ambled off, back to the river, to fight it out with ducks and swans.

'Funny how no one ever says that break-your-arm thing about the geese, isn't it, even though there's not much in it in size between them and swans?' Sara turned to see if she was the one the voice (male) was addressing. There was no one else around, so it had to be her. The man who'd spoken was sitting with the last inch of a pint of something at one of the pub's picnic tables, out on the raised terrace alongside the slipway. Coming up to high tide, the water lapped at the edges of the paving. It would soon be flooding right across, as it did at every spring tide. He was about her age; more actor than accountant, she'd say at first glance. An early summer tan, longish dark hair that was greying here and there, crumpled loose blue linen shirt that had surely never seen an iron and was all the better for it.

She smiled at him. 'Maybe geese are known to be a bit weak in the wing. Maybe it really *is* only swans that could break your arm! There have probably been tests. Any minute now we'll read about it in the papers, one of those scientific reports where you wonder why anyone would waste their time trying to find out what they've learned.'

He laughed. It was a warm, soft laugh – no sarcasm in it, just enjoyment of the moment. 'Definitely. Like the one where women walk differently when they're fertile! I don't know – I wouldn't like to be on the wrong end of either a goose or swan in an arm-breaking contest. But . . . er . . . if your baby wouldn't object, can I offer you a drink?'

Sara hesitated, then thought about what Marie had said that morning about time out just for herself. What was to race back for? A daughter full of post-natal bad-boyfriend gloom, Pandora arriving any minute and certain to crow 'told you so' at her poor sister, Conrad childishly negative about any possible plans regarding his forthcoming birthday (just as he would be if there *weren't* any plans), dinner to finish cooking . . . She felt the warm, lazy, spring sun on her hair . . . it was no contest.

'OK, thanks, yes, that would be good. A spritzer would be lovely and I'm sure Charlie won't mind staying here for a bit longer. And he's not my baby, by the way, he's my daughter's!'

She wheeled the buggy away from the river and went to sit on the bench across from this casually friendly man.

He laughed. 'You're a *grandmother*? Good God, they'd better redefine the term. You look about eighteen!'

She did look young, Sara was well aware of it. Unsurprisingly, given the age difference, when they first got together it had often been assumed that Conrad was her father, not her lover. But then she'd gone on looking like a teenager well into her late twenties, and had learned not to mind the uncontrollable looks of mild horror when people realized the truth. The first had been a barman in a pub in Henley – she recalled it well. He'd said to her, 'OK, so that's a pint for your dad, and what can I get you?'

'He's my lover, actually.' Sara, defensive, had gone for the bravado option. The barman had looked as if he would like to throw the two of them out on grounds of all-out perversity. She'd been that close to finding her driving licence, to show him she was actually heading for twenty-one.

'None of his business. Don't take it personally – the world's full of pillocks,' Conrad had calmly murmured to her, leading her to a seat outside in the sun. That was by the river too, swans, ducks, geese again.

What on earth am I doing here? Sara asked herself as she watched this stranger take the steps to the bar two at a time. It was five o'clock on a spring afternoon, and one way of interpreting this was that she was being picked up. Did the presence of the baby render the situation one of unarguable innocence, or was she being dull and suburban for giving a thought to whether she was being reckless or not?

'So . . .' he said, putting her drink on the table.

'So . . .' she echoed.

There was laughter and a pause in which they looked at each other with mutually surprised intensity.

'I don't usually do this, you know,' he said. 'Only . . .
well I had one of those moments of thinking, hell why
not? I don't just mean about asking you if you fancied a
drink, I mean the whole coming down to the pub on
a whim thing. I moved in round the corner back there a
few weeks ago. The cottage with the pink bench outside
it; do you know it?'

'Ah . . . Alma's old place. I did wonder who'd moved in.
It's a very pretty house, though I haven't been inside it for
a while.' Did that sound as if she expected him to invite
her there? Not that it mattered, but she did seem to have
all the family caution genes, unlike her sister; if she was
anything like Lizzie, she'd not only go and check out his
home's decor but would almost certainly be in his bed
within the hour, airily dismissing any scruples as
bourgeois.

'And I don't usually do this either, by the way,' Sara continued, before he could interpret her comment on his
cottage one way or another. 'When you were getting the
drinks I thought, is this sensible? Or would I have even
had that thought if you'd been a woman?' She laughed,
feeling that she was gabbling nervously. 'Not that women
tend to sit around in pub gardens by themselves in the
afternoons drinking on their own and inviting strangers to
join them.'

'I don't see why not,' he said. 'They sit around in coffee

shops with overpriced lattes having a sneaky look at the tabloids, so why not a pub?'

'Hmm . . . why *not* a pub . . . ?' She laughed. 'A woman drinking alone brings to mind someone mildly mad, wearing a hat covered in wilting wild flowers . . .'

'A crazy hat and scarlet shoes,' he added. 'That whole bunch of old prejudices, as if a woman out drinking alone must be either an alcoholic or furiously drowning personal trauma.'

'One of life's big unfairnesses, and I'll remember that next time I wear my own red shoes and I notice people looking at me sideways,' Sara said, watching Charlie chewing his cloth rabbit. 'Of course, way down the list would be that she could be simply enjoying wine in the sunshine,' she added.

'As we are,' he said. 'No hidden agenda, perfectly simple.'

'Perfectly simple,' she agreed. Their glasses clinked together and a sparkle of sunlight set a prism of coloured lights dancing on the table. Charlie waved his baby fists and smiled.

'Will she be paying rent?'

Pandora stalked round the kitchen table, slamming cutlery down on it almost at random, not caring that it ended up pointing in all directions as if arranged by a five-year-old trying to be helpful. Sara took a deep, calming breath and stopped herself from commenting. These items were only knives and forks and spoons. This was not earth-shattering stuff and not worth getting cross about. Several years ago, when Pandora had been a fourteen-year-old pick-and-mix of erratic, furious hormones, Sara's sister Lizzie had given her a book on surviving teendom. Rule no. 1 had been: 'Only pick fights with teenagers over issues of essential personal safety (theirs and yours), otherwise all conversation for the next five years will be combative.' Five years? Ten now and counting. If sixty was the new thirty, did that mean twenty-four was the new thirteen? It seemed horribly likely.

'If you mean Cassie, no of course she won't be paying rent. Why would she?' Sara went to the fridge in search of the Dijon mustard. The jar, when she dug it out from behind the redcurrant jelly, was virtually empty – only the thinnest smears of the stuff remained around the sides. Conrad again. A horrible little flash of mortality recognition crossed her brain as she accepted that he was way past changing. By this stage in his life he was never, ever going to stop putting empty jars back in the fridge or cupboards, however often she reminded him not to.

There had also been a couple of cold sausages in the fridge. Their fat-smeared plate, lightly crumbed with meaty shards, was still there. He liked to dunk sausages in the mustard, scooping up huge dollops of it. He dismissed all consideration of germs and hygiene as namby-pamby garbage. Another connection he refused to make was to link the idea of a used, empty plate with the dishwasher. This was something else that wasn't going to change. As with surviving life with a teenager, she would have to keep quiet. These things, these little ant nests of annoyance, they weren't worth picking fights over. Or at least individually they weren't . . . there would surely come a time when the sheer number of gripes built up to explosion point. What then? Wait and see, she told herself, deal with it in the if-and-when.

'So Cass'll be living *here* and she won't have to pay *any* living expenses. Is that right?' Pandora stood with her hands on her narrow little hips. She was wearing a long skinny sleeveless purple top and her arms were twiggish like a child's. Her usual row of silver bangles hung loose over her right wrist, and the watch on the other one dangled over her hand. She was scowling, challenging. She was like her work, Sara thought suddenly – all Pandora's paintings were furiously executed, great slashes of anger. Where had this come from? Her childhood had been as happy as Cassandra's, surely? She had a first in fine art, growing interest from galleries, early success and . . . OK, a job in a restaurant, just a bill-payer, a fill-in. But didn't every painter have to do such jobs, starting out? And many at the finish as well?

Sara managed to scrape a spoonful of mustard out of the jar and into a bowl, adding salt, pepper and a pinch of sugar. As she stirred in the balsamic vinegar she began a calm, slow explanation for Pandora.

'Look, Panda. It's what you do as a parent. You accommodate your children when they need it. Cass is finding it all a bit hard to cope with just now and she's asked to stay for a while, that's all. It could even be a touch of post-natal depression, who knows? You know that you can come back and live here too if you ever need to, don't you? But Conrad and I don't need to take money off you or Cass, so why should we? What would be the point?'

'OK.' Pandora picked a sliver of plum varnish off her thumbnail. 'It's just some of us are out there in the *real world* working for a pittance and having to pay rent and always thinking can I afford it about almost every tiny little thing, including a pint of milk and a pizza . . . and, well, everything. And Cass *chose* to have a baby – she must have known what she was getting into. *Some* of us are more . . .'

'More what?' Cassandra stood in the doorway, tendrils of her wet hair escaping from a loosely wrapped towel. She was carrying Charlie, whose baby head snuggled against her shoulder. 'More careful, were you going to say? Go on Panda, don't hold back will you?' Her voice was rising with her anger. 'Cos I wouldn't want to think you'd gone all kind and sweet and sympathetic and were completely different from the sister I'd always known and loved!'

'What's to sympathize about?' Pandora shouted back. 'You've always . . .'

'You girls, *please* . . . will you for once *just shut up!*'

Sara let fly, hard, with the mustard jar. It was an anger-backed, powerful throw. The sound of the window breaking was bliss. It took a luxuriously long time for the glass shards to tumble, to settle into the leaves of the herb plants along the ledge, and as the last silvery slivers tinkled into the sink Sara let go of a long-held breath, feeling the air cool across her overheated lips. Strangely, in the milliseconds before sense kicked back in and she realized what a crazy moment she'd had, a vision came to her of Marie trussed up tightly in her pink basque, tangled with a man on a starchy white hotel bed. But it wasn't Marie's secret lover Angus whom Sara had never met that appeared in the scene, but the friendly man from the pub. She didn't even know his name.

'Mum!' Both girls shrieked at the same time. Sara looked at the broken glass as if she didn't quite recognize what it was, and then at Cassandra, who was wide-eyed and frightened, clutching Charlie tightly to her and with her hand across his head. For a moment, none of them moved; all three frozen in the shock of the moment.

After the crash of the glass, the silence was heavy.

'Stay there,' Pandora quietly ordered her sister. 'You and Charlie stay right away from the glass.' She approached Sara silently, took her arm and led her to the table. 'Mum, sit here, just keep still and quiet and don't move. Cass, go and get Dad, will you? I'll clear this lot up.'

'OK. Is he in the studio?' Cassandra quickly strapped Charlie into his bouncy chair and opened the door.

'No,' Sara told her, feeling flat and miserable. 'He's out by the pool smoking one cigarette after another. He walked the dog, then came home in a funny mood and suddenly decided he was a smoker again.'

'But it's been years . . . Oh never mind.' Pandora went to the fridge and took out a bottle of wine, poured a large glass for her mother and then pulled a dustpan and brush out from under the sink. 'Most of the glass is outside in the garden,' she said. 'That can wait till the morning.'

Sara sipped her wine cautiously. Maybe she shouldn't have any more, she thought. How much more crazy would she get if she drank too much of it? Pandora was being gentle, treating her as if she was suddenly ill. Perhaps she was. She felt stiff, tired and disgruntled.

'Sara?' Conrad raced in through the door, followed by Cassandra.

'Dad, mind the glass!'

He took no notice, crunching across it to get to Sara.

53

'What's wrong? What happened?' He sat beside her and pulled her close against him.

Sara shrugged. 'I broke a window.'

'*You* broke a window? What, on purpose?' He looked amazed, delighted.

'Dad, you sound, like, *proud* of her?' Cass looked confused.

'Leave it, Cass.' Pandora abandoned the dustpan and hauled her sister through to the sitting room. 'You know what they're like,' she said quietly. 'Mum just totally lost it. He *is* proud of her. Look at them.'

'Yuck,' Cassandra murmured, turning away from the sight of her parents wrapped around each other, apparently oblivious to anyone else and to the damage. Pandora sighed. Were neither of those two going to clear up the glass? And what about dinner?

'And before you say anything, Sara my love, I know what this family gathering is all about, so I'll let you off the hook right now, even at the risk that you'll start hurling plates round the room. I really, truly don't *want* a birthday party,' Conrad announced as he poured cream on the lemon tart. 'I know you've been revving up all through dinner to talk about it and it's very sweet of you all, but really, let's just not bother, shall we? I'd feel like a small child. And as my second childhood's rapidly approaching I really don't want to tempt fate by trying the feeling on for size.'

Conrad leaned back in his chair and smiled across the table at her. So good-looking he was still, craggy and arresting. Women still turned in the street to look at him. Unfair that, Sara thought. Why is it that men can be so beautiful in their later years with faces eroded like ancient cliffs, yet women, however copiously they religiously smother themselves with cosmetic protection, just look *worn*? Cheekbones – that was part of it. He'd got cheek-bones like Peter O'Toole's, whereas she, with her round face that had always been thought cute, would simply end up with her skin drooping off her like a bloodhound.

Sara's mind had been a total blank as they'd eaten, and she'd completely forgotten about Conrad's birthday. She'd been vaguely aware that he was twitchy and had a weird 'elsewhere' sparkle in his eyes, but that wasn't particularly unusual. He'd been like that so often over the years. Sooner or later he'd come out with it, maybe an announcement that he'd been asked to paint Keira Knightley floating Ophelia-style beneath Hammersmith Bridge among urban-river flotsam. Or that he'd been offered a knighthood and was going to turn it down. She could wait.

Through the mists of her quasi-absence during this meal, she'd heard her voice talking to Cass about Charlie, sympathizing with Pandora about the gruesome backstage conditions at the very fancy restaurant she worked in, yet feeling completely disconnected. She'd kept glancing across at the kitchen window that was now all taped-up cardboard, and she'd wondered, with mild amazement, where that had come from, the wild urge to smash something? She was the calm hub of this family, the one who made it tick. A shrink would call her the 'enabler' in the house. She was the keeper of the lists (birthday, Christmas, shopping, holiday plans and so on). She wasn't supposed to shatter. *Windows* weren't supposed to shatter.

Conrad was the one whose artistic mood swings took up the breathing space here. Usually, it was all about *him*. The girls seemed barely out of their teens and still brittle, testing the murky depths of life. Just now, shaken by their mother's explosion, Cass and Pandora were still being polite to each other, almost exaggeratedly sweet-natured, passing the salad down the table without being asked, collecting plates and putting them into the dishwasher as soundlessly as they could, as if frightened that a sudden noise would provoke another fit of mayhem. They needn't worry. She was over that now. The attention was on Conrad. It was all right – she was used to that and it felt comfortable.

'Well, what *do* you want to do about your birthday then?' Sara eventually asked. 'I mean it is a special one, surely? Shall we go away somewhere? All of us? Maybe Venice? We had such a blissful time there, I remember.'

Conrad pulled a face. 'Absolutely *not*. I don't want to travel anywhere. I don't intend to go on a plane ever again.'

'Now you're just being peevish. Spoiled, like a kid,' she told him.

'Second childhood, bring it on!' he laughed, reaching across and taking her hand. 'We can have temper tantrums together, now you've brought out your violent side. Only not abroad, if that's all right with you. Let's trash the UK.'

'You can get to Venice by train. It's easy,' Cass pointed out.

'I still don't want to go. All those hours, too close to strangers. Almost worse than flying.' Conrad shuddered.

'OK, well that's your choice made, but what about the rest of us? Does that mean you won't come away with me anywhere if it involves flying, ever again?' Sara asked.

'Darling, you can find plenty of other people to travel the world with. Call on your stable of trusty men. Ask Will. If he'll go and see horror movies with you I'm sure he'd be up for weekend mini-breaks. And what about your oil-stained-mechanic admirer who supplies the veg boxes? He'd be handy for carrying your baggage.'

'Why would I want to go anywhere with Stuart? I've never been further than the pub on the Green with him.'

Was he losing his mind, she wondered? Where had this come from? 'I barely know the guy. And Will's got Bruno to go on holiday with. I quite like travelling with you actually, Conrad. Sharing experiences, having conversations. All that. It's called a relationship.' Why was he being like this? Only a couple of hours ago he was murmuring comfort words into her hair.

'But we've been just about everywhere we've really wanted to go by now, haven't we?' he said. 'We can impose ourselves on your mad sister Lizzie in Cornwall if we want to get away. Or explore the outlying edges of this lovely British mainland. Why ask for the Maldives? We have Stonehenge! Get it? Good that, I thought!'

'Hmm. Going all *New Voyager* on me isn't a top placatory tactic,' Sara warned him, taking up the long sharp knife from the cheese plate and waving it at him. Cass and Pandora backed away, nervously.

'Mum . . . Just . . . like, put it down?' Pandora carefully took the knife from her mother's hand and placed it out of reach.

'Well – he's annoying me, so childish!' Sara said. Conrad smiled at her, blew her a kiss. She tried *not* to smile back, though it was difficult. He was pouring more wine and looking too pleased with himself, knowing quite well he'd got round her, as ever. No party. No big-deal celebrations. That was fine, so long as that was what he really wanted.

'You're as bad as each other, you two,' Cass told them, glancing at the taped-up window. It was one of very few ordinary, small-sized windows in this house of wall-sized safety glass and wood. It was lucky, Cass thought, that her mother hadn't gone mad with a sledgehammer and written off half the building. Perhaps that was next. Lucky she'd moved back in, really, as it looked like she wasn't the one most in need of supervision.

'You're not just telling me you don't want to do any-thing special because I threw that stupid jar, are you?' Sara persisted. 'Is it because you think a bit of organizing might send me right over the edge?'

'No, Sara.' He sounded tired suddenly, she thought. 'No, I really don't want any fuss. Please. Just . . . nothing.'

He was quite capable of being this insistent now, but when it came to the crunch he could well sulk and accuse them all of not caring. He was too used to her being the calming influence. Come to think of it, she probably did tend to treat him a bit like a child, second time around or not. Maybe she always had been the one who did the taking care of: fending off the persistent admiring women who couldn't believe a man as famously attractive as Conrad didn't want to take advantage of sexual offers. And then there were his clients . . . all those egos having their portraits painted. They always started out *thinking* they wanted the manic, quasi-abstract Blythe–Hamilton portraiture, but no one could accuse Conrad of being a flatterer when it came to paint. Somewhere deep down the subjects all preferred attractive to honest, or to down-right cruel, in some cases. She'd been the one on the end of the phone when they wanted to whine that Conrad hadn't stinted when it came to portraying their excess body fat or facial wrinkles.

The knife having been confiscated, Sara broke off a chunk of Yarg cheese with her fingers, leaving big untidy shards of it scattered on the plate. It didn't matter. It was just cheese. Lots of things didn't matter, possibly the least of them the sharing of aircraft space with a reluctant voyager.

'It's fine about flying. And the train. And everything. It's up to you, darling. Suit yourself,' she told him.

He looked at her in surprise. 'Don't you want to know what I *do* intend to do?'

She kissed him lightly as she passed him, on her way to make coffee. 'No, not really. Now I know I don't have to organize anything, why don't you just surprise me?'

He looked slightly nervous at her unexpected abdication. 'Oh all right, Sara. I'll do that. Just don't say I didn't warn you.'

Paint It Black.
(Keith Richards/Mick Jagger)

'Mum you are *so* brilliant. Are you really sure you don't mind? I mean, babies are quite hard work and everything . . .' Cassie was whirling round the kitchen, scattering crumbs from her croissant as she went from fridge to cupboard to kettle, creating maximum air turbulence out of a simple matter of making two mugs of tea.

Charlie sat on Sara's lap, trying hard to reach the bowl of gloopy baby cereal on the table. One fist had already been in it and he'd smeared creamy streaks across the glass tabletop, an activity that pleased him enormously and that he was eager to repeat. Sara tried to distract the baby from his mission, guiding another spoonful of the stuff (which smelled horribly like wallpaper paste) towards his mouth. He turned away, his big wide eyes fixed on his mother, who was now packing her laptop into her bag.

'Of course I don't mind. We went through all this last night,' Sara said, with more conviction in her voice than in her head. 'If you can't take care of him and you won't ask Paul, then aren't I the best person to have Charlie while you're at college? And it's not as if you have to be there all day every day. Don't worry about it, just go – it'll be fun for me!'

Well, how else would the girl be able to continue with her course? Whatever arrangement Cass eventually worked out with Charlie's father, she was still going to need plenty of backup. Guiltily, Sara now wondered if she should have been more persistent with her offers of help earlier. She'd tried, offering Cass some simple me-time, but Cass had usually turned her down. Perhaps if she hadn't, it wouldn't have come to this. If Cass hadn't been so determinedly independent and if Sara had insisted (for Cass's own good) on taking Charlie for a while on a proper regular basis from the start, she and Paul might still be together and coping well with their baby and with each other. As it was turning out, Sara was just glad Cass had chosen a university only thirty minutes' drive away, rather than Leeds, Liverpool or somewhere impossibly distant. What happened when things went wrong for those high-flyers who'd picked US Ivy League universities? The ones who'd flown off full of brainy confidence but who ran into trouble somewhere along the line, simply because emotional trauma didn't stay out of your way on account of your IQ being in genius range. You could hardly keep whizzing across the Atlantic to hug a heartbroken daughter every time a relationship went into meltdown. By the time you rolled up to the campus with a box of extra-strength tissues and a comfort-size bar of Fruit and Nut, the girl would surely be about to leave for a party with an instant new love of her life and tell you it was OK, she was over it, but ta very much for the chocolate.

'It'll just be a couple of days a week till the end of the uni year – so it's only till June, really . . . though I suppose then I'll need some kind of job.'

Cassandra looked so much happier this morning than she had the evening before, when she'd seemed defeated by the pressures of boyfriend, babycare and life. It was a strange meal, the girls being so careful about what they said, and Conrad with all this new mad stuff about not wanting to travel any more, and looking as if he had a secret that he was desperate for someone to ask about. Sometimes, Sara thought, it was a toss-up which, out of Charlie and Conrad, was actually the baby. Maybe this attention-seeking was what people meant by second childhood.

'Gotta dash – said I'd pick up Miranda on the way. Bye-bye my lovely baby.'

Cassandra dropped a kiss on Charlie's fuzzy head,

grabbed her bag of books and car keys and opened the back door. For a moment, she hesitated in the doorway, the sunlight shining through breeze-blown blonde hair. She looked back at her mother and Charlie, eyes glittery.

'Thanks so much, Mum. I really couldn't . . .'

'Cass – just go!' Sara was close to getting up and shooing the girl out of the door. She would be late for her lecture if she didn't leave now, but it seemed important not to return to chivvying her as if she was still a schoolgirl putting off the dread moment of a maths test. 'It's all right, honestly. He'll be fine with me. Now quick, Cass, slide out before he notices.'

And Cassandra was gone.

'So. Looks like it's just you and me for the day, Charlie,' Sara said to him as she carried him to the sink and ran cool water over his sticky hands. He grabbed for the stream of water, trying to catch it. She clasped him firmly as she tried at the same time to reach for a towel to dry him. He seemed to have got water all over him, even in his hair. There was quite a lot down her, too.

'Here – let me.' Conrad came in through the back door and took Charlie from her. Charlie wriggled and swiped at Conrad's face with his wet hands.

'Thanks, darling. I'd forgotten how squirmy babies can be. Here, let me dry him.'

Conrad held Charlie up in front of him and looked into

his face. Charlie stared back, mesmerized, then broke into a broad toothless smile, his blue eyes wide and sparkling.

'He's beautiful, isn't he?' Conrad said quietly. 'Remember Cass at that age? She was still about half the size of the other babies.'

'I know.' Sara slid her arm round Conrad, remembering. 'So tiny. I thought she'd never grow. When she was born, all the other babies in the hospital were so huge by comparison. I know the midwife said the tiny ones catch up fast but it was hard to believe she ever would.'

It had been a terrifying time; Cassandra had been born six weeks early, labour having got under way for Sara during a private view in a Cork Street gallery full of what were described as 'political landscapes'. Conrad had been deep into conversation with Peter Blake about the Everly Brothers, and she had tuned out from their chat and into the depths of excruciating backache, assuming she needed no more than a glass of water and a comfortable chair. An hour later, Cassandra had whizzed into the world in an ambulance on the King's Road as if she simply couldn't wait to get her life started. She'd weighed four pounds – well within an easy-survival range, but her lungs weren't ready to function, she was sleepy and jaundiced and seemed to have used up all her energy getting herself born. Conrad had said, as he watched her breathing unevenly in her incubator, 'It's as if she's taken one look at the world and wondered why she bothered.' Terrified that by saying this he'd jinxed their baby's survival, he and Sara had gone to the hospital chapel and lit candles for her. Neither was religious. If asked, they'd fill in the 'agnostic' box, but sometimes, they agreed, you just had to go for all the help that might be out there.

'Shame I won't see him grow up,' Conrad said now, looking as if he'd only just calculated the age gap between himself and his grandson.

Sara put her arms round him, hugging him and the baby together. 'Oh of course you will! You're well and fit and you could go on for years and years! You'll probably see *his* children!' she laughed, letting go of them and making a start on cleaning the sticky table.

'No, Sara, I won't.' Conrad sat on one of the twisted-elm chairs, still holding Charlie close to him. 'I really want you to know this and not to laugh it off. I don't want to get older than this. I can feel it creeping on and I intend to sidestep it. Outwit the Reaper, play him at his own game.'

'Conrad? Are you crazy? Don't say that – it's that be careful what you wish for thing! And anyway, what do you mean, exactly? How can you possibly just . . .' Sara stopped wiping the table and crossed her fingers, because the awful word was surely one you shouldn't say casually. 'Just . . . *die?*'

Was he going to tell her something terrible? She knew he was, just knew it. He must be ill. Terminally. How could she not know? How had he hidden the kind of symptoms that could kill? Ridiculously, she didn't want to remember this moment as one where she was covered in crumbs and dried baby food, hearing life's worst possible news with a soggy J-cloth in her hand. She went to the sink and bought herself some time, washing her hands, smoothing anti-ageing hand cream all over them, very, very slowly.

'You're so young,' Conrad was saying. She turned round and realized he wasn't speaking to Charlie but to her.

'No I'm not!' She laughed, but it was the nervous kind. 'Not any more! I'm a classic midlifer, surely, heading for trouble?' The man from the pub slid in and out of her thoughts, just quickly, like a single, half-caught, subliminal frame accidentally slotted into a movie. *Get out*, she told the image. *Not now*.

'You're still young enough to start again with someone else, Sara. Young enough to make a whole new life, even have another child if you wanted to. There are plenty of men out there who'd snap you up.'

'Now I *know* you're crazy! Men who are looking for women aren't looking for the forty-something ones,' she said, feeling more scared than she would allow him to know. 'And anyway, why would I want one? I've been happy with you since day one. You know that. And even if

I could, I don't want any more children. That's what I did with you – I'd never want them with someone else.'

'All the same . . .' He smiled, but looked sad. 'I don't want you to waste the rest of your youth taking care of an old man who is going into swift decline. I don't want to be seventy.'

She put her arms round him and kissed him gently. 'I know you don't, darling. I don't suppose I'll want to either, if and when the time comes.'

'We've had a good time, haven't we?' Conrad asked her.

'Yes. The best. But we'll go on having a good time.'

'When I've gone, just remember it was good. And that I'll be OK about going. Don't be sad, will you?' He took her hand, stroked her palm softly with his thumb.

'Conrad, of course I'll be sad! I'll wear deepest black, get Philip Treacy to make me wonderful hats and I'll lie in a darkened room playing early Dylan to remind me of you.'

'Sara, please, you're saying this as if it's a joke. I'm just trying to be realistic here. I'm so much older than you . . .'

And suddenly he looked it. Sara felt scared for him, for her, for the unsaid something that was in the air.

'Hey, hush. We always agreed age would *never* be an issue. Nothing's changed.'

'It has, though. I'm old. I wasn't old then, just old*er*. Now I'm heading for *seriously* old.'

'You're frightening me, Conrad. Just tell me one thing, honestly.'

'Maybe – ask away.'

'Are you ill? Do you secretly know there's something seriously wrong with you? Because I couldn't bear not to know. If there's something, please don't keep it from me; don't try and go through it all alone.'

Conrad didn't hesitate. At least here, he could be honest. 'No. I'm not ill. I'm actually fine. Physically. As far as I know. As far as anyone can know.'

'All right. That's all I wanted to know. Now please, can you stop thinking about the dying thing? You've still got loads of living to get on with.'

He sighed and stroked Charlie's suedey head. 'Sara – I . . . OK, let's leave it for now. I know – shall we go out somewhere? Take this little boy out and show him some of the world?'

'What, just you and me? Yes, that would be good. I'm not working today; my only plan is to go out to see a film with Will tonight. Any ideas where to go?'

Conrad thought for a moment. 'Let's go to the London Aquarium,' he said. 'We can show him the fish. He'll like that, all calm and swimmy and wafting weed and so on. It'll lull him into a nice sleepy mood and then maybe poor Cass will get a good night's sleep for once. Fancy it?'

'Definitely, as long as I'm back by six so I've got time to get ready for seeing Will.'

'Ah – you see, one of your other men. They're like wasps round jam, with you. Like I said, you'll be OK after I've gone! And that Stuart bloke from the college will keep you in allotment produce and logs for the fire. You'll always be warm and fed at the very least!'

Sara laughed. 'I can't live entirely off Stuart's obscene-shaped carrots and I don't think Will's going to be in hot pursuit, somehow, unless he's got a vacancy for a full-time fag hag. Listen, I'll get Charlie's kit together. It'll take a while though. From what I remember, babies don't travel light.'

The weekly box of Stuart's vegetables was in the usual place just outside the front door. Sara, having once tripped over it, now knew always to look when she opened the door on Tuesday mornings. Why Stuart didn't either give them to her at the college or knock on the door when he brought them, she'd never know. In the coldest months of winter when there wasn't a lot growing, he would turn up now and again in a truck before daylight on Sunday mornings and quietly, stealthily, top up the log pile by the front wall, stacking them with precise expertise. Conrad teased Sara about her admirer, said she was cruel for taking his offerings and giving him no reward.

'It's only the surplus crops,' Sara told him. 'Sometimes it just adds up to a wormy cabbage and a dozen apples. I think it's sweet!'

'He *lerves* you!' Cassandra and Pandora crowed when the vegetable deliveries had first begun. 'Mum's got a pash!'

'You should give him a flash of your knickers,' Conrad had once suggested. 'That'll see him off. He's a fantasy rather than reality sort, you can always tell.'

Sara didn't want to see him off and she knew all about his fantasies. They didn't involve her knickers – more the fast removal of same so he could wallop her bum with whatever implement of choice he'd dreamed up as suitable for that day. Was this something he couldn't get at home? Or something he'd got at home so much that his wife had decided enough was enough, she'd be quite glad not to have to take painkillers before she dared to sit down, thank you, and had called a halt. Sara liked Stuart and his slightly pervy devotion. He was several years younger than Conrad, yet shuffled round like somebody seriously ancient. He wore a random job lot of corduroy in all weathers, muddy-coloured and shiny, and he trailed pieces of grubby string from his pocket like an elderly Just William. His hands were ingrained with a mixture of earth from the allotment and car oil from years of endlessly teaching how to change a cylinder-head gasket to women

71

who still believed that Car Maintenance classes were a pretty good bet for meeting a dream man.

Cass and Pandora called him Scary Stuart and laughed about his attachment to their mother, but how much harm could it do that he liked to supply her with boxes of his allotment-grown vegetables and have her company for a quick drink during the odd lunchtime while he told her about his fantasy plans? He wouldn't take any payment for his crops, which, she said, was ridiculous, as a similar delivery from any of the many organic companies would have cost a bomb. A year ago, when he'd started this but wouldn't take any cash, she'd offered him a signed print of Conrad's. He'd refused and said apologetically, 'Actually, I'm not much of a picture man,' which had, Conrad gleefully decided, been the clincher in working out whether it was Conrad or Sara he was keen on. Perhaps Mrs Scary Stuart gave him a hard time. Maybe she preferred her vegetables pre-scrubbed, pre-packaged and microwave-ready.

Sara carried the box into the house and had a look through the contents. Purple sprouting broccoli, carrots, early-season potatoes, a bag of rocket, a posy of violets. She quickly arranged the flowers in a small jug and put it on the kitchen worktop. When the glazier had been, and after she got back later that afternoon, she'd put the jug on the ledge where much of the broken glass had landed when she'd thrown the mustard jar. That should keep the glass safe from further damage. After all, it would be deeply disrespectful and heartless to throw heavy missiles in the direction of an offering from an admirer.

Cassandra drove more slowly than usual, feeling reluctant to get to the college and possibly find that Paul was leaning on the door of the lecture hall, looking for an instant explanation of what, exactly, she thought she was playing at. In a lay-by, switching her phone on for the first time since leaving the flat the afternoon before, she found – as she'd expected – that her inbox was completely filled with increasingly grumpy messages from Paul. She could track his thought processes through the tone of his words as they gradually changed with his realization that she wasn't merely out, she had actually gone. She'd done the unthinkable and abandoned him. Girls didn't do that to Paul Millington. He was one of those prize boys, the ultimate trophy date. When she'd first met him and he'd got her to admit she liked him, he'd joked, 'And hey, what's not to like? I'm rich, pretty and the shag from heaven.' Except, of course, he hadn't been joking.

'Where u babe – got food' was the first missed text, timed just after eight the previous night. No prizes for guessing what he'd been doing before that. The only debatable point was which bar he'd been doing it in.

Union bar or the Lion? Possibly both – that was the trouble with being a rich student – his drinking wasn't curtailed by his bank balance. She pictured him post-pub in the flat, doing the one bit of multitasking he was well practised at: unfastening the pizza box (or a greasy, cooling bag from the Chinese takeout) while opening the fridge with his foot in pursuit of a can of Stella, and all the while somehow flipping through the TV channels in search of any kind of sport that involved at least twenty men and a lot of muddy running.

'Cass – fuk goin on?' was the final message, timed at midnight. She could picture that process easily enough, too. After he'd come in, pleased with himself for bringing home the twenty-first-century equivalent of a felled ox, he'd have given it five minutes then eaten his way through very nearly the lot, leaving a token pancake roll or a third of an American Hot (extra cheese – which she hated). All the packaging would be half falling out of the overflowing rubbish bin. Comfortably full of e-numbers and/or MSG he would have been enjoying having the sofa to himself, with sole custody of the TV, and would not have given Cass and his son any more thought till he fancied going to bed and couldn't help noticing that the bedroom looked strangely depleted without Cass's clothes and the baby's possessions.

Whether or not he noticed (or minded) about Cass and

Charlie's absence, Paul would have immediately seen that the mobile over the cot had vanished. Intricately painted ponies dangled from coloured ribbons plaited with tiny crystals which caught the light and sent sparkles dancing across the walls. Conrad had made it for Charlie. She'd caught Paul having a good close look for that essential Conrad Blythe-Hamilton signature. It *was* there and he'd laughingly suggested they should put it on eBay and use the cash to pay the rent for the rest of the year, and possibly the one after that as well. Cass had given him the benefit of a big heap of doubt and asked what kind of father would steal his baby's toys. So then he'd gone all mock-serious and said, 'No, sorry, you're right. Terrible idea. If we keep it till after your old man snuffs it it'll be worth stacks more!' She hadn't been sure if he'd been serious. Maybe, maybe not. More benefit of doubt had been given, though in a very thin, slightly translucent layer this time.

Miranda was waiting for Cass outside the bus station, her high-spiked pink hair seeing off a challenge from a strong breeze.

'Cass! Thanks for this – I just got here. Feeling a bit fragile today and *soo* didn't fancy the trek up the hill!' Miranda flopped into the Mini, bringing with her a scent of several clashing hair products. She propped her feet up on the dashboard, then slipped off a shoe and picked at shards of blue varnish on a toenail, dropping them on the floor.

Cass laughed at her. 'Good thing I'm not one of those freaks with car pride, Randa.'

'Sorry! Now Cass, what's this about you and Paul?'

Cass fumbled with the gearstick, almost stalling. 'What? What have you heard?'

'Only what everyone's heard. That you walked out on him, took Charlie and all your stuff and vanished in the night! What's the story? He's been texting everyone, trying to find you!'

'Didn't do the obvious though, didn't call my folks, did he? Where else would I go? He's just being a drama queen, probably hoping some girl will come to the flat and comfort him. I bet there were offers, starting with that skinny minger who hangs out with the skateboarders.'

Cass slammed the brakes on sharply, almost driving into the back of a Range Rover at traffic lights she hadn't even noticed. The Range Rover had a Baby on Board triangle in the rear window and she could see the backs of some small heads, probably on their way to school. Would that be her one day, all settled and comfortable with nothing more to worry about than whether Charlie should take up ballet or judo or join Beavers, or whatever it was small boys did these days? She hadn't been a joiner herself, but she'd loved ballet and enjoyed having a flexible, rhythmic body. If Charlie took it up, would he be the only boy in the class? Possibly, but she didn't want him to have gender issues about what kids could do. Paul would want him to do sport, play rugby like he did, but the thought of Charlie's velvety little head being thumped by muscle-bound thugs was too terrible to contemplate.

'So will you get back together? I mean, it's not, like, it's not just you two any more, is it?' Miranda was looking at Cass nervously, as if, Cass thought, being a mother made her something to be treated warily. She was probably right. She felt she was a fearsome, bubbling mix of hormones and protective savagery.

'Dunno. Only if a lot changes.' Cass shrugged. The Range Rover moved off slowly and she followed, cursing school-run traffic at the same time as realizing that in a few increasingly short years she might be part of it. How grown-up that would be. How alien. 'If we don't, though, we'll have to stay friendly because of Charlie. I don't want to spend his childhood apologizing for my choice when it came to his parentage.'

Miranda put her shoe back on and started biting hungrily at the varnish on her thumb.

'Randa, did you have breakfast?'

'What? Like more than some coffee? How would there be time? Does *anyone*?'

'Yes! Otherwise you'll end up fat. Your body will think you're starving it and learn to cling to every last calorie. And you're, like, eating your own *skin*?'

'You know what, Cass?' Miranda laughed. 'You sound like my mum! You've turned into Every-Mother! Oh God, I'm sorry!' She looked stricken suddenly. 'I didn't mean to say that. I don't mean you sound *old* or anything!'

'I feel old, sometimes. Or maybe it's tired. I've turned into that warning about contraception that all careless girls need, haven't I? The one who looks haggard and knackered and has baby sick over all her clothes. Who'd want to be *that girl*? I should go into sink schools and give a lecture. "Look at me, everyone. Do you want to end up like this?" '

'Oh Cass, you look great, no worries, truly. And you know, Paul really does love you. He's just a bit . . . you know, like *boy* stuff. They take a while to adapt. He'll be OK. And he adores Charlie. He never didn't want this baby. Everyone knew that.'

They were nearing the college now. Cass slowed the car so much that the gears complained. She was tempted to stop before she got to the gates and collect her thoughts a bit.

'I know, you're completely right.' She sighed, thinking about how she'd loved the way Paul had lain across her on the bed with his ear against her stretched skin, feeling the baby kick against him, playing gentle songs from his iPod and talking about how he'd take him (or her) to the park and to watch Chelsea's home games.

'When I was pregnant he used to talk about how he'd

teach him (or her) to swim and to ski and to skateboard. Thinking about it now, I don't remember any of these plans being about how we'd all do these things together as a *family*. Family is a bit of a grown-up word for what we are. I don't remember Paul once saying that I'd be there in all this sporty future, playing cricket on a beach or hanging out down the park. It was like he was already planning a life for Charlie as a maintenance child and organizing activities for his access times.'

'Oh come on, Cass; you're just saying that because you need something to pin on him. He hasn't actually done anything *bad*, has he? He's *mystified*! He's just a lad being a *lad*!'

'Can't argue with that,' Cass replied gloomily. If Miranda was hoping to cheer her up, she'd dismally failed with that last statement. Cass had *got* a lad. He was six months old. She didn't want to have to deal with the delayed maturation of another one. Paul was a couple of years older than her – why did the growing-up process take so long for males? Definitely she didn't want another infant to take care of. Her mum had spent years pandering to the flaky uselessness of Conrad, who had got away with domestic hopelessness by being so bloody successful, work-wise. He was like some kind of rock star – overindulged and never quite growing up. It worked OK for her mum, who'd made all the serious decisions and had all the home power by default, but Cass didn't want that for her own life. Who the hell, in their right mind, would? She wanted someone who'd come across with more supportive input. Paul might be a trust-fund spoilt boy, but that didn't mean he could pay his way out of sharing the Charlie care.

She turned the car off the main road and drove in through the college gates, thankful that she'd hung on to the parking permit she'd been allowed when she was so very pregnant yet determinedly dragging her aching, exhausted body to lectures and to the library. And there was Paul, looking at his phone while leaning on the wall outside the sports hall across from the arts block. He hadn't seen her yet – he was texting someone. A girl? Probably. She slid the Mini into a parking spot behind a red Golf and waited for a moment, hoping he wouldn't look up, so that she could sneak into the building and avoid him. He'd have to be faced sometime, just not yet.

Down in the studio at the far end of the garden, Conrad collected his wallet, a jacket and keys. He looked at the huge blank new canvas that had been waiting for him for the past week. There wouldn't be any problem deciding what or who to paint if he chose. The list of ego-crazed celebrities who had fought to commission him in his peak years might have diminished a fair bit, but there was always someone out there who would pay well over the odds to hang themselves in their shiny new gilt-trimmed mansion. They weren't the ones who excited him, though. Back when he'd painted Keith Richards (surprisingly non-fidgety) or Laurence Olivier (forever changing the pose) or Veroushka (fell asleep a lot), he was taking on those who delighted him in their own field. Now what was left? Russian football managers. Young hedge-fund kids who couldn't tell a Picasso from a potato.

Conrad slid the canvas back on its runners into its slot at the back of the studio wall. The decision he'd made by the riverside still stood. He didn't intend to paint again. Ever.

He gently nudged the dog off the sagging old leather chair to take her up to the house. When he was younger and living alone, he'd always assumed he could live quite happily for all his life in this kind of space. It had everything he'd wanted – somewhere to sleep, to work and to relax, all in one stunningly light, airy studio. But then that was before he'd met Sara. He looked up at the big sloping skylight and watched a distant, high plane trailing a slim line of vapour across the blue sky. There were very extreme emotional aspects to travel, he thought. A plane was full of people either *with* those they most loved or very much *without* them – leaving them behind. It was a wonder they didn't explode – all that anguish involved. All the times he'd travelled across the globe to undertake commissions, he'd been one of those who was missing someone. Few things were ever lonelier than clocking up the miles between himself and Sara. He'd found being more than a few hours without talking to her so difficult. He'd had to phone her at every possible opportunity, just to make sure she was still there, just to make sure the luck of her being *his* hadn't run out. How was this eternity thing going to work, without her? A tricky one, that; after-life was only comfortable if you believed in an unimaginable dark nothing-void. Whatever it was, he didn't intend to find out today. There were fish to look at.

The greatest pleasure in life is doing what people say you cannot do.
(Walter Bagehot)

'You know, Conrad, you're only claiming Charlie liked the train because *he's a boy*. I hope you don't have an inner sexist that's going to come out now there's a family male child!' Sara was laughing as they walked along the Embankment towards the London Eye. It felt so good to be out. Charlie was wide awake; unlike most babies, travel didn't appear to make him sleepy. He seemed already to be thrilled by the stimulation of new sights.

'No, I could tell, he definitely loved it! And of course I'm not being biased – so don't think I can't tell that's what you're angling to accuse me of. His mum loved trains too, I remember,' Conrad insisted. 'When he saw that one pulling out from the platform just now as we walked past, I swear he got all jittery and excited.'

'Funny to think of Cassandra in terms of "mum", isn't

it? Surely it's only about twenty minutes since she was this age herself,' Sara said. 'And I don't feel remotely ready to be called Granny. I'm so glad we all decided that Charlie will just call us by our names. Though I suppose . . .' She stopped. She'd been about to say that it was all right for Conrad, he was well advanced into an age when 'Grandad' was very normal as something to be called. People sometimes did it already, albeit in the context of being rude rather than in the fond-family sense.

Conrad had come into the house and complained, only the other day, that he had been ambling along the high street, not really concentrating as he walked, and had wandered into a group of teenagers. 'Grandad' had been the politest of the terms they'd used for him as they'd jostled him out of their way. He had reported all this to her with some surprise, as if he didn't expect to have it confirmed by anyone out there on the streets that he was as old as his birth certificate told him.

Sara now decided to leave the subject alone, in the interests of tact, especially as he got so grouchy at any mention of his forthcoming birthday. Was it really going to be a day they must ignore? She hoped not. She quite liked birthdays. Somewhere out there would be the annual death days, waiting secretly hidden on the calendar, for all of them. A tiny superstitious part of her believed that if you carried on celebrating the one loudly enough, you could perhaps ward off the other, like clapping to show you believed in fairies to keep Tinkerbell alive.

Conrad was pushing Charlie's buggy, looking happy. And so he should, Sara thought. A grandchild was a delightful thing. Charlie was theirs and yet not theirs. Theirs for fun and to love but not for all-time responsibility, apart from on days like this when they were his minders – and it did feel good to be sharing this outing with Conrad. She hadn't really had anything special in mind to do with him if she'd been by herself, nothing more than possibly a trip round Waitrose and maybe taking him to buy some board books to entertain him.

Were grandchildren a last-chance thing about getting relationships with children right for once? With her own, she'd spent so much time when they were little just struggling to get through each day that any bigger vision became a bit lost in the mix. Conrad had been away such a lot, teaching at first as a visiting lecturer wherever he was invited so they could survive financially, and then as he started to get celebrity portrait commissions he'd be away meeting clients, making sketches, working on the projects from life wherever they happened to be located. Later, when he became as fashionable as his subjects, they'd come to his studio. But by then the girls were into their early teens and didn't need or want the hands-on input. The thought of cosy family outings tended to have them going, '*Eugh* do we have to come?' in that awful way that young teens do when faced with the thought that they might be seen out with the parents. Too humiliating, and as they put it, *bo–ringggg*.

'We haven't been up here for quite a while, have we?' Sara commented, looking around. They were approaching the Hayward Gallery, making for the riverside so they could walk along by the water, get Charlie out of his buggy and show him the boats on the Thames. It was breezy but sunny, the kind of day when you suddenly realize with mild surprise that the seasons have slid round to summer, and that days like this have to be appreciated while they're here.

'I loved it the last time, when we came to the Antony Gormley exhibition,' she went on. 'There was almost a party atmosphere out here on the street, with everyone looking around to find those bronze figures way up on the roofs for miles around. Strangers talked to each other, pointing out the figures, getting excited whenever they spotted another one – you don't often get that kind of spontaneous communication outside a disaster or freaky weather.'

'*Event Horizon* he called that,' Conrad was frowning, 'though how can you call something an "Event" when it's just static? It reminds me of back in the sixties when there were all these things called "Happenings", but nothing much did, just people in a field, looning about with acid, sex and music. It was all very self-conscious, "look at me, I'm cool enough to get naked." You could do all that at home.'

Sara prodded him in the side. 'Hey come on now, don't get all antsy about Gormley! And it wasn't static. The people talking to each other were part of the event, surely? Think of it that way.'

'He got lucky,' Conrad muttered.

'He's got talent,' Sara countered swiftly. 'And anyway, you liked that exhibition. In fact you *loved* it. I couldn't drag you out of the Blind Light box.'

'That's because I couldn't see anything. I couldn't find the exit,' Conrad grouched. 'I certainly didn't see the point.'

'Ah! But it made you think!' He could be such hard work, she thought suddenly. Why couldn't he just admit that he'd enjoyed it? She knew he had at the time. Was this another of those 'old' things? There were so many lately, what with the no-birthday thing, the sleeping in the studio and the refusal to travel, and this mad idea that he wasn't going to make it to seventy. Could she face another possible, what, maybe as much as thirty years of him winding down, ever more moody, till he ended up complaining that he didn't want all that hundredth-birthday fuss? No wonder she thought of . . . A fleeting picture of the man from the pub, in the sun with a glass of wine, came into her head. She banished it, fast. Thinking about one particular man in a vaguely fancying way was surely the first step on the Marie-and-Angus route – something which was never going to happen to her.

'No it didn't make me think,' Conrad told her. 'It made me damp and cross and I could hardly breathe in there.'

'Yes, but there was that one thing though.' Sara was determined that he should be positive. 'Don't you remember? The blind man – that was interesting. He went in there with the woman. Outside the box he was dependent on her to be his eyes, but they were on equal terms in that dense mist, neither of them able to see, dependent on each other in exactly the same way. Perhaps he was showing her what he "sees"; the blindness in there being stark white, being completely unable to see in bright white rather than darkness. Or . . . would he know the difference? You see? There was a point to the thing. It made you question. We're talking about it, even now. Isn't that a good thing with art?'

Conrad wasn't having it. 'They'd have been on equal terms anyway, in being run into by screeching overexcited schoolkids in there. Nothing like a dense, choking, steamy fog to get kids all wired up. Though I suppose,' he grinned, 'having schoolkids get excited by an art piece is an achievement in itself. All credit to Mr G. for that.'

He was looking across the river towards the Houses of

Parliament. Sara wondered if his antipathy to Antony Gormley was anything to do with the student who had approached him at the Hayward in the room with the wire figures, the one who had rather nervously come up to Conrad and murmured, 'Excuse me, aren't you Lucian Freud?' Conrad had been amused, flattered to have been recognized as a painter, even if it was the wrong one, and a much older one.

'No, but close. I'm Conrad Blythe-Hamilton,' he'd informed the lad, confidently waiting for the next bit which was usually, when admirers accosted him, something about his once-controversial painting of Mick Jagger as the crucified Christ and asking whose idea it had been for him to pose like that (Answer: Conrad's). Instead the questioner had looked mystified, had simply said, 'Oh. Sorry to have bothered you, mate.' And walked away with no further comment.

'I don't look anything like bloody Freud.' Conrad had sulked all the rest of the day. It wouldn't be kind to remind him about this.

Sara also recalled, guiltily, other details of that day. Much as she'd loved Antony Gormley's exhibits, she'd found herself distracted, her eye caught by a woman in a stunning coat. It was cream, overlaid with pale grey figures, like a very subtle toile de Jouy pattern, and she'd absolutely loved it. In the end she'd simply gone up to the woman by the pile of spent bullets in the corridor and asked her where it was from (Agnès B). She probably wouldn't have done that on the street, but being at an event like that gave the viewers a common bond, even over something as frivolous as fashion. They'd had a girly chat about clothes, while eager culture vultures around them talked of vision and provocation and the challenges of spatial values. It was so different somehow from the starchy private views that Conrad had always hated, where people stood around clutching warm wine and a catalogue and making interested faces at paintings, wishing it was somehow *all right* just to have a normal conversation about absolutely anything else rather than express constant near-reverence at what they were looking at. She couldn't blame Conrad's age on his loathing of such gatherings.

Once inside the Aquarium, Charlie proved disappointingly uninterested in the fish. After watching a few of the more colourful specimens gliding across his line of sight, he lost interest and fidgeted to get out of his buggy. Conrad held him in his arms and pointed out the big sharks in the huge four-storey central tank, but Charlie was now more interested in the constant stream of schoolchildren who bustled about being excited and comparing notes on the worksheets they were filling in.

'He's a bit young,' Sara said. 'I suppose he's only just learned to focus really.' And what are we doing here, she thought, looking at these poor captive creatures? This was just a zoo, but in water. Was it cruel? She couldn't tell. It was certainly beautifully put together. Perhaps it was only cruel if the fish had the kind of brains that knew there was an alternative to captivity. Did lions at the zoo know this? If she was going to get all philosophical about this, how did it work if you applied it to humans? It would be different, because only humans could move away from the life they had to a life they'd chosen.

'You never see any dead ones,' Conrad commented as they walked along the corridor towards the Touch Pool, where the rays were on display in a huge shallow-water pond and could be stroked by onlookers. 'When I was a child, my father kept a complicated tank of tropical fish and almost every week there was some poor thing floating, belly up. You'd think out of all the thousands of fish in here, at least one of them per tank, per day would have snuffed it, wouldn't you? I'd love to lob a dead haddock into one of these so perfect displays, see how quickly anyone notices.'

'Something would eat it. You'd probably find you'd chucked it in with the piranhas. And then you'd get thoroughly told off – I bet these fish have personal nutritionists.'

'You're too sensible, Sara.' He sighed.

'Maybe I am. Come on, one of us has to be.'

'Hey!' Conrad had an idea. 'Maybe they're not real at all, maybe they're holograms!' He put his nose up against a glass tank full of Pacific fish. They were the colours that a magazine fashion spread would describe as 'acid brights'.

'Well, look, they're definitely not holograms in here. You can even do hands-on stuff,' Sara told him, as they entered a room full of hyper-excited schoolchildren spread round a vast shallow tank, every child having a hand in the water. The elegant rays, some as large as tabletops, undulated round the pool, generously allowing themselves to be touched, then making for sanctuary out of reach in the centre when the mauling got overenthusiastic.

'Don't splash!' roared an ineffectual teacher as the children tried to get the rays to swim over their fingers.

'Now this *is* weird,' Sara commented. 'I wonder if the fish like it, having their bodies stroked by grubby schoolkids?' But Conrad was already dangling Charlie over the side, gently putting his hand on the water's surface. It wasn't easy to keep the space, though – there were so many children, all jostling for room to touch the fish.

'Conrad! Please be careful – hang on to him!' She felt a dire certainty that Conrad was going to choose that moment to lose his marbles completely and see what happened if Charlie slid into the water with the fish. Of course he wouldn't hurt him on purpose, but . . . well because there was something so not-as-usual about Conrad at the moment, she wouldn't put any possibility past him. But Charlie was fine; he was wriggly and excited, happily bashing at the water's surface as if he was in his bath. He was too small to reach the fish.

'Pretty, aren't they Charlie?' Conrad was saying to him. 'Very graceful. Look, those smaller ones over there, they're called plaice. We eat those.' Charlie smiled.

'I don't. I'm a veggy-*tarian*,' a passing small girl sneered at him.

'Hush, India. Come away.' Her teacher glared at Conrad as if he was about to pounce and hold the child's head under the water. Conrad glared back as if he was tempted to do exactly that, then looked at Sara and winked at her. She smiled back, feeling reassured that he seemed to be, for the moment, reasonably sane and happy. She relaxed and turned to look at the posters on the wall and read up about the different varieties of rays in the pond. As she was halfway through a description of their feeding preferences, the volume of the child crowd suddenly increased – there were shrieks and squeals and someone angry and adult shouted, 'Hey you! Out of there, *NOW!*' A whistle blew, sharply, urgently.

Sara looked through the crowd of laughing, pointing children who were being haphazardly rounded up by their teachers.

For a moment Sara couldn't see Conrad, then she realized that he was actually *in* the pool, thigh deep and apparently oblivious that he was completely soaked. He'd left his shoes by the buggy, she noticed, so he'd at least had a moment to consider what he was doing. It wasn't a hundred per cent spontaneous gesture, then. He was wading carefully towards the centre, taking no notice of the frantic staff, holding Charlie down close to the water as if this was just the shallows on a tropical beach and he was showing him the pretty shells.

'Conrad! What the hell are you playing at?' she yelled. The room was clearing as the school parties were vanishing fast, ushered out by one of the attendants. The three remaining staff were looking furious but uncertain – one of them kept a hand hovering over the fire alarm. Possibly nothing in their training schedule had equipped them for how to deal with a lunatic who decided to paddle with the fish. They looked at her now. 'Get him out, immediately,' one of them ordered, as if she was the only one who could make him hear.

Conrad looked up in surprise. 'Charlie couldn't reach the fish!' he said, as if climbing over the barrier and wading around in the water was the most logical remedy for this. Obviously to him, it was.

'But Conrad . . .' Sara began, but at that moment Charlie lurched from Conrad's hands and fell forward, his top half sploshing into the water on to a very surprised ray, which flicked its tail, sending a spray all over Conrad. Conrad grabbed Charlie, retrieving the now howling child quickly, and wiped his head on his shirt. Charlie, having worked out how cold the water was, upped the volume of his crying.

'It's all right Charlie boy! It's only a bit of water! No harm done, is there?' Conrad hugged him close and wet stains spread across his denim jacket. Water dripped from Charlie's sparse hair and from his nose. Conrad now waded to the side of the tank and handed the baby over to Sara.

'Quick, you mad idiot, let's get out of here before we're arrested,' Sara said. 'I'm going to get Charlie changed and dry and then I'll meet you outside.' She grabbed the buggy and turned it round, heading for the door.

'Why? What's the rush?' Conrad asked. 'At last he's actually enjoying it!' He climbed out of the tank, sending pools of water all over the floor. He looked around for his shoes and put them back on as if what he'd done had been nothing out of the ordinary.

'No really, Conrad, let's just *go*. I've got lots of spare clothes for him and he needs to get warm again.' Sara almost pushed Conrad through the door and looked for the signs for the loo. She felt scared, as if she'd discovered something alarming and frightening about Conrad.

Perhaps she had, she thought. He'd always been a tiny bit off the wall, but was he really beginning to lose his mind? Was laughing at Charlie the right reaction for almost plunging him into the cold fishy water? Her heart thumped fast at the idea of some version of dementia setting in. Her mother's long-ago warnings came back to her. 'In sickness and in health,' she'd crowed. 'That's hardly going to be a fair division over time, is it?' How spiteful that had sounded. Sara hadn't really ever quite forgiven her for that. Illness could happen to anyone, she'd argued back: Sara herself could die, leaving Conrad alone with young children. She could have been run over in the street only weeks after they married.

Conrad was dispatched to wait outside the building on the steps by the Thames – always assuming, she thought furiously, that he didn't decide he'd got a taste for leaping into cold water. Sara changed Charlie's clothes, thanking the heavens that she'd brought plenty of spares with her and spreading them out over all the available space in the baby-changing area. Charlie seemed to understand her anxiety and cooperated beautifully, not rolling or wriggling but just looking at her calmly, as if trying to communicate that all would, somehow, be well. She prayed he was right.

'You need to carry around so much kit with babies, don't you?' One of the teachers from the ray pool was by the door as Charlie was being crammed into his coat. She was a plump woman with too-long raggedy grey hair that had probably been gloriously auburn in its younger, darker days. Sara smiled uncertainly, feeling crazily paranoid that this woman might be tailing her, spying for a report to Social Services that she and Conrad were unfit grand-parents. A mad thought, but it went perfectly with her mood of the moment.

'And it can't be easy for you,' the woman sympathized, leaning against the doorpost. 'I know what it's like being an older mum and dealing with an elderly relative at the same time; they're like extra babies, aren't they? A liability when they start to lose it, the way your father did in there. And us, stuck in the middle between our own children and our second-childhood parents!' She patted Sara on the shoulder; it was meant kindly but made Sara want to cry. She didn't trust herself to speak, so didn't put the woman right about the various relationships here. What, after all, was the point? She muttered dutiful thanks, managed half a smile, gathered Charlie and his possessions into the buggy and fled.

Back in the past, she and Conrad used to think it was funny when he had been mistaken for her father. His usual reaction was to shock the wrongly assuming person by thoroughly kissing Sara in a highly unfatherly way, just to see the appalled look on a face. He said it was an expression he'd tried to catch when painting but had never quite managed. But suddenly, it just wasn't remotely funny. At the door to the building she was hugely relieved to see Conrad safely there in front of her, looking relatively sane and content, leaning over the river wall smoking one of his horrible French cigarettes and not seeming the tiniest bit concerned that he was soaking wet. The way he was being today, it would have been no surprise to have found him way above her, up on the London Eye, sharing a flight capsule with a dozen Milwaukee tourists and waving down at her.

'Blood 'n' guts, flouncy costumes or a silly, frilly chick flick?' Will asked as he and Sara approached the cinema. 'I didn't want to presume so I didn't book anything.'

'Er . . . ooh I don't know! I just need something I don't have to think about too much, unless there's a special one you've got in mind?' It was a busy night – the day's warmth had brought people out for the evening. Dusk was falling now, though, and those who'd thought a date at an outside table at the pub might appeal were looking for somewhere warmer to spend a few hours.

'No, I'm easy,' Will said. 'It's just great to be out of the house. Bruno's spring-cleaning and he's got all the curtains down. He's hired a steam cleaner and boy, is he getting his money's worth. Over the weekend we weren't allowed on the stair carpet because he'd overdone the water, and we ended up sleeping on the sofas. Lucky we've got a downstairs loo, is all I can say. The windows got all steamed up, and no, I don't mean like that! Bit of Jane Austen, then?' he suggested, looking at the hoardings outside the building. 'Looks like they've got a special revival week of them. Must be to do with school exam time coming up, or something. Don't kids have it easy? Spoonfed. Still, at least you'll know the story, then you can nod off once you've checked out the bonnets and not miss anything crucial. Had a busy day? You're very quiet.'

'Sorry Will – I'm feeling a bit absent,' she told him as they joined the ticket queue. In her head all she could see was Conrad on the way home from Waterloo. It had been a fairly full train with passengers standing. All the same, there'd been plenty of space around the seats where they were. Nobody wanted to go near Conrad, who was unconcernedly reading the *Standard* while the puddle from his wet clothes trickled across the carriage floor as the train lurched along. 'This is perfect! I'm like the nutter on the bus,' Conrad had whispered to her, laughing. 'It certainly buys you space, being mad, doesn't it? Handy tip.'

'Please don't even think of doing anything like this ever again,' she'd warned him. Did he have the choice, though? Had he really been completely aware of what he'd been doing?

'Why? Do you think I'll catch pneumonia?' he'd asked. 'Quite a good way to go, that. They used to call it the "old man's friend" if you'd already got something badly wrong and happened to catch it. It would wipe you out quite painlessly, compared with the alternative. Probably still does, now we're all getting resistant to antibiotics. When I was a kid there really weren't any, and now they're next to useless. I'll have seen them in and seen them out. Like Concorde.'

The big wall poster over the booking desk of Keira Knightley looking wistful went blurry.

'My darling, you're crying before we even get in there! Whatever is it?' Sara drifted back to reality and to Will. He put his arm round her and led her out of the cinema. She snuggled against him, inhaling the delicious scent of frangipani. Will always smelled wonderful. He and Bruno were very keen on potions and lotions – their bathroom was close to a replica of a department store's Clarins outlet.

'Look, whatever it is that's making you cry, it's not going to be improved by a weepy movie. Let's go and get a drink, or something to eat instead. You can tell me all about it – or not. Pizza Express?' She was quite hungry, so they opted for food, a better option than a bag of cinema pick 'n' mix. She thought of Conrad and how he hated the way people always stuffed themselves at the cinema.

Having grown up with rationing and in an era when people only ate meals at mealtimes, at home and at a table, he detested the possibility of sitting beside a stranger who was noisily munching a stinking hot dog followed by what he called a 'crater' of popcorn.

'I never cry,' Sara sniffed as Will poured her a big glass of wine.

'Of course you do, babe. We all do. And if you don't, you should try it, as often as possible. There's a good reason for tears,' he told her. 'It's to do with endorphins or some such. Like exercise . . .' He shuddered. 'Not that I'd know. Bruno's the body freak.' He patted his rotund stomach, which wobbled beneath his lilac cashmere sweater. Will always favoured pastels, claiming his mother had told him they suited his pale colouring. His hair was even whiter blond than Boris Johnson's, so, depending on the colour combinations, he often resembled a bag of sugared almonds.

'Anyway, you're supposed to let it all flow and then you'll feel better. Plus your eyes get a sparkly wash and look pretty. So . . .' He sipped his wine and pulled a face. 'Euw . . . this Merlot has seen better days. Probably not many of them though, it's obviously still a mere infant. So are you going to tell me what's up? Is it that gorgeous man you live with?'

'*Is* he gorgeous?' Sara asked him. 'I assume he still is

because he always was, if you see what I mean. I don't think *he* thinks so any more. He says he feels old. He's *going* old.'

'My God, *he* feels old?' Will gasped. 'If I look half that good at his age I'll be going round telling everyone I'm twenty-seven. How old *is* he, if you don't mind me asking? I mean I know he's no teenager, everyone knows that, but he could be anything up to about sixty-five. And that's hardly anything, is it, not these days. Look at the Rolling Stones. Or perhaps not . . .'

'Sixty-five? No! He'll be seventy in a few weeks,' Sara told him. 'Except he's decided not to be. Don't even ask how that works. He's gone funny. He keeps saying he's not going to get any older. I'm scared about what he means. He says he's not ill, but . . .' Strangely, this didn't seem disloyal, talking to Will about him. Why was that, she wondered? If she talked to Marie like this she'd feel all wrong. But then Marie would make her talk about her sex life. What there was of it. Will didn't do that. He was more likely to ask about how she stocked her fridge – condiments on the top shelf or in the door racks? Or about cushions – was purple a good accent colour with a turquoise sofa?

Will laughed. 'Well, is that all? Sara, you're a woman! You should know *exactly* what he's saying here! I'd say he's intending to go backwards, that's all he means. My old mother went up and down from fifty-five to fifty-nine for a good twenty years. Why, what did you think he meant? That he's going to jump off Richmond Bridge?'

Sara watched a young couple at the table opposite. They sat in silence, stolidly munching their way through a heap of garlic bread. Something about their utter stillness told her that even when they'd finished eating, they still wouldn't embark on a conversation. She'd always assumed those long silences were something you didn't get till old age. Maybe age had nothing to do with anything, ever, after all.

'Will, don't say that! Suppose that's exactly what he *does* mean? I've never had anything with Conrad before that I don't dare to talk about . . . but this one, well it's the big One to Avoid. And today . . .'

She took a deep breath and told him about Conrad paddling at the Aquarium. Will, by the time she'd finished, was almost choking with laughter.

'Is it that funny?' She was puzzled.

'*Funny?* Of course it's bloody funny! What did Cassandra say when you told her he'd waded out into the deep like John the Baptist and dunked her poor infant among the fish? Hysterical!'

'Ah . . . well we didn't tell Cass. I made Conrad promise not to.'

'*What?*'

'I was scared, Will! I know it just comes over as an amusing little story but at the time, the way he was, it was like he'd completely lost the plot. He just wasn't *connected*. I don't want Cass to think we can't take care of Charlie. Oh God, perhaps we can't! Or at least, perhaps *Conrad* can't. How can I think of him as safe to be in charge of a baby after this?'

Will looked more serious now, thinking. 'Hmmm. Well if you really feel like that, then just . . . don't let him.'

'He'd be mortified . . . so upset. But you're right. Charlie's safety comes first, obviously.'

Will smiled and stroked her hand. 'But look, sweetie, he's an artist. They do mad things. They do it because they can, or for attention – you shouldn't need me to tell you that. If Tracey Emin climbed into the penguin pool at London Zoo, even if it was just to pick up a glove she'd dropped over the wall, she'd turn the whole episode into a conversation piece and have it written up in the *Sunday Times* ponce pages complete with photos and the usual guff about her abortion. Think of Conrad like that, apart from those bits, obviously. He's turned into . . . a . . . what do you call it, a human *installation*. An event. See? He's just being *him*. Nothing spooky, nothing dangerously mad. Trust me, darling, and wish him a happy sixty-eighth birthday when the time comes. OK, counselling session over for now. My turn later cos I've been agonizing over whether Bruno would think a surprise trip to San Francisco would be a yay or a nay and I want your input. But for now . . . are you going for your usual Margherita? Or are you going to be *completely* crazy too, maybe as off the wall as choosing lasagne?'

Art is not what you see, but what you make others see.
(Edgar Degas)

'No, it's fine − it doesn't matter at *all* about the colours being true to life. Whatever you feel. If you want to paint him completely in purple then of course you can. You see, that's the point, Melissa − art is about expressing what's inside *you*. There *are* no rules. Any medium, any shade, any size. Each decision is what makes up your inner artist. Do you see?' Sara tried to look encouraging. Most of her students relished the idea of absolute free choice when it came to artistic impression, but with this one it was hard work. Sometimes half the lesson had gone before she'd decided whether to use a pencil or a brush.

Melissa didn't look as if she *did* see. Or as if she ever would. It sounded a bit cruelly intense, addressed to this most anxious-to-please of Sara's Wednesday afternoon Beginners Art class, who were sitting in a circle in the

Adult College studio (actually a former science classroom, all Bunsen burners capped off by Health and Safety) with their easels set out like wagons round a pioneers' campfire. There were twelve class members, the majority of them post-pension age, making the most of cut-rate access to the classes and determined to get out and about while they could. Some spent almost every waking hour on college premises, flitting from Conversational French to Yoga to Batik by way of Cake Decoration and the Poker Club.

Just now, the class were concentrating intently on the naked life model. Poor Melissa – one of only three younger-generation class members – was a tragically in-decisive soul, and would prefer to be doing something that had a comfortable set of regulations to obey. Why her hyper-keen probation officer hadn't suggested a useful skill like Basic Cookery instead of pointing her firmly in the direction of Art, Sara had no idea. Possibly it was to do with the theory that Melissa would feel the glow of creativity in an area unconnected with relieving high-street clothes shops of their goods without paying for them. It was a pity, because Melissa, who had led a chaotic life, would feel secure in the comfort of an exact recipe to follow, something she couldn't really get wrong, and surely you couldn't get much more of a creative glow than by eating what you'd made? Sara watched as Melissa opened a tube of Prussian Blue gouache and another one of Crimson Lake and squidged dollops on to her palette, then hesitated again, dithering over the choice of brush.

'Big brush . . . or a little skinny one . . . big, little, fat or thin?' Sara heard the girl murmur to herself. She backed away, wondering how Melissa ever made decisions in shops over what to steal. Perhaps taking skirts in every available colour had been what led to her many arrests. She turned instead to look at Mrs Mottram's heavily scuffed charcoal drawing. Alan the model – one of the college's caretaking staff, enjoying a lazy but paid break – shifted slightly on his chair and scratched his pale bum, the only bit of him that wasn't deeply tanned. Pamela Mottram, a tall, rod-straight sixty-something with a Hermès horse-head scarf tied bandanna-style, scowled at him for daring to move, and he winked at her.

'Cheeky sod,' Pamela whispered to Sara. 'I wouldn't mind but he's not got a lot to wink about, has he?'

'Oy – I heard that!' Alan twisted round and grinned at them. 'You should try handling the goods before you pass judgement, darlin'. You might find I'll grow on you, in a manner of speaking!' A ripple of sniggers went round the group.

'I don't doubt it,' Pamela told him. 'But you haven't got anything I haven't handled before *and* in a grown-up size, so would you kindly resume the position please?' She added some vicious strokes of thick dusty charcoal to her flamboyant sketch as the model settled back on his chair and turned the pages of the *Daily Star* to the sports section. The room settled into a comfortable silence as the students concentrated on their efforts.

Sara glanced across to the corner of the room where she'd left Charlie sleeping in his buggy. You couldn't just put babies out of your mind and concentrate on what you were doing, even when they were sleeping. No wonder Cassandra found it hard to get her college work done. All the time, one ear and half a brain were tuned to the slightest movement, the first stirrings. Stuart from Car Maintenance had put his head round the studio door earlier, making going-for-a-drink gestures at Sara, but when she'd pointed at Charlie he had almost fled from the room. 'Another time . . .' she'd heard him call as he dashed off down the corridor. What she'd actually meant was that they'd have to take Charlie too . . . not that she couldn't go. She'd been about to say yes, if he'd stayed long enough to listen. It would have been good to have had a quick wind-down after work before going home to sort out supper and second-guess whatever mind game Conrad had got planned for the evening. If Cass and Paul really had separated, would Stuart's reaction be that of just about every new potential boyfriend the poor girl attracted? She really hoped not.

'He's a good sleeper.' Melissa now pointed her paint-brush in the direction of Charlie. Purple paint dropped in blobs on to the parquet floor.

'That's because he was up twice in the night,' Sara told her. 'Poor Cassie had a ten o'clock lecture this morning and spent half the night trying to settle him.'

'You can get stuff for them,' Melissa said, giving Sara a sharp look, as if about to offer class-A drugs in baby-dosage. 'Stuff to make them sleep. My sister always does for hers. She says she's got to have a life too, and that it's not all about the baby.'

'But they're not little for long,' Sara said carefully, not wishing to condemn an unknown woman's child-rearing methods of choice, however tempting it was, for surely the point should be that it *was* all about the baby? 'Cass knows it's just a stage. It's funny, it only seems about a week since that was me, trying to get her to sleep through the night.'

Conrad had suggested dipping a finger in brandy and letting Charlie suck it, as his generation's parenting had decreed – whether secretly or otherwise. Not very much changes over the years, she thought, wondering if, resentfully camped outside the gates of the Garden of Eden, Eve had despaired over the sleeping habits of her own babies. Did she blame God when they woke her all through the night and resent this extra aspect of his mean-spirited eternal condemnation of her, simply for fancying a bit of fruit and the answers to some questions?

The blanket over Charlie was shifting. He was waking and would need some milk. This was going to involve a trip to the staffroom to use the microwave, so it was a good time to send the students to the canteen for tea and a biscuit. She was pretty sure they liked this bit of the lesson the best, especially the older women, who treated the breaks as a social event and a chance to chat up the most eligible widowers, luring them with two-for-one theatre-ticket bargains or offering to cook them supper, saying it wasn't worth doing a full-scale roast for one. The men were easily wooed by offers of home cooking, and the most greedy of them played off the women against each other. Marie reckoned the canteen was elderly dating heaven.

'How long have we got?' Alan the model asked Sara. 'I mean is it worth my while getting dressed, or would Mrs Mottram be persuadable in the fetching-me-a-cuppa department?'

'Certainly I'll get you some tea,' Pamela told him. 'And I'll remember to bring you something to stir it with,' she added, grinning, as she picked up her bag and went to the door.

'Now that's what I call a classy goer,' Alan said, admiringly. Sara laughed. A more unlikely pairing she could hardly begin to imagine.

'Ah there you are, Sara darling – are you coming up for a cup of tea?' Marie breezed into the studio, passing the last of the outgoing students. She looked at Alan, who was now wandering naked among the easels, commenting on the success or otherwise of those who'd tried to capture his likeness.

'Oh, no wonder you're staying in here, Sara!' Marie chortled. 'And this is an aspect of you we never get to see, Alan! I'll picture you like this next time I see you in the corridor bleeding the radiators.'

'Marie please – don't tease him! Do you know how hard it is to get nude models? Especially ones as pleased with their own bodies as Alan. The difficult bit is getting him to put his clothes back *on*.'

'I just like to please the ladies. Gives them something to think about in the lonely night-time hours, if you catch my drift.' Alan smirked.

'Stop it now! Save it for Pamela!' Sara laughed. 'Come on, Marie, let me get Charlie and we'll go and chat.'

She lifted the now wide-awake baby from his buggy and picked up his bag of essential supplies. Charlie wriggled in her arms. Slippery things, babies, she thought, remembering Pandora at this stage, intent on hurling herself backwards every time she was picked up.

'Ooh let me carry him, Sara! I don't get to play with babies very often.' Marie sighed. 'I don't think my boys will ever get round to breeding. They're too into Wii games and beer. When did playing with toys become something that went on beyond the age of eleven? I certainly wasn't still asking Santa for dollies and daft games when I was older than that, were you?'

'Definitely not! Maybe it's a boy thing. Even Conrad plays computer games. He pretends he doesn't but I've caught him loads of times sprawled on the sofa in the studio, switching off just too late to stop me seeing.' That was what she'd caught him doing the night before, when she'd come home early from not going to the movies with Will. He was down in the studio, escaping, he said, from Cassandra and her friend Miranda, who were having one of those girly intense chats that involve lying on a sofa each and saying, 'And *then*, like he says to me . . .'

Sara handed Charlie over to Marie, who tickled his tummy and made him smile. Marie made everyone smile – she had that big-eyed happy kind of face that warmed and encouraged people. No wonder she'd so easily snaffled this Angus person.

'I've had more titillating texts from Angus. It's still all on, though next week now, not this,' Marie told Sara excitedly as they went up the stairs to the staffroom. 'He's getting me so warmed up, I can't wait! He's got a friend's flat in Chelsea that he uses when he's down from Edinburgh. Better than a hotel, I think. Less, you know, *staged.* Don't you think? And no embarrassing inter-ruptions from room service and so on.'

Sara laughed. 'Well, I suppose so. It's not something I've thought about. If it *was* a hotel . . . actually I quite like hotels, but it would have to be one you already knew was good. A room you'd stayed in before and really liked, so you didn't get any nasty surprises such as a shower that's a bit manky or *ugh* chintz! I don't think I could do anything sexually fun in a room that was all green swagged velvet, ochre walls and floral sofas!'

'Oh I don't know, the way I feel about Angus right now, I could do it in the back of a Mini. *Anywhere* just so long as it happens!'

And what about Mike, Sara wondered, what about that long-devoted, stolid husband of Marie's who never did anything that wasn't first of all intended to make her happy? Where did he fit in? He was probably putting up a shelf right now, or replacing the sealant round the bath. Not romantic, but done with love, all the same. None of my business, Sara told herself. And besides, with Marie all wound up like this, so happy and excited, it could be argued that so long as he never found out, he was actually getting the benefit of this hyper-good mood. There would be a lot of men out there, living with women at the same menopausal stage as Marie, who would envy Mike his ever-smiling, cheerful partner. Way better, they'd claim, than living with a hormonal time bomb, a moody viper veering between bouts of depressive sobbing and expensive therapeutic shopping. He was a sweet man, even if his idea of a fun trip out was a visit to B&Q to top up his supply of drill bits.

The staffroom was, for once, pleasingly underoccupied. Marie carried Charlie to the tattered leather sofa by the window and Sara found his bottle and put it in the microwave.

It wasn't quite as true as it had been, what Sara had said about not thinking about sex with someone new. Sleepless the night before, she had found herself drifting into a fantasy about the man she'd had a drink with by the river. How easy it had been, chatting with him for that short time, how very relaxing it was to be with someone whose life history and life burdens she didn't know about, and who had nothing at all to do with hers. A slightly shocked part of her recognized that he would have been an ideal candidate for that sexual holy grail Erica Jong wrote about many years before: the zipless fuck. Sex without any complications, no obstacles – emotional or otherwise. Except surely there were *always* complications. Premises, for one. How *not* spontaneous would booking a hotel room be? It would surely take all the edge off and put all the pressure on. Did the zipless thing ever really work, unless you were her sister Lizzie, whose sexual mores had never left the sixties love-in, or Marie, who, after a silver wedding's worth of absolute fidelity, astonishingly failed to see a downside to this exhilarating love she'd recently found?

'I bet you have thought about it. You must have. Everyone has.' Marie looked at Sara sharply, making her blush, as if her mind was being read. 'I don't mean I'd recommend a full-scale affair.' She backtracked. 'And that's not what I'm having.'

'Would Mike agree with that statement?' The microwave pinged and Sara took Charlie's bottle out, shook it and tested the temperature.

'Don't be silly, of course he wouldn't. But it's not about Mike. This is *separate*. It's for me, like going to the spa and having a day of pampering. I love Mike to bits, I can't imagine ever living with anyone else . . . but . . . this Angus thing just jumped out and bit me when I wasn't looking. Remember, I told you how we met at the Teach To Write conference, I was there when he did his talk. I watched him . . . he looked at me a lot and after the question session, we just drifted together as if we'd known each other for ever. It was always going to happen.'

'Why didn't you sleep with him at the time, then?' Sara asked her, quietly in case the few staff reading newspapers or talking together had bat-like hearing.

Marie laughed. 'His wife was there! I don't think she'd

have been very thrilled if we had! As it was she didn't take to me. Her radar was working overtime. I thought, hey why is she being like this, and tried to be friendly, but when she asked me if I'd got my dress from Primark I just *knew* she wasn't ever going to be a sister.'

'And *did* you get your dress from Primark?'

'Oh yes, of course I did! But that's not the point, is it? You know the rules – if you think you might like someone a huge lot and become proper friends with them, you say, "Oh that's lovely, is it Prada?" And then they do a big shrieky laugh and say, "No actually, it's Primark!" feel incredibly flattered and you then marvel at their amazing ability to pick out a fabulous bargain.' Marie bustled about, fetching tea and biscuits for them both, then whispered loudly, 'Got to go send a quick text, back in a jiff! Keep my seat, I'll be out on the stairs trying to concentrate on not sending it to Mike by mistake! God, can you imagine?'

The staffroom was filling up now. Sara relaxed in the depths of the sagging leather sofa, feeding Charlie his milk while various members of the teaching staff cooed over him. Charlie enjoyed the attention, allowing people to distract him, breaking off to smile at the ones he liked the look of. Stuart came in and hovered by the microwave, glaring across at Sara and the baby as if the child was a love rival.

'Stuart! Thanks for this week's veg box!' Sara called across to him. 'Why don't you come and meet Charlie?'

'OK, just for a minute. Don't want to interrupt. Hello Charlie,' he said, rather grumpily. 'I suppose if Sara's got *you*, she won't want to come to the pub with me any more.'

'Of course I will, don't be daft!' Sara protested. 'I'm just looking after him for Cassandra while she's at university. It's not a full-time thing, this grandmother business, just occasional.'

Stuart smelled of old cars, motor oil and mustiness, with an underlying hint of shower gel. She wondered if his wife found that mixture a comforting, home-familiar aroma. Possibly she even found it erotic. Or did she hate it and light scented candles or even have those plug-in room fresheners all over their house? Maybe she didn't notice. There were a lot of things you didn't notice about husbands and partners when you loved them and lived with them. It was a bit like overfond owners of cats, who managed to ignore the pungent whiff of unneutered tom. Over the years, friends who'd got drunk enough to be frank had occasionally expressed amazement that she could live so apparently easily with Conrad's constant travels to paint commissions, which meant he missed birthdays and anniversaries; and there were all those hours he spent in the studio when he'd seemed to lose track of day or night, missing appointments, social events, a couple of dinners at his own house that he simply didn't turn up to, through all of which Sara stayed calm and happy enough. Other people's husbands had always seemed a predictable and unappealing lot by comparison. Now she wondered if they might simply be quite restful. She'd be willing to bet they didn't pounce on you to discuss death while you were cleaning a table, or paddle in public fish tanks.

'Got some new totty joined the class,' Stuart told her as he perched on the sofa arm, leering a bit. 'A little blonde-of-a-desperate-age with a perfect derrière.' He cupped his hands round an imaginary something that Sara guessed to be a size 16. 'She's big, round and curvy in exactly the right places. I can't wait to see her leaning over the Fiesta's radiator, delving with the dipstick!'

'Stuart! You never give up, do you?'

'Well, you turned me down. A man has to get his fun somewhere. And besides, what else has she come to the class for?'

'Ah, the old theory – women only go to car maintenance in search of a big choice of geeky dates.'

'And what do they get?' Stuart laughed. 'Lots of women just the same as them and . . . me! Not all bad news then! Talking of which, must get going. I hope she comes back from the break even later than me, though. I can threaten her with the cane. Talking of which, fancy some nice fat cucumbers later this summer?'

Sara hesitated, wondering about an answer that would be straightforwardly non-suggestive. Stuart could find a double entendre even in a nursery rhyme.

'It's just that I've got the seeds in and I reckon I've over-done it. You can have too many, with cucumbers.'

'OK, thanks. That'd be lovely,' she told him.

'No worries. I'll do you some nice long ridgy ones.' He winked. 'We can work out terms of payment another time. Gotta go . . . got to show that new woman which way up to hold a spanner.'

What was keeping Marie, Sara wondered as Charlie was just, after what seemed ages, getting to the last drops in the bottle. Sending a text to her lover was taking a hell of a time. Maybe they were finalizing their tryst details. She shifted Charlie into a more upright position as a male voice in front of her said, 'Is there room on this sofa for one more? Oh – hey, it's you! Hello again!'

Sara looked up, startled. And there he was, the man from the White Swan garden. She could feel her skin warming uncomfortably, and she wondered if he'd bolt if he sensed her night-time thoughts. How was one supposed to keep a dignified demeanour and make polite conversation with someone you'd imagined trailing his fingers over every inch of your skin?

'Oh! Hi! What are you doing here? Have you joined the staff?' Her voice sounded normal enough, if a bit shrill.

She moved Charlie, who had slumped somewhat, into a more comfortable position, put Marie's bag on the floor and the man sat beside her. He was wearing ancient jeans with the hems fraying and another linen shirt, dark blue this time, with the sleeves rolled up. No watch, just a small friendship bracelet made from plaited embroidery threads in shades of blue. It crossed her mind (with a surge of disappointment) that possibly, as Conrad rather quaintly put it, he *travelled on the other bus*.

'I'm working!' he told her, smiling. He did have lovely teeth. She stopped herself from staring at them; it was hardly seemly to gaze like that at a man's mouth. 'I'm a journalist. Freelance. I'm writing a piece for the *Guardian* on the social aspect of Adult Education classes. It's not about the people who are here for extra academic qualifications that they need for work, but those who rely on it for friendships, networking and so on. I've just been checking out Advanced Yoga – there are people in there who must be pushing ninety who can tie themselves in knots. Terrifying!'

'You should come and hang out in my art class,' Sara laughed. 'Today it's eager pensioners giving hell to the naked life model. Not that he minds. It would take more than a lively eighty-year-old to upset Alan.'

'Ah . . . you're an artist?' he said. 'I should have guessed.'

'Guessed? How?'

'Just the way you dress. Something about what you wear. You have an original, stylish look. I thought that the other day. I liked your blue skirt – all layers and pointy bits. And . . . aha! Today you've got red shoes! Didn't we decide it was the sign of a madwoman?'

So he *was* gay, she thought. He'd noticed her clothes.

Feeling flattered but slightly uncomfortable at being so observed, Sara looked at today's dress as if she hadn't quite noticed it before. It was a shades-of-pink floral 1940s tea dress, a junk-shop discovery she'd had for years, worn with a pale green cashmere cardigan, slightly shrunken. She'd changed the buttons for tiny heart ones in rainbow colours. Her shoes were scarlet strappy wedges, found in a charity shop and probably circa 1973, though with a 1930s look. Underneath was a white antique cotton petticoat, with drawn-thread work and ribbon.

'I don't know your name,' she said at last. 'If you really are coming to see my class I possibly should be able to introduce you to the others. I'm Sara.' She hesitated about adding her surname – here at the college she used her maiden name. Admitting to being a Blythe-Hamilton tended to invite the question: 'Are you any relation to Conrad?' She wanted to keep Conrad out of this, whatever 'this' was, so – 'Sara McKinley,' she said.

'Ben Stretton,' he said, taking her hand with pretend solemnity. 'And I'm delighted to meet you.'

Sara laughed, feeling slightly light-headed. Charlie pointed across the room and bounced excitedly on her lap as he spotted Marie returning. Sara caught Marie's eye and saw a whole lot of questioning going on behind her gaze.

'She thinks we're up to no good,' Ben whispered as Marie came towards them.

'Marie thinks everyone's up to no good!' Sara told him. 'Sadly, she's nearly always disappointed.'

'Only *nearly* always? Well then, there's hope,' he said.

Men, Sara thought. So confusing.

He leaned towards her and murmured very quietly, 'And you know what they say about red shoes, don't you?'

'Yes I do,' she said, inhaling a heady mix of laundry scents and some kind of sharp, delicious citrus. 'That old saying: red shoes, no knickers.'

She would leave him to guess whether it applied to her.

Life is a lot like jazz – it's best when you improvise.
(George Gershwin)

Sara looked back at the house from the pathway through to the river. It was a strange building, all slabs of dark glass and long, weathered cedar struts. They'd only managed to get planning permission for it because it was sufficiently hidden among trees and behind high fencing not to flaunt its shocking modernity among the tasteful, discreet Georgian/Edwardian mix of the rest of the area. Someone had once commented that it looked like a low-profile outpost of MI5. Another had sniffily decreed that it resembled an airport terminal. When she and Conrad had had it built the architect had been thrilled that at last he had clients who didn't want to temper his wildest design, didn't start off by saying, 'Yes, as ultra-flamboyant as you like,' but then keep coming back and sneakily lopping off the madder bits, deciding that really what they wanted was something that looked more like a house than a piece of jagged, glassy sculpture. He still claimed it among the proudest achievements in his portfolio, and occasionally students of architecture would get in touch and nervously, apologetically, ask if they could come and have a look. Conrad didn't mind – his opinion was that with architecture, wherever a building worthy of a second glance was situated, then that was the gallery. You shouldn't expect to hide away art.

Halfway down the sloping garden and up in an elderly oak was a tree house in a similar overall shape as the house that the architect had had built for Cassandra and Pandora. The weather had taken its toll and pieces fell off now and then in storms, but one day, Sara thought, perhaps it could be repaired for Charlie to play in. The girls had already been a bit old for it by the time they moved to this house, but it had proved useful as a place for them to go to sulk after family rows, to kiss their first boyfriends in and to climb into to cry in peace when teenage life went as wrong as it inevitably did.

By contrast, Conrad's studio, close to the boundary wall, was less contemporary and had a pitched roof, with an inset north-facing window, and was modelled on nineteenth-century artists' studios that pitched up in various hidden corners of West London. Conrad had always wanted one and took as his model those that were hidden away beside Chelsea football stadium, bent on having something as similar as possible in spite of it being so unmatched to the rest of the property. His studio was big enough to include a spiral staircase leading to a platform sleeping area above a shower room and small kitchen.

Sara wondered, these days, how he could bear to sleep in there so frequently. It had an overall grubbiness to it: it was strictly off limits to Xavier, the sweet young half-French cleaner. Conrad said he didn't want things moved about. Meticulous Xavier, who tutted about the merest fleck of thread as he hoovered, and told Sara off for the way she loaded glasses into her own dishwasher, would have paled and fainted at the ephemeral clutter; the smell of turps was completely overwhelming, ingrained into the walls and floors. Sara liked the smell, but was sleeping with it any good for Conrad's lungs? Maybe over the many working years he'd become immune to it, or even needed it, like a smoker being oblivious to the reek of stale fumes on clothes and hair.

Sara's own art medium of choice was gouache, but a strong scent of turps still reminded her of when she'd first met Conrad as a student, when after their first proper date at a blues club in Soho he'd taken her back to his flat in Kensington and seduced her on a plum velvet sofa in a room full of half-finished, still-wet canvases. There had been a pink and purple fringed silk shawl beneath her body, almost certainly one that her predecessor had left behind in the hope that Conrad would think of her fondly and invite her for a follow-up sofa session; she could still remember how the rows of tiny mirrors stitched on to it had dug into her flesh. They'd left little half-moon scratches and circular weals on her skin and she'd hated to see them fade, superstitiously thinking that if they vanished completely, all would be over with Conrad.

Everyone had warned her he was a rampant womanizer, forever taking up with his students for a month or two and then cheerfully moving on, an eternally good-natured non-settler. He'd told her she was different, right from the start, right from the moment when she'd walked into him in a blind rage at Hyde Park Corner and he'd taken her to the Athenaeum hotel for tea and champagne, sympathizing over the theft of her bag. She wasn't so naive that she'd believed him entirely; he'd probably told all his girls they were different. But he had never given her cause to suspect that having found her, he was still looking for something else.

There'd been plenty of 'something else' on offer over the years. Sara could always spot them at parties: the gleaming, eager women who had just happened to read about him in the culture magazines or the weekend colour supplements, or had recently admired one of his paintings at a friend's house. They were always shiny and excited and would drift their perfectly manicured fingers across his arm and laugh a little too much at any inconsequential piece of nonsense he uttered. Often he'd push that to the limit, coming out with something totally nonsensical, or contradict himself from one sentence to the next, just to see how far he could push their fawning gullibility. He would smile and do the polite thing, and if they stayed too long beside him he'd pull Sara closer and say, 'And this is Sara. She's the love of my life.'

It was only eight in the morning but Sara had been awake since six, and the day promised to be a warm, sunny one. She and Floss went out through the gate to the towpath and started walking towards the park, the spaniel excitedly snuffling out dog smells among newly sprouting nettles. It was too early for Stuart, her frequent walking companion, to be out, and besides, she wanted to be alone with her thoughts. Stuart would want to entertain her with news of his latest piece of spanking apparatus, following up with his usual request that he be allowed to try it out on her. She much preferred him when he told her how to mulch courgettes.

Tempting as it was, Sara chose not to take Floss in the other direction, for less than a mile that way was the White Swan pub and the row of pastel-painted cottages where Ben lived. At the college the other day, he had said to call in any time. But people just said that, didn't they? Would he really want to see her 'happening to be passing' at an hour when most people were racing about on their way to the working day? He was a freelance journalist, too – he was probably still asleep. And there could be a Mrs Ben, who would definitely not want to be meeting her husband's new friends at this time of the day. Besides, he'd said he'd be coming to her art class on Wednesday afternoon. It must be quite a long piece he was writing, needing more than one research visit to the college.

As she walked, Sara watched a couple of early rowers out on the Thames. Perhaps they were on their way to work. Possibly they'd discovered this was the one sure way to beat the school-run traffic and the army of Chelsea-tractor mummies. Where, she thought as she went into the park, did you park a skiff for the day? And in winter, did you row back in the freezing dark with lights on the front of the boat?

'Hey Sara! Good morning!' Marie's husband Mike was sitting on a bench just inside the park gate. He had Marie's white poodle on a pink lead and in his spare hand a cup of something frothy from Starbucks in the high street, it being too early still for the café in the park to be open. Sara felt guilt twinges immediately. How much better it would be right now if she didn't know about Marie's secret tryst with Scottish Angus. She wished she knew nothing of the laced basque; the French knickers. It was hard not to think she had a stake in adultery's success. Or otherwise. Seeing Mike, she felt really bad about it all. What was it with women, that they had to have a confidante for everything? Marie talked to her, she talked to Will, Cass talked to Miranda.

'Mike – hi. You're out early.'

Mike got up, poured the rest of the coffee on to the grass and dropped the cup into the bin beside the bench. The poodle started bouncing and yapping. Sara and Mike let the dogs off their leads and set off along the shingle path together, heading for the duck pond. The dogs raced away, like little children fresh out of school.

'Couldn't sleep,' Mike grumbled. 'Well, correction, *Marie* couldn't sleep. Kept fidgeting and muttering. So I thought, might as well get up. Take the dog out. She's been like this for days, flipping and flapping in her sleep. Marie, that is. Not the dog. And whatever she's got on her mind, she's not telling me about it.' He gave Sara a sharp look. 'She said anything to you?'

'No!' Sara said, too quickly. 'Er . . . well I saw her at the college yesterday as usual, just during the break, you know, for a quick cup of tea . . .' She was gabbling. She took a breath. 'She seemed fine. She said she was teaching her class how to write from multiple viewpoints or some-thing. Tricky stuff, anyway.'

'Oh she's fine all right.' Mike grunted. '*Too* bloody fine if you ask me.'

Sara bit her lip. She knew exactly what he meant. Marie was so flushed with new love she couldn't help showing it. You might as well tell freshly poured champagne not to sparkle as tell Marie to calm down. Her eyes shone, her skin (no longer olive, just perfectly sun-kissed) glowed. She was losing weight by the day. Mike, on the other hand, was looking defeated before the battle had begun. He had become tubby lately, shambolic and bulging in clothes bought several sizes ago. His hair needed cutting and was looking Brillo-ish: matted and neglected. Sara fought back an urge to tell him to get a grip if he wanted to hang on to his wife, take care of himself and . . . well, at least clean the wood dust from his obsessive DIY ventures from beneath his nails. Women were quick to pass judgement on each other, 'She's let herself go' being the ultimate condemnation, the worst female crime; but in Sara's opinion it was the men who were more likely to decline into scruffiness as they got older. It was such a long time since they'd been children – why did so many need telling that it might be a good idea to take a shower?

'Thing is,' Mike continued, 'I sometimes . . . well no, it's not possible.' He laughed, but it was a harsh and bitter sound. 'I sometimes wonder if she's *met someone*.' He stopped on the path and looked Sara square in the face. 'She'd tell you, wouldn't she?'

Sara watched the two dogs up by the pond, avoiding having to see Mike's unhappy eyes, full of pain. He wanted so much for Sara to reassure him, to tell him that Marie was . . . actually, what? How could the everyday Marie – or any woman of her age – be accurately described? Ecstatic to be entering her menopausal years? Thrilled to be experiencing claggy swamps of sudden flushing? Loving the newly erratic nature of her periods and their delightfully unpredictable heaviness?

No. Exactly.

Floss was wading into the pond. She'd be stinking and filthy with mud. Sara looked across at her, willing her to do something conveniently distracting, catch a duck (even at her age), get bullied by a swan and need instant rescuing. Nothing.

'Well, yes I suppose she might tell me,' Sara admitted, because this was factual but didn't give anything away. 'But you know, we meet people all the time in our job. Teaching adults is like that. With teaching children, you don't exist for them beyond the school gates, but in adult education one or two see you as some kind of lifeline, someone who will help them find the path out of their humdrum lives on to a whole new route.' She laughed. 'It can go to your head, that kind of power! Maybe life's just going well for her right now, no hassles, no real problems. She hasn't mentioned any problems to me, anyway.' This much was true.

'It's not like that, she's all, I don't know, just . . .' Mike wasn't having it. Sara had failed here – he wasn't remotely reassured by her breezy tone and she wasn't surprised.

'Look, I'm sure all's well,' she interrupted. 'Why not . . . I don't know . . . it's a cliché, isn't it, but why don't you just tart yourself up and take her out somewhere lovely for dinner? Or away for a weekend? Sometimes we women just need a change of venue. And at least it'd be just the two of you. No teenage sons sprawled about all over the house, no distractions. You could talk to each other . . . properly. Or just go bird-watching or something.' She was floundering now.

'Agony-aunt stuff,' Mike chuckled, picking up a fat stick to throw that surely the poodle would never be able to carry back to him. 'You're good at it. If that's all it takes, will you let me take *you* out? For lunch sometime? I mean . . . I don't want to come over all New Man, but a bit of guidance on this midlife female stuff would help.'

Sara realized she must be looking pretty horrified. She didn't mean to: she liked Mike. It was just the thought of him imagining she'd discuss Marie with him seated at a table in Giraffe. Realizing how he'd come across, he all but physically backed away, hands raised as if she was about to attack him. 'Just as friends, that is. Not that . . .'

'It's OK, Mike.' Sara managed to compose her face into an expression that was more convivial. She could see him digging a deep, deep hole here. 'I do know what you're saying; look – just . . . keep the faith. Come to the house and have some coffee sometime, OK? And don't worry. All will be well.'

Pandora's hands were sore. It was the cutlery that did it. There was some knack to picking up the dirty plates and making sure the knives weren't within grazing distance of your wrists and fingers, and she couldn't get the hang of it. Giovanni, the manager, wasn't helpful – he just pointed his staff at the tables and shouted orders. He seemed to assume that if they were young and female, waitressing was a skill that came naturally. The only person who got anything resembling good manners out of him was the sainted big-name chef under whose verbal abuse Giovanni grovelled and smarmed, before coming back to front of house to snipe at his staff. Pandora had cuts, quite deep ones, between the thumb and finger on her right hand, and even though they were healing (and boy had they ever bled at the time), on each shift something serrated caught the skin and started the stinging up again. And doing the breakfast hour was the worst, because the cut she'd got during last night's late clearing was still giving her twinges in her sliced skin.

'I hate this, I hate this' was her mantra. The early morning customers had started noticing that she was no longer thinking it but murmuring it out loud. Giovanni had asked one of the other girls to ask her if she was on drugs. As bloody if. Did he really think she would be so moody if she was? Didn't you take drugs to lift your spirits, not to make you feel like the drudge from hell? What did he want at 8 a.m. with the walk-of-shame party girls still in their heels and hair glitter, making a latte last for an hour, and the cabbies going upmarket with a Danish and espresso and thinking they were *somebody* in this so cool East London eaterie?

'Hey! Girl, cutlery! Out of the garbage!' Too late, Pandora realized she'd dropped yet another half-dozen knives into the food-waste bin. She'd have to delve in. She looked down at the turgid mix of last night's pasta and chicken and streaks of salad and stinking Parmesan. It should have been emptied but would be there till the afternoon. It was too much. She closed her eyes and tried not to breathe in. She picked out the knives, one by careful one, flung them in the dishwasher and ran her hands for a long, long minute under the hot tap. Giovanni glared at her and tapped his watch impatiently.

'*What?*' she shouted. 'I'm allowed to wash my hands, aren't I? Basic hygiene?'

Giovanni slowly shook his head. He was going to fire her. She'd seen that look with other staff. She thought not; she'd get in first. Her fingers fumbled for the ties at the back of her long white apron. She was out of here, soon as the knots were sorted. What kind of life was this for an artist? That's what you got for doing it the way your dad said it was done. All that starving in a bedsit was for other times, other customs. This wasn't working for her. If Cassandra could move back into the lovely, comfortable family nest and be spoiled rotten, then so could she.

Sara was out on the pool terrace with tea and toast and the *Guardian* crossword, her eyes closed and the sun on her face. To hell with wrinkles, she thought; you couldn't beat this delicious feeling of spring sun warming your skin and hair. How could it be bad for you? This was the first really sultry morning of the year, one when you didn't think, oh this will be fine, but only for ten minutes, or that you hadn't got quite enough clothes on to feel no chill. She sat at the old teak table, watching a pair of wrens doing the food run to a nest under the studio eaves, and, concentrating hard between Heathrow-bound jets soaring overhead, could just hear the eager squeaking of the baby birds as they sensed their parents' return visits.

Conrad must still be asleep. The blind was pulled across the glass roof of the studio, and there was no sign of movement at all. Horribly, it crossed her mind that one day she could go in there, maybe at midday wondering why he hadn't surfaced, and find that he had died in the night. She tried hard to push this awful notion out of her head – it was too beautiful a morning to blight with such thoughts. And after all, why should it happen? He was in pretty good condition, and not all that old in the scheme of modern life. He could outlive her. All the same, now she'd had the thought, she knew that never again would she be able to go and wake him with a mug of tea without some dread at what she'd find. Perhaps he *did* know something about a possible brush with death, though he seemed to have given up on the idea of talking about it. He did that . . . got all involved with things (past projects included possible purchase of an E-type Jaguar, a six-month stint in Antarctica to 'clear the palate of colour', sending the girls to school in America), worried at them for a week till he'd talked himself through every aspect, then never mentioned them again.

The peonies alongside the studio were about to flower. The bursting buds reminded Sara of Marie laced into her basque in Selfridges. It was going to be today, her tryst with Angus. She had phoned the night before, urgently whispering 'Suspenders or hold-ups?' at Sara, who imagined Mike in the background, innocently watching *The Bill*. Maybe he'd overheard her – perhaps that was what he wasn't admitting in the park earlier. What would it feel like to be Marie, Sara wondered, that mixture of deep apprehension and excitement, going to meet the man who would become your lover. Those hours before it happened . . . in fact, would they be hours or would she ring the apartment bell and be hauled by Angus straight to bed with barely more than a hello? Marie had said they were going for lunch at Le Caprice first. What would they talk about, Sara considered, knowing what was to come in the afternoon. Would they whisper giggly, suggestive quips to each other over the warm duck salad? Share oysters, messily, sexily? Or make polite conversation about books and the art of fiction, or slowly, accidentally, put each other off the idea of torrid sex by talking about their families and steadily destroying the ambience? Poor Mike – if Marie was bubbly and light-headed before her date with Angus, what was she going to be like after it? Sara hoped she'd be able to tone her mood down by the time she got home. She'd insisted this Angus thing was separate, but was anything ever that separate when you'd lived with someone so long that they sensed every butterfly-wing-beat of change?

'We must get a fence built round this pool!' Conrad's voice, coming from the house and not the studio, startled her. 'Charlie will be crawling everywhere soon. You'll need safety measures.'

He sounded wide awake and emerged through the open sliding door entirely naked, carrying a towel. Without any hesitation, he stepped off the side of the pool and vanished under the water, emerging to execute an elegant crawl and swim to the pool's deep end. Sara flicked drips of splashed water from her bare arm.

'Where did you spring from?' she asked as he stopped to tread water under the diving board.

'The downstairs shower. I just woke up, came up here and fancied a swim – went in through the side door. Come in and join me?'

'No thanks, I'm full of toast. Maybe later though. And what do you mean, I'll need safety measures? You'll be here too.'

'Not for long though – I could drop off life's perch any day. I reckon I'm about ready. Like I said, I've had a good time, nice party and all, but it's time to leave.'

'Please don't start on that one again, Conrad.' Sara touched wood and crossed her fingers, just in case.

'OK. But hey, sure you won't come and swim with me?'

'While I still can, you mean?' she teased, reaching down to feel the water. It wasn't icy, but the solar heating hadn't really kicked in yet. 'Hmm . . . it's a bit cold. I don't think so.'

'Pity.' He grinned and flipped under the water. Surfacing again, he said, 'We don't often have the house to ourselves just now. And we'll be a long time dead. Quite soon in my case, like I said . . .' He had that sex-speculation look in his eyes – one she hadn't seen for a while. Sara felt mildly annoyed. What was he getting at? That the lack of recent sex was down to Cass having moved back in only a few days before? Hardly – the sex drought was surely all about him having taken to sleeping in the studio and only visiting what used to be their bedroom when he was looking for clean clothes.

And then she thought, hell, why not take chances when they come? Who was it said you should always make love as if it was for the last time? Because one day, as Conrad had hinted, it surely would be. The spring day was fabulous, they were lucky: alive, energetic, healthy and he was right . . . She kicked off her shoes and felt the sun-blasted heat of the stone terrace on her toes. She stripped off all her clothes quickly and jumped into the pool before the thought of the cold water changed her mind, her breath taken by the shock of the chill. Conrad swam alongside her and ran his fingers along the inside of her thigh, kissing the back of her neck.

'Your bed or mine? Or what about in here? Though I have to say,' he laughed, 'this water could be warmer!'

Sara took his hand and swam away, towing him with her

to the shallow end. She walked up the steps and looked back at him. 'OK, studio,' she said, collecting her clothes from the back of the chair, and quickly pulled her dress over her wet, cool body. Conrad followed her out of the pool, pulled her close against him and kissed her.

'I've missed this . . .' she murmured to him.

'Hi*iiii*! Thought I'd find you out here, gorgeous day like . . . Oh!' Sara's sister Lizzie had a voice that could slice tempered glass. 'Aha! What are you two up to?' She looked the naked Conrad up and down. 'Hmmm . . . I get it. Here . . .' She picked up a towel from the table and threw it to him. 'Cover up, Conrad. I'm a highly excitable woman.'

'Lizzie! How did you get in?' he asked her, idly drying his hair with the towel.

'Side gate. Does no one ever lock up around here? If you left gates open down in the far west, you'd find your mower and your garden table on offer at the nearest car boot sale before you'd blinked!'

'It was bin day. We have to leave it open for them,' Sara told her.

'So you two were skinny dipping! How romantic!' Lizzie squealed, hugging her sister. 'Ugh, you're all soggy still! Hope you don't mind me just turning up like this, Sara. It's just . . . we have a bit of a home crisis and I thought, well where better to sort it out than here with my nearest and only sister? It's Jasper. He doesn't want to

141

go to school any more. So, well, I don't want him skulking about at home doing nothing and pretending he's "finding himself", because that would involve lying in bed till past noon every day. He's decided he wants to paint and the obvious solution was, why not come here and stay with you for a while and he can see what life's like with a *real* artist?'

'Oh Lizzie! You're such a sweetie and you never change! Didn't think to phone first? Or email? You might have driven over two hundred miles just to find we'd gone off to Spain or something!'

'I *did* phone! I called last night from the Travelodge at Yeovilton – didn't Cassandra say? I told her we were on our way and she said it was fine!'

'Hey, it's all right. And it's *so* good to see you,' Sara reassured her, leading her into the house. 'Cass must have forgotten. She's got a lot on her mind, but you're here now . . . and – so where *is* Jasper?'

'Er . . . he came in the gate ahead of me, saw you and Conrad canoodling naked in the pool and bolted to sit in the car. He said you were "*sooo* like, *barrassin*" or words to that teenage effect. Such a privilege to get that many words out of a seventeen-year-old. I was quite shocked.'

'You didn't have any such scruples though, did you Lizzie? Were you hoping to catch us in flagrante?' Conrad laughed.

'Yes darling, in fact I wondered about joining in. I bet

you could still take us both on, Conrad. I remember one time in Ibiza back in '75, just before I had Tamsin. I was with Pablo and ooh, names escape me these days . . . was it Michael or Pierre . . . or possibly both?' Lizzie's eyes went dreamy and distant. Conrad took the chance to sidle out of the kitchen to go and get dressed, blowing Sara a regretful kiss as he went.

'Oh spare me, please! Your old-lover stories go on for hours and in too much detail!' Sara laughed at Lizzie. 'And of course Jas can stay for a bit. But only if he doesn't mind babies. Cassandra's moved in for a while with Charlie.'

'And . . . er . . . while I'm this side of the Tamar,' Lizzie went on hesitantly, 'would you mind very much if I stayed for a little teeny while as well? It wouldn't be for long . . . only until I can . . .'

'Oh Lizzie, not again!' Sara looked at her sister's face, which revealed something strongly resembling a hint of guilt. 'Don't tell me you've left Jack! How many husbands can a woman get through in one lifetime?'

'As many as will have me, darling,' Lizzie said. 'Though at my age it's certain to be a fast-diminishing number and they're usually other people's. I'll go and give Jasper the good news. If I can prise him out of the car and off his mobile, I'll get him to bring our stuff in. You are a darling, Sara, thanks so much for this. What did I ever do to deserve such a generous baby sister?'

★

'You're smiling,' Sara said to Conrad. He was still panting slightly. She put her fingers lightly over his heart and felt for a safe, steady rhythm. It was thumping a bit, unsurprisingly, but seemed regular enough. Would she always do this now after sex? Just to make sure that this wasn't going to be the final way out for him? People joked about men dying with a smile on their faces, but she couldn't even remotely see the amusement value here, not now.

'Why wouldn't I smile?' Conrad turned towards her. His blue eyes were bright and full of happiness. She wasn't going to comment on the recent scarcity of sex, not say anything to spoil the moment, something trite and whiny like 'it's been ages'. Even if it *was* rare, it was worth the wait. How, and here she thought of Marie again, how could new sex with even the most devastating stranger be better than this?

She felt tingly, floppy and as if she wouldn't be able to move for hours. She pulled the patchwork quilt over both their bodies and stared up through the sloping glass roof of the studio to where, far above, a plane was passing, leaving a skinny line of white across the blue. She imagined passengers on it, looking at the little electronic map on the monitor and thinking, oh, London's down there.

'This is like being really young again, way back when we first got together, isn't it?' she commented.

'What, leaving your sister and Jasper to settle in and sneaking down here for a quick one? Lucky they didn't follow!'

'Lizzie knew better. I'm sure she could tell, the way I quickly told her which rooms she and Jasper could have, practically threw the mugs of coffee at them, then scarpered. She knew all right,' Sara giggled. 'Just like my parents did that first time you came to stay in Devon, and we went out to the barn saying we were going to see if there were owls.'

'And you went back into the house with hay all over the back of your clothes. Not much of a giveaway, that!'

'Like I said, we were young then.'

'Well, *one* of us was young then,' he corrected her, laughing. 'You're now at the great age I was when we first met. Though . . .' he leaned over to her, softly kissing the edge of her mouth, 'you still seem nineteen sometimes. Especially at this moment, with your features all soft and full of love. I should paint you like this. If I could even begin to capture that look, I'd do it right now.'

He wasn't smiling any more. 'You look sad,' she said, stroking his face.

'No, I'm not sad. I'm just concentrating on what you look like,' he told her. 'If we could take one sight with us into the next life, it would be this one.'

'You're doing it again. The death thing,' she said, sitting

up abruptly. 'Don't talk like that, Conrad. Don't spoil the moment. You're not going anywhere, right? I don't want to have to hear you blathering on about heading for death for the next twenty years, OK?'

'Sara . . .'

'No! Just . . . *stop it*! You're frightening me – I'll start thinking you're going to do yourself in or something. Oh God, you're not planning to, are you? How cowardly would that be? You copping out and leaving us all? Promise me you won't even think about it!'

'All right,' he said, simply. 'I won't think about it.'

Sara snuggled against him again, feeling better. And yet . . . when she analysed exactly what he'd said, she couldn't quite make herself feel as comforted as she needed to be.

Art is making something out of nothing and then selling it.
(Frank Zappa)

'I'm going to put a No Vacancies sign in the window,' Sara told Marie, as she flung her bag on to her favourite sofa in the far corner of the staffroom. 'It's exhausting having so many people in the house, especially when one is a baby, another is a teenager and two are eternally squabbling sisters. Conrad is an absolute delight to live with by comparison, even considering his funny little ways and his peculiar hints that he's up to something weird and wonderful that might involve jumping off a high building.' She sent a quick mental plea to the president of the immortals here, warding off the fleeting possibility that she might have hit the spot with this thought.

'*All* men have funny little ways. Mike won't wear shoes in the house but never considers that leaving them right in front of the door, so you have to move them to open it, is *not* a sensible thing to do. And he polishes his Black & Decker gadgets as if they're heritage silver. Mad. So which are the squabbling sisters? Pandora and Cass, or you and Lizzie?' Marie asked, examining scarlet marks on her left wrist. She stroked her skin gently, smiling dreamily.

'Not me and Lizzie – we're past that, thank goodness, though I'm not saying she doesn't drive me nuts. She's ten years older than me – why do I still think this should make her a fully fledged grown-up? She'll *never* be grown-up! This is the third husband she's left – plus several of other people's . . . No, it's Conrad she picks little niggles with these days, not me. She thinks he's gone . . . what was it she said? Oh yes, "tame", that was the word she used. She thinks he should be out hell-raising like a "proper artist". I don't know quite what she means by that, but for some reason she's always had it in her head that painters should collectively go in for serious excess, like rock stars. He'd rather lie on the sofa and watch *Casualty*.'

'Doesn't she know that aged rock stars – well, the ones who aren't Keith Richards – mostly end up playing golf and taking up fishing?' Marie said. 'You can't get less "excess" than that.'

'Exactly. You tell her. I'll be right behind you.'

The two of them had the room to themselves so far. The rest of the teaching staff were out making the most of the lunch break or hadn't yet arrived, which wasn't surprising – the room wasn't a particularly inviting one. You wouldn't choose to spend unnecessary time in it. The walls were painted Institution Beige; tables and cupboards were left over from the days when the building had been a school, and the sofas and chairs should have been confined to a skip years before. Council resources didn't exactly run to redecoration or refurbishment for mere casual staff. But Marie had excitedly pleaded with Sara to come in especially early so she could, as she put it, Tell All. Sara wasn't entirely sure that 'all' was something she really wanted to hear, but Marie wasn't having any argument. Right now, she looked keyed up enough to explode, reminding Sara of schooldays when girls who'd lost their virginity would come in glowing with new knowledge and a desperate need to brag.

Sara was feeling a bit distracted. Ben had told her that he was coming into the college again this afternoon for more research into his *Guardian* piece. Much as she loved Conrad, she was surprised how strangely giddy she felt, anticipating seeing Ben again. This too reminded her of schooldays – had the boy she fancied really turned up at the school gate to meet her, or was he hoping to run into her much prettier best friend? The thought of seeing Ben made her smile uncontrollably, and gave her an inkling of how Marie must be feeling. Ridiculous. It was almost like having a silly teen crush on someone. This was something she definitely *wasn't* needing in her life. You don't do this at my age, she told herself as she pulled her attention back to Marie's newly tumultuous sex life, proof, if any was needed, that you *did* do crushes at their age.

'OK then – out with it, Marie.' Sara relented, filling the kettle and then looking through the cupboard for a couple of mugs that were the least cracked and stained. 'You've been smirking in that "dying to tell you" way ever since we got here. You'd better tell me . . . though how much detail I can cope with, I'm not sure! I take it things went all right with the flying Scotsman?'

'*All right?* That would be the understatement of the century!' Marie sighed, dropping heavily on to the sofa. Sara heard one of its last few springs give way. Poor sofa – could it take the strain of Marie's overexuberance?

'So how was the lunch?' Sara teased. 'Was Le Caprice as good as ever?'

'Lunch was fine. Lunch was lovely, what bit of it I could eat. Lust is wonderful stuff – such a brilliant appetite suppressant.'

'You should suggest it to WeightWatchers for their list of sure-fire diet tips,' Sara told her. 'Did he mention his wife, or was home life definitely off the menu? I always wondered if you just pretend they don't exist, those inconvenient real-life people.'

'We talked about books and films and things, but

absolutely *not* about our families and children and all that stuff that would make it *ordinary*. If you do that, it takes the romance out of it.'

'I'll bear it in mind in the unlikely event that I'll ever need the info! I'll know where to come for expert advice.' Sara poured boiling water on to the two tea bags, watching the sepia tones bleed darker and darker from the tea, enjoying the smoky swirl of colour. 'So – did the basque go down well?' she asked Marie.

'Oh *yes*! And so did Angus!' Marie closed her eyes, smiling ecstatically, remembering.

'Eeeuw! Stop right there – too much detail! I only meant . . . actually, I don't know what I meant. Did he appreciate the effort you'd made, is all, I suppose? Was he surprised when he found you were sort of *gift-wrapped*?'

'Surprised? Well not very, actually. We'd discussed it all in lots of detail by email. The airwaves or ether or whatever must have been sizzling! The nipple-rouging thing backfired slightly, though.'

'*What?*' Sara poured milk into the mugs. She suspected she should have sniffed at it first, checked it wasn't off. Too late now. She handed tea over to Marie and perched on the arm of the sofa, carefully in case it gave way, in a position where she could see if anyone came in to interrupt their conversation. It was hardly typical staffroom chat, after all. A bit of grumbling about various partners' thoughtlessness over birthday-present choices was usually about as personal as it got in here. Only the week before, there'd been a long discussion about why any man would imagine his partner would be thrilled to unwrap oven gloves.

'Angus had told me he likes really pink nipples,' Marie said, peering down her own low-cut top.

'It's OK, you don't need to show me . . . I'll imagine Bengal Rose from the gouache colour chart,' Sara laughed.

'Oh, I wasn't going to get them out, not in here!' Marie giggled. 'I was just thinking about what I did. Mine are a bit pale so I thought, well, I'd enhance them for the occasion, as it seemed to be a special request. So after you'd gone home when we'd been in Selfridges that day, I went into Space NK to have a look for something suitable. There I was, just browsing and trying a few shades of glossy blusher on the back of my hand, and this nice girl, about your Cassandra's age, started talking to me about skin tones and saying maybe I'd need this shade or that one. I didn't like to stop her and say, oh it's not for my face, I want to make my nipples pinker for my lover. I mean, you don't, do you? I wonder what she'd have thought if I *had* said it, though. Young people have no idea, do they? Like that sweet girl I bought the basque from. If they only knew . . .'

'So did it work? The blusher?'

'Oh no – you see that's the thing. I ended up with some lip gloss that was *exactly* the right shade for my mouth. Not at all right for my tits. He said it tasted funny too, like cheap sweets . . .'

'OK – enough again!' Sara held her hand up. 'So you'll be seeing him some more?'

'Oh yes!' Marie smiled. 'But I think possibly we'd better forget the handcuffs next time . . . they've made marks. Mike was asking what I'd done. I told him it was a bracelet. Which it was really, wasn't it? It wasn't exactly a lie.'

'No, Marie, it wasn't really a lie,' Sara reassured her. She felt a bit sad. Here she was, stuck between Marie's delight in her part-time lover and the deep, uncertain misery of Mike's reluctant suspicion. What to do? The sensible answer, of course, was *nothing*. And yet . . .

'Look, Marie . . . I saw Mike in the park yesterday and he asked me things about you. I probably should have phoned you immediately to warn you but . . . well, if I had, and he was around, he'd have twigged that it was because he'd spoken to me, and thought there was something in what he'd said.'

'*What?* What did he say?' Marie looked stricken, wide-eyed and scared. 'He can't possibly know about Angus! Did you . . . ?'

'Marie, of course I didn't say anything! I wouldn't! It's just he's noticed you're looking good and to be honest you are rather going round with a secretive smirk on your face! Look, I know you think he wouldn't notice you unless you were dressed in nothing but a B&Q tool belt, accessorized with chisels, but he's not entirely stupid, you know. Just . . . please, take care, won't you?'

'I will, I will, I promise. I don't want to hurt him, that would be the *very* worst thing. I absolutely don't want to lose him – the Angus thing isn't about *not* being with Mike,' Marie wailed. 'God, what have I done? Oh, I wish . . . !'

'Wish what? That you'd never got involved with Angus?'

'Oh Lord no! I just wish I didn't have the kind of stupid face that gave all my secrets away! How is an honest woman supposed to get away with a harmless spot of extra-marital?'

Sara laughed. 'Well forgive me for being boring here, but is an honest woman supposed to have extra-marital? And is it ever harmless?'

'Oh Sara, you just wait! If you really think it couldn't ever happen to you then you're tragically lacking in imagination!'

Jasper was a very quiet boy, Cassandra thought, but he was

comfortable in his silence and easy enough to be with. She could see him now, lying on the lawn under the willow tree way down the garden. His toe was twitching in time to something on his iPod and he didn't look as if he planned to move from this spot for some time to come. Cass needed to read some more of the Hardy, and had things to look up on the Internet. Charlie was awake and wanting to be entertained. He would only take so long of batting around the dangling duck that hung from his play centre. Pandora had gone out to try to find a local part-time job in a bar, and wouldn't be back for ages, especially if she started looking round the shops.

Lizzie had gone to visit some old friends in Chelsea and hinted that if things worked out, she might not even be back at all that night. Old people who'd been hippies seemed to have no second thoughts about sleeping with all and sundry, Cass reflected. Lizzie made no secret of what she called her running total. If anything, she boasted about it. Even at her age, she seemed to expect to add a few more victims to the list. Over supper the night before, she'd congratulated Cass on leaving Paul, but said she hoped it wasn't just because he slept around a bit. 'Young people should put it about. When else can they? You should do the same, darling,' was her advice. 'Get it out of your system while you're young, otherwise you'll be for-ever wondering what it was you missed out on.'

'You're still checking up on that, are you? Making sure *you* aren't missing out? God, it's sure taking a while!' Conrad had teased her. Poor Jasper, Cassandra thought now, as she looked at the long skinny boy-figure stretched out on the grass, no wonder he was silent. How many times must he have heard his own mum airily dismissing sexual fidelity as bourgeois, heard her declaring that the world was so much the brighter for a little light sexual adventure. No pressure then, Jas. The only way he could possibly rebel would be to stay stubbornly celibate.

'Jasper?' she called down the garden. No response. She picked up Charlie from his rug on the grass, where he was doing his best to learn how to crawl, and carried him down to the oblivious teenager.

'Jas?' She prodded his shoulder gently with her toe. Jasper jumped as if she'd clouted him with a hammer.

'Wha'? Ouch!' he grumbled, shading his eyes from the sun as he looked up at her.

'Sorry. I surprised you, OK, but I didn't hurt you. Don't overreact! I just need a small favour, Jas.'

He sat up and took the earplugs out. This, she thought, looked promising.

'What is it?' he asked, suspicious.

'Nothing too tricky. Just, would you mind taking care of Charlie for me for an hour? I've got uni work to do and I really need a bit of space to concentrate. Charlie likes going to the park . . . and there's swings and stuff. I know he's too young for them . . .'

'But you think I'm not?' Jasper grinned suddenly. Cass wondered if he looked like his father – she couldn't remember Lizzie's current husband, Jack, very well. He didn't much like leaving Cornwall. Lizzie said he considered the rest of England to be enemy territory. Then another thought crossed her mind: that's if Jack *was* Jasper's father. Old people – *soo* like *irresponsible*. She cuddled Charlie tighter to her.

'No! Charlie loves to look at other children and there'll be plenty of them there. They do this thing, babies, they give each other the evil eye when they pass in their prams. Checking each other out, you know?'

'Cool. Early infant warfare!' Jasper stood up and brushed grass off his jeans. 'Yeah OK. I'll take him out for you. Will he get, like, *hungry* or . . . ugh I don't have to do the nappy-change thing, do I?'

Cassandra laughed. 'No he's just been fed, changed, all that. He'll be no problem as long as he's got stuff to look at. No worries. Come on, I'll load him into the buggy for you.'

Ben must have forgotten. Or maybe saying he'd come in today and check out Sara's class had been just a casual, polite remark. It didn't matter, really it didn't. She wasn't really looking at the door every two minutes, she wasn't really uncomfortably conscious that her blood pressure was nowhere near its normal low level. He'd said he'd come and see how the students interacted for this piece he was writing, ask them what they got out of their time here. He hadn't had time last week when she'd seen him in the staffroom, said he had someone to meet at the station but would come back. Today. This afternoon. She'd been waiting for him and the class was well under way. Not that it mattered, really, though hadn't she chosen what she was going to wear with a lot more than the usual casual hurry? She had decided on a silky pink Toast dress with a deeper pink soft tulle lining, and a mink-coloured wrap top, loosely tied at the front. She was also wearing a delicate necklace of purple and tawny glass that Conrad had given her. She'd washed her hair that morning which meant it was a bit all-over-the-place, but it felt soft and silky against her neck. But otherwise, no extra effort. Definitely not.

She must, she thought, have a face far more discreet than Marie's, otherwise Marie, in the staffroom, would have seen something in her that would have given her plenty of cause for comment. I'm two-faced today, she thought to herself, completely two people. She thought fondly of Conrad, picturing him now seeking refuge from Lizzie and her endless reminiscing about her glory days in the late sixties. He'd be out on Petersham Meadows with Floss, listening to birdsong and trying not to let hay fever spoil the moment. Years ago, he'd predicted this time would come. 'One day you'll meet someone your own age, and you'll fall for him so thoroughly, so catastrophically, you'll wonder why you were ever with me,' he'd said. They'd been at the top of the Empire State Building at the time. She'd kissed him and laughed, dismissing his statement as mere attention-seeking, fishing for reassurance. It must have been ten years ago, when he was approaching sixty. Perhaps there was a ten-year age-wobbler thing that he got. That time it was the dread of another man, this time a flirtation with the notion of death.

'You see, I don't think fruit *can* be fire. Fruit has a chill to it. You don't get *hot fruit*. Fruit's mostly water. Or you could say air. And it grows out of the earth. Whatever it is, it's definitely not *fire*.' Pedantic Pete was finding fault with Melissa's still life. The class were working on the theme of Elements – any interpretation of this that they chose. Today's element was Fire, and several had brought a selection of items they wanted to paint; others were taking a more abstract approach. Cherry, who had her own determined agenda in this group, was ignoring the topic – as usual – and was steadily working on a large acrylic painting of her cousin's wedding from photos she'd pinned up all over her easel. The rest of them were keeping clear of her – too close an approach and she'd start on the story of how the pregnant chief bridesmaid had had to run outside halfway through the service for a wee in the graveyard.

Pamela Mottram was flamboyantly painting something in shades of vibrant pink while humming a tune that sounded vaguely operatic, and Melissa had assembled a still life of fruit but had spent most of the class time rearranging it on a plate, unable to make a decision about composition. She had eaten several of the strawberries and the rest were becoming squashy, juice flowing off the plate and on to the floor. She'd piled slices of peach on top, with blueberries over those, interspersed with mint leaves.

'I'm making it look like a real fire. The way the colours of the flames go, dark at the bottom, then paler and flickery with blue and green?' Melissa argued with Pete. 'Only I'm using fruit. It's ... it's ... *representational*,' she claimed triumphantly, looking to Sara for backup and pleased with herself for having thought of an end-of-argument term.

'Looks like half a friggin' trifle to me,' Pete grumbled, well beaten on syllable count, but otherwise unconvinced. 'You wanna pour some cream and custard on it and we can all have a bit.'

Sara stepped in to keep the peace. 'Hey, look, there's no need to argue over it! Melissa's had a really good, original idea. I love the way the colours are bleeding together, the way flames do, constantly changing . . .'

Lively debate was one thing, and to be encouraged, but downright personal criticism would thoroughly shake the confidence of someone as flaky as Melissa. Sara wondered how she'd managed to get out of the greengrocer's shop with a selection of fruit that pleased her. She must have been in there hours, dithering between blueberries and blackcurrants. Expensive selection, too . . . though now she came to think of it, Melissa had brought them in all jammed loosely into one carrier bag. Given her previous track record, possibly the goods had not actually been paid for. Or was that harsh?

Just as Sara was turning her attention to Pamela's efforts, the door behind her creaked open. Ben. At last! So . . . now what?

'Oh Ben! Hi – I'd forgotten you were coming!'

Now why had she said that? Such a lie! How stupid. How flustery, silly and girlish, and why had her heart rate rocketed?

'Good to see you again, Sara.' Ben came over. He was looking at her intently, and for a moment she wondered if he was going to kiss her. Just in a meeting-a-friend sort of way, but all the same . . . Sara was aware of sudden silence in the room and a dozen pairs of curious eyes of the collected members of Beginners Art staring at the two of them. She could see Pamela Mottram squinting across, shamelessly inquisitive. She had stopped painting to watch them, and, noting Pamela's keen-eared stillness, the others followed suit, making Sara feel as if she was on some kind of stage. Why were they staring? She'd told them he'd be coming and would want to talk to some of them. They hadn't taken this kind of keen interest at the time.

'You didn't come to visit me,' Ben said, as if Sara had seriously disappointed him. He was talking quietly – Pamela Mottram and Pedantic Pete glanced at each other and, suspicious of such intimacy, stepped closer, pretending to be appraising Melissa's work, yet again.

'I didn't know I was really expected to. I assumed the invitation was just a neighbourly throwaway remark!' she told him.

'I don't do throwaway,' he said. 'Have you got a car with you or can I drive you home after this? You could come and see what I've done to your friend Alma's cottage, tell me if you think I've improved it or wrecked it. I make very good tea and I can promise you Jaffa cakes.'

'Ah . . . well there's an offer I can't refuse. OK then, I'd love to, though I have got my car and a bit of clearing up to do here after the class, so shall I just turn up as soon as I get finished? I've got a house full of people to go home to . . . it would be good to have a breathing space between this and them.'

This was not a date. Not that she wanted one – she was married and old(ish), not a teenager. Nor was she as sex-crazed as her sister. All the same, she felt skittish and happy. Then she remembered why he was here. It wasn't about her, not at all.

'You must come and meet Pamela Mottram.' She led him across the classroom to where Pamela was smirking with a disturbing knowingness. 'Pamela is very much a fixture of this college. Just what you need for your *Guardian* article, I should think. The class is working on a series about the elements . . . today's is fire.'

'Pamela, this is Ben, Ben Stretton. He'd like to talk to you about the social aspect of this place, how the students interact, that sort of thing.'

'Hello Pamela,' he said, smiling at her and looking at her energetic rendition of pink spikes on the paper. 'Oh, and I like that. It's . . . er . . .' He hesitated, looking at Sara rather desperately, and she could see he felt like Prince Charles faced during a gallery visit with some incomprehensible exhibit. In this case, though, she couldn't rescue him. Pamela's interpretations of themes could take any form. One could only take a wild guess. 'It looks like arrows? Or, er . . .' He was evidently struggling.

'Penises!' Pamela boomed. 'They're penises. The fire of passion! They're Aflame with Desire!'

'Right . . . er . . . great!'

★

'No. No she doesn't want to speak to you, she's doing some work. She said if you phoned the house to tell you to get lost.' Pandora lay on the purple sofa, flicking between TV channels while very much enjoying giving her sister's boyfriend a hard time. There was something so deeply satisfying about passing on someone else's fury. It saved you having to work up plenty of your own, but at the same time maddened the other person to a delightful degree. She could hear the desperation in Paul's voice. It was a good voice, lazy, articulate and, what was that line in *The Great Gatsby* that she'd recently read? Yes that was it: his voice was full of money.

She'd met Paul a few times, and had hung out with him the day Charlie had been born when they were all up at the hospital when Cass was in labour and alternating between shrieking that no, of course she didn't want drugs – she was having Natural Childbirth, wasn't she – and then minutes later squealing for an epidural. Paul had been pretty calm, quite capable and unflapping until Charlie was actually born, then he'd gone sweetly tearful and delighted and the way he'd been hugging Cass when all the parents and Pandora went in to see them had made them all feel very aaaaaah, lovely. Perhaps she was being unfair to him now, because she hadn't actually got any kind of problem with him. This was Cass's gig. Panda was only doing what she'd been asked to do.

Would anyone ever again be like this with her, she now wondered. It was a while since she'd had someone being one hundred per cent loving towards her, desperate to see her. Months, a year nearly, had passed since Ollie had gone travelling, saying he'd only be a couple of months, and leaving the words 'and then when I get back . . .' hanging in the air with the rest of the future not quite promised. He was never coming back now. The blonde girl in Toronto had a fabulous flat, fabulous body. Panda had seen the Facebook pics, read the comment tags and the between-the-lines messages in the way they looked together, all partied out and cuddly and loving: Ollie had new friends, a new life, a new woman. 'Over' was the big word that hadn't yet been said, but Pandora was no idiot. She and Ollie were, no question, an ex-relationship.

'Well if she won't talk to me, how can I sort it out with her? She's blocked me from her mobile and her emails; what am I supposed to do?'

'I don't know, Paul. Can't you just write an old-fashioned letter and say, "Hey Charlie is my baby too and I've got rights" or something?'

'I've got responsibilities as much as rights,' Paul said. 'More than, even.' Pandora was surprised and impressed by this. Did Cass have the first clue how lucky she was? What an idiot of a sister. Work it out with him, girl, why don't you.

'Can I talk to you about it? And about how to get through to her mad brain?' Paul asked. He sounded so sad, poor boy. Well, *boy*, Pandora thought, he was her own age. But boys mature so much more slowly, which meant that in *real terms*, a bit like dog years or something, he was way younger, surely, barely mid-teens.

'You *are* talking to me,' she said, feeling a bit more sympathetic. 'I really don't know what to say to you, though. All I know is what I've just told you. She hasn't got anything to say to you, and if you called I was to tell you to go away. She's doing some college work.'

'No, I mean talk to you properly. Like, face to face? Just about Cass and Charlie and what to do. You're her sister; you know her best of anyone. Please? I could come and meet you in a bar somewhere?'

There was a long silence while Pandora worked out what was the best thing to do. If she said no, that would be yet more rejection. He'd give up eventually, feel there was no chance. Cass was only being moody and idiotic. She shouldn't slam the door shut on him permanently, not when there was a child involved.

'OK,' Pandora heard herself agreeing. 'Tomorrow? Maybe the day after? I'll meet you at All Bar One. But if you ever tell Cass . . .'

'I won't tell Cass. This is just between you and me, promise. And . . . Pandora?'

'What?'

'Just, you know . . . like, cheers for this?'

Desire is the very essence of man.
(Benedict de Spinoza)

Sara hadn't had the best afternoon's teaching; or rather, it could be argued that her class hadn't had the top value in terms of an afternoon's learning. Luckily she hadn't needed to say much, because the class members, for once, seemed to be thoroughly focused and had a pretty clear idea of what they were doing. The room was peaceful, with them all quietly absorbed. All she'd had to do was a lot of vague wandering about in a daze, passing the odd unhelpful comment to students who looked more than a little surprised to be interrupted. Ben was still on the premises, and had taken Melissa and Pamela out to the students' canteen to talk to them about what they'd gained in terms of friends from the college. Sara pictured him buying them tea and macaroons, while the rest of the class members painted themselves into a near stupor.

The students could tell that Sara was mentally elsewhere. Every now and then she'd catch one of them staring at her with a wondering look. She felt bad about her lack of concentration, at one point absent-mindedly telling Pete the Pedant that she thought his rather ambitious semi-abstract rendition of the Great Fire of London really did capture the essence of an erupting volcano.

'It was me doing the volcano, not him,' grouched Evelyn, a disgruntled woman with a look of the late Thora Hird, who smelled slightly of Scotch and rarely came out from behind her easel to make any comment in the class at all.

'Sorry . . . of course it is. Sorry.' Well, it was an easy mistake – it was tricky, keeping up with the class members' varying styles. To their credit, they all had their own arty quirks and preferences, but sometimes, especially with the more bizarrely abstract among them, it was like being in an infant class where you had to smile and say, 'Ooh lovely . . . and that is . . . ?' with the risk that they'd be horribly affronted that you couldn't immediately identify, say, Windsor Castle painted from directly over-head, or the rocks off Land's End. Sara looked at her watch, looked at the door, willed the time away. At last, close to the end of session time, Melissa and Pamela returned.

'He says to tell you he'll see you there.' Pamela twinkled

at her as the students collected their belongings together and drifted homewards. 'Nice man, would suit you very well,' she added.

'I don't need a man,' Sara laughed. 'I've got a husband!'

'All the more reason. Every wife should keep a spare,' Pamela insisted. 'Life is too dull without someone slightly forbidden as a bit of extra; someone to feel a passion for.'

'Aren't you supposed to feel that for your own partner?' Sara asked her. 'Isn't that the point of being with them?'

Only the two of them were left in the classroom now. Melissa turned and waved goodbye from the doorway. She was munching a slice of peach from her still life, looking pleased with her afternoon's efforts. 'Thanks Sara!' she called. 'See you next time!'

Sara waved to her, smiling. 'You did really well today, Melissa! It was such a great idea!'

Pamela picked up her bag. 'That shivery passion is a bit exhausting on a full-time basis,' she told Sara. 'That's why God decreed that it's better kept for off the domestic premises. Over the years I've always had someone I've had a fancy for; most women do. Even when it was just the man I used to see at the bus stop in the mornings, on the way to work. When he was there, my heart used to beat a bit faster. When he wasn't, I was unsettled till at least lunchtime. Whether you do anything about it that would give your marriage vows a shake-up is down to you.

Doesn't stop you feeling that way. Trouble is, most folks don't admit it, and so continues the myth of happy-ever-after in some fairy-tale dreamworld. But if you've got someone else in your head now and then, the one you're actually with gets the benefit of your imaginings, if you see what I mean.'

'Did you do anything about the bus-stop man?' Sara asked her. Was that impertinent, she wondered. Pamela wasn't of a generation that was used to that kind of talk, although, come to think of it, she couldn't be much older than Conrad.

Pamela laughed. 'Heavens no! We never so much as spoke! That wasn't the point, you see! I'll see you next time. And whatever you do, have a bloody good time; remember, you'll be a long time dead.'

It wasn't easy, this ending-your-life malarkey. Sara must never, ever suspect that he was in on his own death. She'd be devastated. With that in mind, and in the interests of being certain the life-insurance people wouldn't wriggle out of paying top whack to Sara, Conrad needed to think of some way of dying that wouldn't look even remotely like suicide. The grasping bastards wouldn't hand over a cent if even a hint of self-destruction came up.

He practised scaring himself at least halfway to death, driving much too fast down the M4 on his way back from a visit to Gerry, his publicity-mad agent, and considered a few possibilities along the way. Crashing the car into a concrete pillar could go badly wrong, might not result in instant oblivion and could well hurt very, very badly. He wasn't good with pain. Even a mildly sprained ankle once had him whimpering in agony. One of the things he most dreaded each autumn was the annual flu shot. Having the cute young practice nurse lewdly smirking 'Just a little prick' at him didn't offset the faintness and nausea he felt when faced with a hypodermic. He had managed in his long life never to have broken a bone, and didn't want to be hauled crushed and shattered from his car by well-meaning paramedics who weren't allowed to give him more than the minimum dose of painkiller in the interests of saving the NHS a few quid.

It had been an odd lunch. Well, any business lunch in-adequately fuelled by alcohol was odd, really. He should have gone by train, then he could have got roundly drunk and blanked out a lot of Gerry's incessant hectoring. Gerry was keen for him to do every publicity opportunity that came up. Well, he would be, wouldn't he? It made him look good, kept the buzz going with collectors and would big him up to newer potential clients, get him back in style and see off all those Young British Artists who went everywhere clutching a MacBook Air and a look of Hoxton hip.

A lot of possible press was coming up, with this birth-day. Did the posher press really have nothing better to publish than look-backs over a painter's life work? How many Day In The Life and In My Studio pieces could these damn fools need? And how undignified was it that Gerry was touting for the slots like a media tart? Gerry had been busy at the gallery, updating the website to make sure this landmark birthday was included, circulating press releases to all and sundry. Too many had responded positively. At this rate the house would be a traffic jam of photo shoots and keen young journos knocking into each other. Sara was good with them – forever patient.

She'd make an excellent widow, he thought fondly. She'd just get on with it, all calm and capable, and even when she cried, she'd do it prettily. She always had. She looked like a sweet Madonna when she wept, tragic and still with pearly tears running tidily down her pale, delicate face. The funeral would run like Mussolini's rail-ways; Pandora would design beautiful invitations to the memorial service and Cassandra would howl and wail very gratifyingly for days and days. All right, it was a shocking piece of bailing-out on them all, but it would have to be done if they were to be saved a dismal future of passing him round to be cared for and mopped and wiped. If they could see that ahead, they'd thank him for setting them free from it. All he saw these days were people that bit older than him, once magnificent, energetic, capable men falling to pieces, crumbling like overdried biscuits. Decrepitude was waiting like a mugger, ready to nab his vitality, any minute. The most cruel would be the desiccation of intellect. That was something else he couldn't bear – to see once scathing minds become limp and formless.

'I feel like you've been sending out sodding begging letters to all these press oiks,' Conrad grumbled to Gerry over the Dove and Olive's hefty steak pie. 'I don't *want* all this fuss. I've sold enough. Painted enough. I've quit. I'm well past normal retirement age, for heaven's sake. Can't I stop now and have some peace? In fact can't I just Rest In Peace in the death sense? Time to go while the going's good, as it were?'

'Bollocks.' Gerry wouldn't have it – which was only to be expected in a man who had made a large chunk of his gallery earnings from Conrad over the years. 'What do you want peace for? Dead or alive? What would you do with it? Artists don't retire. Look at Freud. Is he being all bonhomie in a golf club? No. Bacon? Never stopped. Look at Peter Blake. Committed, absorbed, fresh, still got something to say. The way you're talking, anyone would think it was just a *job*.'

'It *is* a job like any other. Just because everyone thinks it's your "calling", and it takes a bit of something that not everyone's got, it doesn't mean it ain't work.' Conrad could hear himself sounding stubborn, childlike. 'And it definitely becomes *just* a job when you have to be nagged into doing it. The minute you think, "Shit, I'd rather stay in bed," that's the end. I can pay the bills with what I've earned, what I *still* earn from print sales and copyright licensing. And I *might* just take up golf.'

'Now I know you're taking the piss,' Gerry sniggered. '*You* on a golf course? I think not. You wouldn't understand the rules, or the concept that you have to play the eighth hole after the seventh but before the ninth. You'd build sandcastles in a bunker. But what I'm saying here is if you don't get your finger out now, the next bit of press you'll get will be your sodding obituary! You don't want that, now do you? You want to keep going, have the buggers stocking up your wares against the day you snuff it and they can stick another zero on the value of their investment.'

'And now you're talking like a stockbroker,' Conrad grouched. 'If you think I'm going to keep going like some kind of factory, just so some grasping bastards can make a fortune after I've snuffed it . . .'

'Ha! Changed your tune there, haven't you? A second ago you were saying it's "just a job". Now you're being all precious. Can't have it both ways, matey.'

It had crossed Conrad's mind, even as he heard Gerry

nagging on, that the view from this pub garden was well worth the trip, if nothing else. The strange non-perspective of the softly rounded Oxfordshire hills, the spring-vivid shades of green on the varying ripening levels of the rape fields, interspersed here and there with silver-leaved crops of poppies. How many dead bodies did these perfect colours hide, he found himself wondering. Not people – though possibly *some* people – but rats and rabbits, mice and moles. If he were to paint part of this scene, he'd put them in. They wouldn't be the first thing you'd see . . . it would be the rotting, fetid truth under nature's pretty skirts. A favourite theme of his. Here he was – he surprised himself – thinking about working, in spite of what he'd decided. How inconvenient. He stubbed the last centimetre of cigarette out and tried to dismiss creative thinking.

'Dead birds,' he said to Gerry. 'Why is it you never see any dead birds unless they've either fallen from a nest or a cat's dragging one in? Why isn't the woodland floor covered in them? Is it foxes, do you think? Carrion?'

'*What?*' Gerry looked despairing.

'Nothing, just thinking aloud. Look – I really don't mind about the obituary thing. Soon would be fine.' Conrad shrugged, lighting another Gauloise. 'In fact, I might just write it myself. That way I make sure I get to say what I want them to print and it's one thing less for

Sara to have to deal with when the time comes. I hate to think what the *Telegraph* will come up with.'

'Good God, man, don't be ridiculous! Look at you! A picture of rude blooming health. Though if you're seriously back on smoking the vile weed it won't help your chances of making the century.'

'I have *no* intention *at all* of making the century, as you put it. Far from it,' Conrad snapped. 'And that's another good reason for writing your own obituary. You don't get God-awful phrases like "he had a good innings".'

'You are being *totally* ridiculous,' Gerry scolded. 'I think the posh papers can do better than that, don't you?'

Now, racing at scare speed along the M4, Conrad wished he'd bought a flimsier car. This Mercedes was fully equipped with every airbag, crumple zone, side padding and roll bar that the safety wallahs could chuck in. Very German tank, he thought. How hard would he have to hit something in it to guarantee instant and painless oblivion? And suppose it bounced off a concrete pillar and took out a family saloon containing . . . a family? No – too dreadful to contemplate. This was to be his ending, and his alone. He couldn't risk it. He would have to think of something else.

The most direct route to Ben's cottage took Sara past her own house. The most sensible thing to do would be to leave the car in her driveway, say a quick hello to whichever family members were in residence, collect Floss and walk her the half-mile along the towpath. Instead, she found herself parking at the corner of her road out of sight of all windows and scurrying down the alleyway to the riverbank, almost holding her breath and with her heart thumping as if she was on a clandestine mission. For heaven's sake, why? she asked herself as she strolled at a more relaxed pace beside the water. What on earth was all the secrecy about? She'd met someone she liked, that was all. A friend; someone she'd admit she fancied a teeny bit. According to Pamela Mottram, nothing could be more ordinary or normal. But Sara had gone off to the cloak-room after she'd made sure the studio was tidied. She'd brushed her teeth. As she'd looked in the mirror and applied lip gloss, brushed her hair, sprayed on perfume, she thought, what kind of meeting was she expecting today that needed scrubbed teeth? How, overnight, had she turned into the kind of woman who kept a Muji miniature toothbrush and paste in her handbag? She'd picked up that little trick from Marie, who said you should always go out prepared for anything. Sara kept telling her-self that the 'anything' she was going out for definitely wasn't something that needed preparing for. It didn't stop the adrenalin whizzing about, though.

Ben was in the long front garden of the pink cottage,

cutting flyaway tendrils from a rampant jasmine that surrounded the door frame. 'Aha – at last!' he said. 'I'd almost given up on you. You're lucky I didn't eat all the Jaffa cakes.'

'Sorry – I couldn't get away any quicker. The class left a hell of a mess of paint in the sink and . . . well, one of them wanted to chat a bit.'

'You smell nice,' he said, leaning close to her. 'Clarins Eau Dynamisante?'

'I'm impressed! You know it well?' she asked, following him into the house. The front door opened into a white-painted sitting room. A huge blue sofa occupied the far wall and three remote controls for a selection of steely gadgets were lying on the arm. The fireplace had a glass-fronted woodburning stove with a neat pile of logs on each side of it. She thought of Stuart and his wood deliveries. If Ben needed a supplier, perhaps she could sort out the contact for him.

'Yes – my daughter wore that scent for a while.'

Ah. A daughter. With a daughter, as a set, tended to come a wife. And there, presumably, she was: on top of a hyper-shiny black lacquer piano, in a photo frame, pictured on the deck of a sailing boat with a pair of teenagers, one boy, one girl. She was pretty: smooth tanned skin, big straight teeth, laughing face and long dark hair, scooped up and loosely clipped. Wisps of it fluttered round her face. She looked quite young, no make-up, one of those slim, fine-boned sorts who would never get jowly or have upper-arm qualms about buying a strappy party frock. Sara was willing to bet the woman was also quite tall and she felt immediately short, round and inelegant in her vintage fabrics and ditzy too-young tie-front cardigan.

'Is this your daughter?' She pointed to the crop-haired blonde teenager in the photo.

'That's Abigail. Couple of years ago now, actually. About the time we were talking about a divorce.'

'Divorce? From . . .' Sara's finger hovered over the smiling woman.

'Yep – that's my wife. Caro.' He was standing just behind her, looking at the photo over her shoulder. She could feel body warmth and moved away a little, conscious of an urge to do the opposite.

'We're still on good terms,' he continued. 'Well, as you can see from the photo. We'd been separated for a while but we'd still take the kids sailing together now and then. You get used to how you sail the boat together, you know? Who pulls which ropes. Which side of the boat . . .'

'Yes, I get the idea,' Sara interrupted. She couldn't look at the woman any more. This sounded too intimate. Were they really talking about boats or . . . She then said, as the two of them moved towards the kitchen, 'It's like in *High*

Society, where Tracy's yacht is a kind of metaphor for their sex life.'

Ben laughed. 'No! Definitely not! I meant it literally about the boat. God no, our sex life wasn't on at that point. Well, together it wasn't anyway. Caro was having a fine old time with her new man. They'd practically moved into the Oxford Malmaison.'

'I was talking about the film, not your . . . Oh never mind . . . !' Sara felt flustered. Why on earth had she said all that? Mad.

The kitchen had been extended sideways so what would have been a long narrow galley was a big square with a scratched old oak table by French doors at the far end, looking out over a tiny back garden leading to a white-painted brick wall with rows of shelves that held rows of pots full of seedlings.

'What are you growing out there?' Sara asked, keen suddenly to get away from the topic of spouses and sex. She was, obviously, just here as a friend. This was just tea and Jaffa cakes. Ben didn't look as if he minded too much about the Malmaison business, but then he had said it was over. He switched on the kettle, found mugs in a cupboard, tea bags. He had a massive brushed-steel fridge, too big for the kitchen really, as if it was something he'd fought to get custody of in the split-up and was determined to hang on to. What on earth did a lone man fill it with? She heard a clink of glass as he closed its door and decided it probably contained bottles of beer and just-in-case champagne.

'I'm growing morning glory and nasturtiums,' Ben told her. 'Climbing stuff; but I don't want them to climb, I want them to hang down the wall and cover it.'

'Oh I do that!' Sara said. 'I've got a big trough hanging on a wall over the pool and I plant it up with nasturtiums every summer. Looks great!'

'Pool?' Ben looked at her. 'Swimming or fish?'

Sara wished she hadn't said anything. Only one house in the area had a garden big enough for a swimming pool. And everyone knew whose house that was. And today she wasn't being 'wife of'; she was being Sara McKinley. Not quite single Sara, just not quite *married* Sara.

'Oh you know, just a regular garden-type pool.' She shrugged.

'Oh, *that* sort. Frogs and fountains, right? OK, let's go . . .' Ben had a mug of tea in each hand. 'You bring the biccies.'

For a mad giddy moment, Sara half expected him to turn left up the open-tread staircase . . . but of course he went back through the open front door to the lush garden and the pink-painted bench and table that Alma had left behind when she'd moved.

'Alma said the furniture out here belonged here,' Ben

explained as he moved a big pot of thyme to the floor beside the bench. 'She said she'd painted it the same colour as the house and it had all sort of taken root, like trees. And she also told me that in the sheltered accommodation where she was going there were always more than enough places to sit. Benches all over the place, were her exact words.'

'She said that to me too!' Sara told him. 'Did she also mention that every last one of them has a commemorative plaque screwed to the back of it, so if you were out for a walk you couldn't sit down without being reminded how close you were to death?'

'She did. But she also said she didn't mind really, that death cosied up and became your friend when you got past eighty-five. I wonder if that's true? I think, hey when I'm past fifty-five, will something happen that means I'll be able to freewheel contentedly to the end or will I just go on forever feeling as if I'm seventeen?'

Sara sipped her tea. It had a slightly smoky flavour. This should be the moment when she could say that she lived with a man who was many years past fifty-five and he didn't seem any different from how he'd been when she'd first met him – or at least not till recently, when he'd clearly had something death-like quite fixed in his mind . . . She decided not to mention Conrad. Today she was, as she'd reminded herself earlier, just *herself*. And it did feel good.

'I think some people have an age at which they're happily stuck. Like those women you see who you can just tell peaked at their best in, say, 1970, and they'll go on with too-long hair, wearing hippy beads and weeds till they drop dead,' she told him. 'I walk past shop doorways that mirror my reflection back and I sometimes think, good grief, who's that middle-aged woman? I don't know her. I'm not seventeen though, in here,' she tapped her head, 'I'm in my twenties or so.'

'You do have a very young look. Like someone who is expecting lots of adventures in life still, not as if most of them have already happened.'

Sara laughed. 'And that's good, is it? To be still expecting so much?'

'Well it can't be bad! Better than thinking it's all over! Like I said, you've got that youthful, art-school aura. So . . . what do you paint? I take it you do, not just teach it?'

'Well . . . I *did*, but not so much any more. I used to paint quite naive scenes, landscapes, events, very bright and colourful stuff.'

'I'd have guessed that! I don't see you with bland water-colours, somehow.'

'Oh but watercolours don't have to be bland! Look at Dufy, for instance. But anyway, I used to exhibit quite a lot but not in a huge way.'

'Sold much?'

'Oh yes – and for cards and posters and things. It just faded out really, though lately I've been thinking of doing more again. Exhibiting is all very much fun, you have a jolly party and everyone thinks you're wonderful for a couple of ego-boosting days, but there aren't many things more depressing than having to go and collect the unsold stuff, the leftovers. And in the end, you've got a big collection of framed work that you think, oh is it worth giving it one more outing, only for it not to sell again. You wonder if you're just not good enough. It's hard not to think of the unsold work as useless rejects.'

'But it might sell, somewhere else, different people.'

'Yes, I know, and it often does. It's just chance. I should have gone the corporate route really, paintings for hotels and all that. But my style's a bit way out, a bit naive. I think it all ground to a halt when I had thirty paintings ready for quite a good exhibition in Bath. The night before delivery, the gallery had a fire and it was all cancelled – so I was left with this big stash of work and nowhere for it to go. The momentum kind of . . . vanished. I probably thought, hey it's a sign! Very immature, you'll probably think.'

'Well, not *immature* . . .' he teased. 'A tad pessimistic, perhaps! My sister's opening a gallery, up in Notting

Hill. Perhaps she could persuade you to drag your collection out and give it another airing?'

'You haven't a clue if they're up to standard!'

He smiled. 'Oh I don't know . . . there's something about you; call it style. Personal style, not painting style – but there's sure to be a crossover. Do you have a website?'

'No – but the photos are all on a CD.'

'May I see them? Would you be interested in gallery space?'

Sara felt flattered, even though she knew he was laying it on a bit thick. How could he possibly have a clue she was any better than an average Sunday painter? OK, so she was an art teacher. But she taught uncritical amateurs and enthusiasts. The college was hardly Central St Martins. She had to admit, though, that possibly because of her student Melissa's enthusiasm, or maybe it was the idea of escaping the house full of people, lately she *had* sometimes craved the feel of a paintbrush, the exciting milky blurring of colours on paper. She could see herself reclaiming the ancient scratched table that she used to occupy at the far end of Conrad's studio.

The late afternoon sun had made Sara feel lazy and settled. It must be getting late, she realized. There were people at home who would be wondering where she was.

'Single?' Ben suddenly asked.

Sara looked at him sharply. 'Are we still talking about

what's in my head, like the virtual-age thing?' she asked, putting off the moment of admitting the truth.

'Real life,' he said quietly. He was very close. Feathery eyelashes.

'No,' she smiled. 'No, I'm married.' She was surprised how reluctant she'd felt to say it. As if the statement ended something that hadn't even started. And of course it hadn't, had it?

'Right.' He said nothing for a moment, looking as if he was doing some intense thinking. She waited for him to speak.

'Sara?' He looked very serious, suddenly. She felt her insides go tight. What was going on here?

'Yes?'

'Sara – I just want to ask you . . . Would you like the last Jaffa cake?'

Jasper had pushed Charlie's buggy in a long circuit of the town, which had been pretty useful for finding out what was where in this place. He'd found some pubs that looked lively enough: not the dark one with all the vintage fringed lampshades and purple velvet sofas. That was too much like home. His mother claimed she was going for the Biba Era look (whatever that was), but he just found it dusty, joss-sticky and gloomy. That bar would surely be full of after-office geezers in suits by six thirty every night, but there were some scuzzier pubs that looked like students hung out in them. According to the chalkboard outside one of them, bands played three nights a week, although one of those nights was advertised as Goth Night, so he'd probably avoid that.

He'd found plenty of fast-food places, too, which made him feel excitedly urban but in a slightly shaming way. It was the thrill of the unfamiliar. You had to go twenty miles to find the nearest McDonald's down where he lived, and you got your pizzas from Tesco, not brought round to you on a bike. This was definitely something he'd keep to himself. His sun-streaked surf-boy hair and clothes would be fine; the look still defined you as cool enough (just), but he had an idea that expressing delight at the possibility of Kentucky Fried Chicken or a choice of several venues for iffy pizzas would one day get him surrounded by mocking thugs, all pointing the finger and shouting 'Hick!' at him. He didn't want to get beaten up just because he'd never before bought a sandwich from Subway.

Charlie was asleep now. Jasper hoped that was all right. He didn't know anything about babies and wondered if Charlie was sleeping because he was bored. He'd liked the park. Jasper had got him out of the buggy and sat on a swing with him, keeping it low and gentle, and Charlie had seemed to love it. Then he'd taken him down the slide, but a mother with three screamy brats had given him a bollocking and told him he was being irresponsible and anyway didn't he know the playground was for the under-twelves? He hadn't argued. He could have picked one, pointed out that Charlie was clearly under twelve but at his age needed just that little bit of help to make the most of the facilities, and who would deny him that? He'd just smiled instead, trying to win her over with calm silence and the kind of mad grin that Steve McQueen aimed at the camp guards in *The Great Escape*. It hadn't worked in the charm sense, but it got her off his case. The mother had gathered up her children very fast and raced across the park with them to the café, where she sat on a bench and glared at him till he put Charlie back in the buggy and wheeled him out of the play area.

Jasper had taken the little road down by the church and was alongside the river again. If he followed the towpath here, he'd get back to the house, no problem. Cassandra would be pleased. He'd kept her baby out a good long while and he hoped she'd be happy about that. She hadn't called him, so she must be. He checked his mobile. Nearly six o'clock.

He passed the pub and was coming to the row of cottages where there was . . . ah. Something told him to slow down. If asked later, he wouldn't be able to say what it was that had made him stop and wait. Well . . . it might be something to do with his aunt Sara kissing the man she was with. It wasn't a real kiss, nothing like tongues or sexual intent or any of that stuff you *really* don't want to think about the olds doing . . . Even though his mother and Jack were forever going on about sex, somehow you just had to do a mental hands-over-the-ears number and pretend it couldn't happen to anyone over thirty (and even thirty was pushing it, he admitted to himself).

Jasper slowed up and lurked behind a chestnut tree, hoping nothing would happen next that he'd really prefer not to see, yet unable to stop watching. He'd clocked that the man had his hand on Sara's body – about hip level, intimate enough but nothing you could say was totally out of order. It was just a goodbye kiss, bit of a clinch/ hug-type thing, and the moment passed really quickly. Then she turned away and walked towards the gate. It was, if he analysed it, no more than his mum and her women friends did, just a mutual quick brush of mouth on skin, but the way she smiled as she came out of the gate, well that was something else.

Jasper waited, moving further into the foliage. Sara walked off along the river, going pretty fast, but he was taller, faster. He could catch her easily. He could even call out – she'd wait for him. But then they'd have to make conversation for the next half-mile . . . Jas turned the buggy around and walked back to where a side lane led up to the main road that ran parallel to the river. Better this way, he thought. Then by the time he got home, Sara might have done something about that loved-up look on her face. God, was she just like his own mother? Staying here was supposed to be a rest from all that. This sex-obsession stuff, it must run in the family.

Love is a game that two can play and both win.
(Eva Gabor)

Sara was up before everyone else, showered and dressed before seven, leaving Conrad to sprawl starfish-style across the bed on his back and enjoy some extra snoring time without her being there to nudge him and make him turn on his side to stop. No wonder he'd liked sleeping in the studio, it must have had a lot to do with not being elbowed sharply in the ribs at three in the morning, she thought as she brushed her hair and watched him, by way of the mirror, being blissfully unconscious and flickering slightly like a dreaming cat.

It wasn't about avoiding sex after all, it seemed. Not if the night before was anything to go by. She smiled to her reflection at the memory of a fast and deeply pleasurable bout of passion that she'd initiated and in which he'd been more than happy to participate. If thoughts of death were really on Conrad's mind, he seemed to have suddenly worked out that there were mortal pleasures he had to make the most of while they were available. And it was so lovely to have him back in this bed with her. She had hated being alone. Having it to herself used to be a bit of a luxury, the times when he went away to paint. But when your life partner *chose* to sleep somewhere else rather than it being a necessity, it was like being abandoned. Even though the weather was now early-summer warm, there was a definite chill to a huge bed when you were the only one in it.

The house, these days, only seemed to be properly hers at this silent time of the day and Sara treasured her hour or two of peace when she could read the paper before Pandora nabbed the crossword, and drink plenty of wake-up coffee uninterrupted. But as she went down the stairs today she could see the first traces of all the clutter that resulted from too many people occupying the place. It was like visiting a wonderful beach and finding, as you approached, that it had shocking quantities of washed-up rubbish hidden among the dunes and rocks. It wasn't a small house, by any means. Upstairs had four bedrooms (plus another which had become an office and contained no bed) and three bathrooms, Sara and Conrad's room being across the stairwell, apart from the rest, linked by a metal walkway, like a bridge. Despite its size, the essentially open aspect of much of the ground floor meant that everything that wasn't where she wanted it to be was exposed to general view the whole time.

Since Cassandra had gone to university and Pandora had lived in her grimy but arty East End bedsit, Sara had become used to the house having the sleek, junk-free adults-only look that its architect had intended for it, and which meant minimum time spent tidying up. She liked knowing that books she'd put on the shelves would be where she'd left them. That her tall glass vases of pieces of twig and long-stemmed agapanthus wouldn't be tipped over by a teenager (Jasper) who turned round carelessly while wearing a rucksack – as had happened the day before. It wasn't that she wanted to sit around posing in something that resembled a swanky, sterile furniture gallery, but she could do with not being the only one who picked up the heedlessly scattered possessions from all over the place.

Why were they all so oblivious to the concept of a certain amount of order? She'd long ago lived through the stage where small children hurled their toys at random. Everyone in this house should have grown out of that by now, apart from Charlie, who hadn't even reached it. And yet how quickly, how thoughtlessly they regressed. Coats flopped over the post at the bottom of the stairs because Pandora, who was sleeping in the studio, couldn't see the point of hanging hers in the cloakroom ('Why? I'll be going out again soon . . .'). Shoes were trailing from the front door all through the hallway as if their owners had simply stepped out of them as they walked. Heaps of sundry possessions (iPods, CDs, items of clothing) were trip hazards on the lower stairs, waiting for someone to remember that they needed to carry them up and find them a home.

Beyond, through the open double doors to the sitting room, the seat cushions on the big purple sofa had been left squashed and all over the place, because whichever of the younger ones had been sprawling on it the night before had merely got up when their TV viewing was done and moved seamlessly from there straight upstairs to bed, without so much as a cursory backward glance. The pink sofa was covered in Charlie's toys, the blanket from his buggy, a pile of books that Cassandra had been reading. The rug was half hidden under magazines (music ones – Jasper). In the kitchen, Panda's computer was charging on the table, plugged in with its wire trailing across to the socket on the worktop. Not what you'd call safe.

Sara cleared some space on the worktop, mopped a puddle where the dog's water bowl had been kicked over but no one had bothered to clear it up, made herself some coffee and carried it out to the terrace, but there was a coolish breeze, this early. Floss ran out past her, peed on the grass then raced down the garden to the studio where she barked to be let in, still not having cottoned on to the fact that Conrad was now sleeping in the house again. Pandora had said couldn't someone keep the dog in, so that she didn't get Floss waking her at what she called 'the devil's dawn'.

No I bloody can't, Sara now thought as she went back into the bomb-site house, feeling annoyed that her blissed-up mood from the night before was in danger of turning to grumpiness. The only bona fide child on the premises was Charlie. Only he had an excuse not to help keep the place looking habitable. The rest of them were adults: did they still think the tidy fairies came in the night and cleared the surfaces? Truth was, of course, they didn't care what the place looked like – for the younger ones it was no longer 'home', so the clear-up rules of the benign dictatorship Sara had imposed during their growing up no longer applied now they claimed visitor status.

Even Cassandra, who had left Paul partly because he was an unreconstructed slob, seemed to have reverted eagerly to domestic anarchy; she might need nudging about that. Lizzie too was hopeless. In Cornwall she lived with so many items of casual decoration (collections of shells, curiously marked stones from the seashore, jars of beads, dresser shelves crammed with beach finds) that it was hard to tell whether she was doing just a careless plonking-down of stuff on every surface, or whether it was all thoughtfully placed and arranged. She had a lucky talent that way; always had, Sara remembered. She'd bought ten folding chairs from a car boot sale, all hideous, flimsy and cheap, but by the time she'd painted each of them a different shade of blue and added junk-shop cushions patterned with Siamese cats (which should have looked hideous but worked in a kitsch way), you looked at them and thought, oh what a fantastic idea, why don't I . . . ?

Conrad's view on furniture was that it should last. Sara put it down to a generation thing. Their chairs were beautiful, expensive craft pieces, made from twisted elm and commissioned from a genius in Norfolk. They would last for ever and look wonderful for ever . . . so long as people like Jasper didn't try to swing them on the back two legs, risking breakage of both chair legs and his own neck. You couldn't be overprecious about these things, she told herself, after the third time of reminding him over dinner not to do it and fighting back an urge to wallop him. It was people who mattered, not *things*. But *she* mattered too, she told herself. She was *not* anyone's skivvy.

Ace cleaner Xavier would leave if they weren't a bit more together. He was already tutting and disapproving for half of his working hours. If it wasn't that he clearly fancied Pandora (trailing around after her, smiling, telling her she spoke French *très, très bien*, even though he almost always spoke English), he'd probably have left after his first encounter with an inadequately rolled-up dirty nappy that Cassandra had left on the downstairs shower-room floor after she'd got distracted by a phone call from Miranda. Xav's face had been as horrified as if he'd come across a badly dismembered goat, and he had needed extra coffee and a doughnut.

It was hard, Marie told her, to keep a cleaner if you were going to be in the house for much of the day. Hers had left a week after Mike took early retirement. 'They don't want you hanging around,' she'd told Sara. 'They like the place to themselves so they can sit on the sofa and call their mates on your phone and watch daytime TV while having a crafty shot of your vodka. We pay them for the three hours and they scratch the surface in just under two, and everyone's happy enough with that.'

What would Ben be doing now? Back in the kitchen, Sara idly wondered about this while the croissants warmed. She collected the newspaper from the mailbox by the front door and went back to the kitchen to read it with her breakfast. Would he be out in his little terrace garden checking the progress of the nasturtium seedlings? Working, maybe, writing against a deadline? Or still asleep? She had an odd moment of wondering what he looked like sleeping. Some people, she thought, look almost childlike and sweet. Conrad looked his age when he slept. Still beautiful, but all the lines and crinkles settled into place, furrowing themselves that bit deeper when they weren't supported by his smile or conversation. Close up, lovely as he was, he looked like cloth that someone had crumpled while damp and left lying around so the creases dried in. Probably her own skin did, too. She would never get a L'Oréal Age Perfect contract, that was for sure. But what, she wondered, would it be like to wake up next to an unfamiliar sleeping man after so many years with Conrad? How odd would that be? What an act of trust it was to be asleep with someone. Almost more intimate than sex.

'Hey you're up early; why didn't you wake me?' Conrad startled her, sliding his hands round her and kissing the back of her neck. She felt guilty, nervous in case he could read her thoughts. And what about the night before? The guilt was surely even worse about that. Wasn't it horribly sinful that she'd been thinking about Ben while making love with Conrad, or was off-the-premises fantasizing a perfectly normal sex aid? She would have to discuss that with Stuart, next time they went to the pub at lunchtime. He was delightfully uninhibited when talking of sexual matters, even if it did tend to lead to him eyeing her up from behind and checking out the whippiness of twigs fallen from the trees around the Green. And maybe it wasn't really disloyal, merely a bit of highly effective fantasy. After all, she (and presumably Ben) had absolutely no plans to indulge in the reality. It counted as no different from having lascivious thoughts about George Clooney. If *that* was a sin, more than half the women of the developed world were on the fast track to eternal damnation. The recording angel would get RSI trying to keep up with the crime lists.

'I just wanted a bit of time to myself, before the hordes descended and trashed the kitchen all over again,' she told him. 'They're like locusts; no, worse – they're like wildebeest stampeding. Have you seen the state of the place? Is it only me who can load the dishwasher? I could spend all day chasing round after this lot. Between them and the Charlie care – which I don't at all mind – I don't even get a moment to think.'

'Why do you want a moment to think about anything?' Conrad asked. 'Thinking's overrated. I'm giving it up.'

'Oh are you?' she laughed. 'How's that going to work then?'

'I don't know yet. Haven't thought about it . . . get it?'

'Yeah, yeah, hilarious!' she conceded.

'OK – but today . . . why don't we just go out somewhere? Just walk out on it all. We'll tell whoever's here to sort it before Xavier throws a wobbler and we'll just leave the rest of the buggers to it.' Conrad poured boiling water over a camomile tea bag in a mug. 'I'm supposed to be seeing someone from the *Telegraph* or *Observer* or whatever, to answer some inane questions Gerry's fixed up for them to ask me. I can't be arsed so I'm going to cancel, pleading a subsequent, more entertaining engagement. So let's think of one, then it won't be a lie.'

'I suppose an exhibition's out of the question?' Sara teased. Conrad hated going to see other painters' work, unless it was of those who'd been dead several hundred years. Sculptors he didn't mind too much, but contemporary painters only made him growl. 'I can't see what they're saying any more, only the childishly simple techniques they're using to say it,' he would mutter.

Sara saw the sleep years drop away as he talked to her. Enthusiasm, life light, that was what gave you youth, she thought. He used to be able to catch that in his painting. If he really couldn't do that any more, maybe he was right not to take on so much work. He already knew he was over the cusp of fashionable now, these things going in cycles as they did. Gerry might be determined – for profit reasons of his own – that there was one more upward curve in the wheel of Conrad's fortunes, but how much worse would it be to work on something with only half his heart in it?

Sara looked at the used wine glasses beside the sink – there hadn't been enough room for them in the dishwasher the night before. The sink contained a plate and knife from Pandora's late-night sandwich, a saucepan of congealed cheesy stuff, a sludge of greasy cold water. There were mugs on the worktop with half-inches of tea in them and probably several more scattered around the house. What was there to stay home for? She and Conrad would go out and then when they came home, well, who knew? Maybe the tidy fairies would have visited. By magic.

'Yes – let's escape. I think that would be fun. But first, as soon as I've eaten this croissant I'm going to walk Floss in the park for half an hour, just to clear my head.'

Sara didn't keep to any kind of regular timetable when it came to walking the dog. She took Floss out at any old time, morning or afternoon, and besides, very often it was Conrad who took her. All the same, seeing Mike on the same bench as before, with the poodle and another carton of Starbucks coffee, it was almost as if he hadn't moved. He'd had his hair cut and didn't look quite as wild and mad-professorish, but otherwise was his usual unkempt self. He slightly reminded her of Pigpen in the Snoopy cartoons, shedding clouds of dust everywhere he went. Having thought this, she tried hard not to laugh and somehow ended up giving him a far broader smile than she'd intended.

'Morning, Sara; what a lovely smile!' he said, getting up.

She glanced at the ground, half expecting a shower of saw-dust and plaster from whatever DIY project he was currently on. She recalled Marie saying something about him replacing the banister rails. The poodle yapped and pulled at its lead, then growled at Floss, who scuttled behind Sara.

'Hi Mike,' she said. 'Gorgeous day, isn't it?' She was, for politeness' sake, going to have to do the park circuit with him now. Knowing what she knew about Marie, this felt hazardous.

'It is indeed somewhere in the vicinity of glorious,' Mike said, walking along beside her, nudging into her. She moved slightly sideways – the path was not a wide one but there was plenty of space for two to walk without bashing into each other; did he need to be that close?

'And the day is all the better for seeing you.'

Sara sensed that something wasn't quite right here. She'd moved across the path, but as they walked he was still slightly touching her. Distraction was needed – this wasn't accidental. It was too early for the café to be open, which would have been useful. She could have pleaded the need for a cup of tea and possibly lost him that way. Shame it was closed, she'd often thought the early dog-walkers were a missed business opportunity. In Bushy Park there was a van serving hot dogs and bacon rolls – just the thing if you'd been striding energetically through the bracken throwing a ball for a bounding pet. No such luck here.

'So how's your old man?' Mike suddenly said, then laughed. 'And of course he *is* old, isn't he? Sorry! I shouldn't have said that, should I? I just meant that compared with the sweet young thing that you are . . .'

'Conrad's fine. Couldn't be better,' Sara said abruptly, moving off the path and on to the grass. She let Floss off the lead, picked up a stick, and hurled it as far as she could. What was Mike playing at?

'Really? Glad to hear it. Though of course, a girl like you . . . and I hope you don't mind me saying but compared with him you *are* a girl . . .' He coughed and looked uncomfortable. 'Oh God, I'm terribly out of practice at this.'

'Practice? At what?' She considered whether it might be a good idea to turn back for home now. They were coming to the woodsy part of the park, where there were fallen trees, tangles of elder, hawthorn. She loved it because the scents of the undergrowth were so strong, so rank and fetid. It was repulsive (moist overtones of rot and death) and yet attractive (new growth, ripening). It was also quite dark, secluded, full of wild flowers hidden between crumbling branches, sticky with fungus. She didn't feel unsafe alone, but with someone whose intentions were a bit unpredictable . . . But this was Mike. Overweight, puffing, somehow gender-neutral because he was her friend's husband. How could she even think he was remotely a threat? All the same . . .

'I'm out of practice at *women*.' He sighed, stopping in the middle of the path. 'At how to be complimentary. I'm doing it wrong, aren't I? I sound like a sleazebag.'

'You do, a bit,' she admitted. 'Sorry, but to be honest you were getting a bit alarming there. What's going on?'

'Well I hoped you might tell me, but I know you won't. You girls all confide and keep your secrets, and a mere mortal man doesn't get a chance. I *know* Marie's up to something. I can't compete with whatever it is she's getting somewhere else that's making her smile like a crazy woman, because we stopped all that lovey-dovey stuff years ago. You do stop, don't you? I mean you can't keep it up year after year. And you'd look silly, holding hands in the street like kids.'

Sara thought about Conrad stroking her leg under the table in restaurants, about how he never walked past her without leaving a light touch on her body somewhere. It was like a cat, leaving a gentle scent, a hint of territory-claiming. On some occasions, such as when she was in the middle of a good party conversation, it had distracted and annoyed her a little; now she just thought how lucky she was; no wonder Marie was delighted to have so much attention. It was obviously sadly lacking at home.

'What's so silly about holding someone's hand? Most women like that sort of thing. You could just start it up again, give it a go,' Sara suggested, heading down the shaded route. Mike wasn't going to pounce on her. She wouldn't have to fight it out with him in the nettles, knee him somewhere painful and go home covered in scratches and an itchy rash. How could the thought have ever crossed her mind?

'She'd wonder what I was up to.' Mike sounded very pessimistic. He was annoying her, anticipating defeat before the fight began.

'Mike – if you really think there's something wrong, then just *make the effort*. There's honestly nothing I can tell you.' (This was true, because what, exactly, *could* she tell him that didn't add up to a heap of hurt? Of course she wouldn't. And one day it would be over and all would be well.) 'But I really think that you shouldn't just *give up*. That's defeatist. The more you act like a sad doormat, the more Marie will walk all over you.'

'Sara, you know last time in this park, you said you might come out for lunch with me?' Mike brightened up suddenly, taking hold of her wrist. The path was narrow here, and muddy. She was sure-footed, used to the parts where it went slidey. She wriggled her arm out of his grip. Maybe this path hadn't been such a good idea after all.

'Actually, I didn't say I would, Mike. I just thanked you

for the thought, that's all,' she told him, trying to keep her voice soft and calm. 'What I *did* say was why don't you take Marie out somewhere lovely? *Woo* her, for heaven's sake! Make her feel loved! Give her the benefit of your wildest fantasies!' The end of the undergrowth was in sight, where the path opened up into broad grassland again. There were plenty of people around and Sara felt slightly foolish to have even considered Mike a mauling menace. Poor guy, she thought, he just wanted to be loved. Didn't everyone?

Conrad's journalist must have been warned that he was elusive and slippery and arrived at least half an hour early. As Sara got back to the house with Floss, a pink VW Beetle pulled up outside the front door and out clambered a small, harassed-looking girl clutching a white iBook, a notebook and a handbag, all of which she dropped on the ground while she was trying to manipulate her key to operate her car lock.

'Ohhhhh! I keep doing that!' she squealed as Sara opened the front door. 'And it's not my computer! Oh God, if it's broken . . .' She scrabbled about on the ground, trying to pick everything up. A wallet, two Tampax and a lipstick fell out of her bag. She leaned under the car to retrieve her pen, showing far too much exposed bum at the top of her low-cut jeans.

'Let me help you,' Sara said, pushing Floss into the house before the dog could add to the chaos by trying to eat the scattered possessions. The girl looked as if she was going to cry. Sara handed her her wallet and a couple of crumpled receipts and wondered why Conrad hadn't phoned to cancel her visit. So much for going out.

'And I'm late!' the girl wailed. 'I hate being late! I'm *always* late!'

'No you're not. Actually, you're half an hour early.' Conrad would be furious, having hoped to do a runner. Possibly not phoning her was yet another aspect of him being flaky: had he simply forgotten? He had never been one of those people who could barely get out of bed without looking in his diary to see what time he was scheduled to clean his teeth. And to be fair, although her scheduled visit had been written on the kitchen black-board, someone had half-rubbed it out and overwritten it with a shopping list that requested beer and chocolate. Who, exactly, were they asking? Three guesses, she thought. There were sounds overhead: footsteps, water running. The house was gradually coming to life. Lizzie hadn't come home the night before and Cassandra's car had gone. She must have left while Sara had been in the park and taken Charlie to college with her, so it must be Jasper upstairs. Had he moved in for good? Perhaps she could suggest he job-share the cleaning with Xavier.

The journalist, realizing she hadn't completely screwed up, immediately became so still and calm, apparently stunned by this statement, that Sara was reminded of a squawking parrot that suddenly has a cloth thrown over its cage. Then she perked up again.

'I'm *not* late? The bastards! They did that on purpose so I'd get here on time! I'm Nicky, by the way. So Conrad's expecting me. That's good, good. I haven't got the day wrong, then!'

'Er . . . no.' Though Sara suspected from her tone that she had got a day wrong before. 'Tea? Coffee? Do excuse the mess in here.' Sara led her into the kitchen and cursed her idle family for leaving the entire house unfit for public view. How lucky that this wasn't also a photo shoot. She could see Conrad on the pool terrace and managed to steer the girl out through the glass door. 'Conrad?' She called. 'Your interviewer. Nicky.' She gave him a be-nice-to-her look.

'Shit! I was intending to go out and avoid you!' he told her bluntly. 'I wanted to cancel. In fact I still do. Why don't you go home and just make something up?'

'Oh!' The girl looked stricken. 'But . . . I . . . it wouldn't be honest!'

'Honest? *Honest?*' Are you *sure* you're a journalist? Haven't you heard of Google?'

Sara left them to it, went back into the kitchen, quickly

209

made coffee and took it out to them, then went upstairs to the little office room, stepping over Jasper's big wet footprints on the carpet. Music blared from his room . . . some rap thing. She switched on the computer, quickly looked through a few emails, then slotted in the CD-ROM which had photos of her paintings. She looked through them carefully, copying the ones she liked best into a new folder, all the ones she thought made up a good cross-section of colour and style. Then she burned them on to a new disk and closed down the computer. Conrad would be occupied for a while. This was as good a chance as any to drop the photos in to Ben. Stupidly, she didn't have a phone number for him, or he for her, so she'd have to take a chance, though whether the chance was on him being home or not she couldn't quite decide. In a way, it would be a good thing if he was out, then she could just slide them through the letter box and not look as if she'd been hoping to see him. Because that, she thought as she glissed on a bit of eyeliner and brushed her hair, really wasn't the plan at all.

She was perfect for the job, this journalist. Natalie? Nicola? Nicky. She knew nothing about him, was as ignorant of the art world as you could get. Conrad ran a few names past her, trying her out. Dinos and Jake Chapman, Sarah Lucas, Gilbert and George. Blank. Nothing registered but increasing panic in those big green eyes. Mention of Tracey Emin raised a tiny glint of recognition but nothing more.

He made a decision. 'Thing is, Nicky,' he told her, 'I'm not actually going to do the being-seventy thing.'

'Oh.' She slumped over the table, looking defeated, and closed her notebook. 'I've got the wrong person, haven't I? You're not the artist with the big birthday, the one who paints famous people looking all odd. You're the one who's given that big tree picture thing to the Tate, aren't you? God, I'm so *hopeless!*'

'No, no – that's David Hockney. Big blond bloke. Glasses? Yorkshire?' Nicky's eyes flickered a bit, brain cogs were almost visibly creaking.

'It's OK, I *am* the one with the birthday. It's just that . . .'

'Oh! Oh God you're ill! I'm like, *so* sorry!' Her eyes filled with easy tears. Conrad felt rather touched, but then realized she'd probably be just as tear-struck if a stray cat walked through the garden clutching a slaughtered rat. She was very pretty, very sweet. In the days pre-Sara he might well have bedded this girl before the interview was half over. He considered the idea in a purely intellectual, distant way. Lovely slender legs, slightly gangly. Her feet were arranged untidily beneath the table, shoes off and her toes pointing inwards. She, of course, would be horrified that he was picturing the feel of her smooth pale skin, imagining her making a lot of ecstatic noise while wrapped round him on a bed. If she had any clue about what was in his mind, he could picture her back home later with her flatmates (there were sure to be flatmates – she was the type to share. All shoes and handbags and a jumble of make-up and diet books) telling them, 'There this like *old* man, like *seriously* old? And he was like *coming on* to me?' He hadn't thought like this for a long, long while, and it crossed his mind that she was probably Pandora's age, if that. Wrong.

'It's all right. I'm not ill,' he told her. 'I just . . .' No, this was wrong, too. He absolutely couldn't say he intended to die. But something about not-painting had to be said. Unlike ninety per cent of the population, Gerry would never believe anything that *wasn't* written in the press. If she wrote this down, there'd be no going back. 'I won't be working any more. That's all. There's no point, you see, writing your piece. There will be no more Conrad Blythe-Hamilton exhibitions, no more commissioned work, just . . . nothing for you to write about, really.' She stared at him for a long, thoughtful moment.

'But you're really famous,' she said, accusing him of an unknown something.

'Not that famous, obviously, or you wouldn't have confused me with Hockney!' he teased.

'No, no I'm just no good with faces,' she laughed. 'Or names, for that matter. I'm working on it. But . . .

does anyone else know you're not working any more?'

Good, she'd swallowed it. 'No, my dear.' Conrad tried to look confiding. 'I'm only telling you. This is just between ourselves, all right?'

'Oh, absolutely!' she murmured. 'So now, tell me about your early life.'

Good, he thought, that was the no-more-work bit successfully sorted. Job done – he looked forward to a ritual burning of brushes. He would never need them again; unless you were Take That or Frank Sinatra, you really looked a twat if you then went for the big come-back option.

Ben wasn't home. Sara felt strangely sneaky, approaching the pink front door with her envelope and ringing the bell. She could already tell there was no one there – houses keep a kind of protective guard when their owners are absent. From inside the cottage she could hear the sound of a washing machine on a fast spin, so he'd been in till recently, anyway. She pushed the envelope carefully through the letter box and heard it thud softly on the doormat. Her mobile number was on an enclosed card. As if he'd already got it in his possession, she took her phone out of her pocket and made sure it was switched on. Just in case.

God and other artists are always a little obscure.
(Oscar Wilde)

'This is mad. You could have talked to Cass at the college – she's there today *and* she's got Charlie with her. What do you think I can tell you that you can't find out from her?' Pandora sipped her Rioja and studied Paul across the wooden table. The bar was busy with lunchtime office workers, mostly female. They were all very tidily dressed – lots of sleek black trousers and slinky-neat wrap dresses. There were power earrings and vein-blood nail polish and big, big handbags, all the trappings of women who knew just how to play the full feminine game. She felt an out-of-place scruff in her long turquoise T-shirt, beads and silver bangles and old jeans. Her pink Converse shoes had paint splashes on them, and stains from the restaurant's eternally leaking grease. The wooden floors made the place very echoey. It reminded her of school: there were so many girls in here talking – no – *twittering* at once. She half expected her old maths teacher to come in, clap her hands and boom 'Silence!'

To cut across the racket of chatter, she'd almost shouted to Paul, and what she'd said seemed pretty aggressive, too. She tried smiling at him but it didn't feel right – from his side of the table she probably resembled an ape baring her teeth. In fact this whole situation felt wrong, to be here sitting opposite her sister's boyfriend having a secret meet-up. The motives were good, though. That was something she must remember. She kept picturing how Cass and Paul had been, that day in the hospital with their new baby. If she could help them to hang on to that, she'd do what she could.

'She doesn't want to have anything to do with me. That's why I can't talk to her,' Paul told her, sounding defeated. 'She just won't. End of. I don't know why.'

Pandora was silent for a while. Did he really not know? He was an intelligent bloke, supposedly. Well, didn't you have to be to take on a maths MA? He was very good-looking, if you liked the sporty type. He played rugby, mad keenly. She didn't really go for hefty muscles but Paul was lucky – he hadn't (yet?) acquired that thick neck and meaty-shoulder look that she'd seen in occasional inter-national matches on TV. Perhaps that came later, then when they gave up the game the next stage was their whole body mass turning to blubber. How unattractive. Pandora was conscious, suddenly, that her expression was possibly registering dislike. It was terribly inconvenient, this way she had of revealing all over her face what she was thinking. More than one person, on the receiving end, had said she'd make a good actor. She said she wouldn't, because it was always what she *really* thought that showed – not what she was pretending. If she could do the pretending, she wouldn't upset people.

Like with the baring-teeth thing, she imagined how she would look from across the table. Not good. She didn't feel real dislike; it was nothing personal, nothing at all to do with Paul himself, just her thinking with a painter's eye: she was picturing a hugely flabby, naked man, lying on a sofa with a remote control in one hand and a Greggs steak pie in the other. A bit Lucian Freud, she thought, suddenly itching to have a paintbrush in her hand and to be smelling oil paint rather than the surrounding hundred designer perfumes. Except L. Freud probably wouldn't have included the pie. That thought at least brought a genuine smile to her face.

'Do you really want her back?' Pandora was almost surprised at her own question. 'I mean, come on Paul, how much do you *really* like suddenly being a grown-up with a family? Because I think that to Cass, you've seemed like you're already opting out on the deal, not joining in like you promised you would. And now she's left, be honest, doesn't a little bit of you think, oh great I'm free again? I can go back to being a lad?'

Paul visibly flinched. 'You don't pull your punches do you, Panda?'

It was Pandora's turn to flinch. No one outside her immediate family called her Panda. It was a pet name among them, intimate, childlike. Even Ollie hadn't called her by that name (irritatingly, he'd considered Doreen to be an amusing nickname. *Not* funny). But then Paul was now, by way of Charlie, a sort of relation. He *was* family. Which was a relief, really, because that meant it was all right to be sitting here in a bar with him. Apart from the secrecy bit, obviously.

'No, I don't hold back,' she agreed. 'But didn't you want *honest*? Or did you come all this way just so I'd say, "Oh poor Paul, how awful for you, I must get my vile, selfish sister to come running back to you." Is that what you expected?'

He grinned, suddenly, his blue eyes sparkly, laughing at her. 'Well no – I knew you might be pretty fierce! You're really scary, did anyone ever tell you?'

Pandora treated him to her foxiest smile, the one no one ever expected. '*Everybody* tells me that, Paul! But no, really, tell me what you want me to do. I can't promise anything, though. Cass and I – well, we don't always agree on stuff.'

'Yeah, but deep down . . . there's loyalty, isn't there?'

Pandora laughed, loudly enough for a group of the lunch-break women to turn and look at her. She got a swift impression of shiny, smeary make-up, of over-straightened, overstreaked hair gleaming with serum. Women as slicks of sticky product, surface oils. The longing for paint swished back again, stronger now.

'Loyalty! God, Paul, you sound so public school! The way you just said that, like you're talking about Queen-and-country stuff! I bet you were in the CCF at school, running round the woods at fourteen with your bayonet fixed and camo paint on your face.'

Paul said nothing. He looked a bit hurt. 'Sorry,' Pandora said. 'Have I touched a nerve?'

'Actually I opted out of anything military on principle, if you really want to know. Which I doubt you do. But all the same, what's so hilarious about loyalty?' He said it very quietly. 'Cass thinks I fancy other girls and that I'm forever off with them. I don't and I'm not and I wouldn't. I work on my course stuff. I do sport . . . OK, maybe too much of it, but she's always known that's a top priority. And maybe I hang out in the Union bar a bit too much – I can either fix that or she can come too. There's no good reason why not, especially while Charlie's still so small. That was what we agreed – that we'd be the same as normal for as long as we could. I just want the chance to have another go at getting it right. I want you to make sure she knows it − that's all I'm asking. That's if you can summon up enough *loyalty* to . . .'

'Paul, I'm so sorry . . .' Pandora could feel her eyes filling with unexpected, very unwelcome tears. Where did they come from? There were girl things that Pandora just didn't do. Cutesy dresses, hair maintenance, heels, mascara and . . . tears. 'It's just that I haven't had much experience of men who do fidelity long-term.' She could have added 'not with me, anyway', but managed to keep that much to herself.

'Oh shit, I've made you cry!' Looking horribly alarmed and embarrassed, Paul grabbed her hand across the table. 'Sorry!' he said, overloudly. The cosmetic women on the next table turned and had a good stare, silent and unapologetically curious. Magnified by Pandora's tears, the eyelashes on the nearest of them looked to her like a row of sharp black spines, as if someone had stolen them from a porcupine's underbelly and marketed them as a hot fashion item. Agonizing, she thought; so ugly, these rigid-looking splinters. And right now, she felt lucky she hardly ever wore make-up, as she mopped her unshadowed eyelids with a tissue. She might look a bit pink and blotchy, but she wouldn't have slimy, shiny slug trails of goo all over her face, no ugly smudgings of under-eye charcoal.

'It's not you,' Pandora reassured Paul, extracting her

hand from his. The warmth of it had surprised and slightly shocked her. From somewhere inside had come a longing to keep clinging to his hand, absorb that comforting heat. But it wasn't really Paul's hand she'd wanted, just . . . well, someone who loved her. She was over Ollie (just about) but not over being loved. Did that *ever* go? The thought that maybe it didn't, but that maybe she'd be stuck with the wanting and not the reality for evermore, almost sent the tears into full flow again.

The girls on the next table turned away, no longer interested now it apparently wasn't a lovers' spat. Glass would not break, drink would not be thrown. Pandora sniffled into a torn tissue and said to Paul, 'I'm OK really. It's just, oh life and stuff. I'm broke, boyfriendless, got nowhere to live, nowhere to paint and the only job I've got is two nights in the local pub where Goths gather. But hey!' She attempted half a smile. 'It's not all good news!'

'You'll find someone,' Paul said, finishing his drink. 'Sure to.'

'You know what?' she said. 'You must be quite a romantic, deep down. Of all the things I said were wrong with my life, the lack of love is the only one you picked up on. Like the others didn't matter. Actually, I suppose in the big forever life plan of things, none of them matter.' She laughed, but it sounded unconvincing and squawky.

'*Especially* not the lack of a man thing. But hey, I'll talk to Cass for you. No worries. Just stay cool, don't hassle her and I'll help you sort her out. At the very least, you've got to be able to see Charlie. I might be a fairly crap sister at times, but I'll always be a top aunt for him. I promise.'

The house was still a complete pit. Sara opened the fridge and picked out salami and tomatoes and a chunk of cheese, then wandered around eating them while making a moody start on clearing the kitchen surfaces.

'Where the hell is everybody?' she asked Conrad when he came in and took a beer from the fridge. 'How can they disappear and leave it like this? Why do I get left with it all while they wander off? They'll be back later, expecting there to be food. There bloody won't be, that's for sure.'

'Just leave it then.' Conrad shrugged. 'Go out, leave them a note, tell them to get it done or bloody else. Jasper's around – I can hear what he calls music. Panda said she'd be back later. The two of them can have a go at it together.'

'They can but they'll mind, even though it's mostly their stuff. I feel really *put on* and I hate that feeling. I'm not here for domestic slavery. You know, Conrad, what I'd really like to do is paint again. It's a feeling that's been creeping up on me. I think it's rubbed off from one of my students, Melissa – she's completely new to it and her enthusiasm is so brilliant. She's reminded me how it feels to get excited about the colours and the feel of the brushes and so on.'

'The opposite to me, then.' Conrad looked a bit moody. Was it, she wondered, because she would be invading his space? In the past they'd shared the studio quite easily.

'I'd really love it if you moved your Dinky Car collection off that grotty table at the end of the studio so I can reclaim my old work area. Would that be OK? Would you mind sharing the space with me again?' She poured a glass of iced water from the fridge and followed him outside to the pool.

'You *really* want to paint again?' he said. 'But you haven't for ages. Apart from the keen student, what's really brought this on?'

She felt a bit shifty and shaded her eyes with her hands, cutting out the bright sunlight but really avoiding Conrad's look. She could feel her phone in her skirt pocket. Why had she even mentioned this? Too late now. 'Well . . . OK, I met someone. At the college. He's called Ben, lives along the river here and he's got a sister – at least I think he said it's his sister – who's opening a gallery and she's looking for someone for the first exhibition, though I'm sure they'll have tons of possibles to choose from. Anyway, I gave him a CD of my work. If he likes it . . . well . . .'

'Oh he'll like it, all right,' Conrad said quietly. 'What wouldn't he like?' Sara said nothing. She knew from his tone he didn't mean the painting. She wished she hadn't said anything. But how could she not? If anything came of this – in exhibition terms, that is – Conrad would wonder why she hadn't mentioned it sooner.

'Well, I suppose it's really the sister who's got to like it. But hey, I'm sure it'll come to nothing,' she said eventually. 'I was thinking it was just a chance to offload all those leftover paintings from the Bath exhibition that never happened.'

'Does he know you're married to me?'

'Er . . . no. I mean, he knows I'm married, but you know that at the college I'm McKinley. So he wouldn't know about you.'

'He asked if you were married then, did he? The subject came up?'

'Conrad – what is this? Why are you cross-examining me?'

'I'm just curious. That's all.' She wished he'd smile. He looked moody and suspicious, which was very unlike him. Why didn't he tease her? Why didn't he say, 'Oh I suppose he's yet another of the admiring husbands?' like he did about practically every other man she knew?

'It could be that he'll really like my work, you know. Have you thought of that?'

'Yes of course I have. I said so, didn't I? That he'd like it? So he's seen it then? When was this?'

'No of course he hasn't! But soon he will, I hope. I sent him a CD of photos.'

Conrad picked a yellow snapdragon flower and played with it, opening and closing its bunny-rabbit mouth. He didn't look at her.

She moved closer and put her arm round him, hugged him. 'Conrad, I wear a wedding ring. Which bit of that would say "this woman's available"?' At which point her phone rang. Sara felt her heart rate double. She didn't recognize the flashed-up number.

'Hello?' she murmured, very much wanting to rush into the house, be somewhere private.

'Sara – it's me! Lizzie! Can you come and get me?' Her sister's voice was both a relief and a disappointment.

'Lizzie – where are you? Where've you been all night?'

'Long story, darling! I'm in Chelsea. I bought some big vase things and I can't get them home. *Please* come and get me – I can't afford a cab all that way! I'm on the King's Road, near the Town Hall.'

Sara thought about the alternative – cleaning, clearing, mucking out the Augean stables, placating Conrad . . . 'OK – I'll be along. But try and get to the Putney side of World's End will you, or you'll have to chip in for the congestion charge.'

★

Lizzie was sitting between her pair of tall vases on the grass at the edge of Parson's Green.

'You look like some kind of weird table decoration!' Sara called to her as she stopped the car just off the King's Road. 'Are you sure they're big enough? What will you do with them?'

'I don't know yet,' Lizzie said as she clambered to her feet. She looked tired, weary, Sara thought. She opened the Golf's boot, shoved the back seats down and moved a bag of garden-centre compost aside to make room.

'How did you get them to here from wherever you bought them?' Sara asked. 'You couldn't have carried them, surely. They've got to be nearly three feet high and not the easiest shape to lug around.'

'Marvin dropped me off here,' Lizzie told her.

'Marvin? And he is?' Sara wedged the compost bag between the vases to stop them rolling around and closed the boot. Lizzie was already in the car, leaning back on the headrest, eyes closed. She smelled a bit . . . stale, in need of a shower. What had she been doing? What on earth did Jasper make of his old-hippy mother, staying out for random nights with possibly random men?

'Marvin and I go way back,' Lizzie said, not opening her eyes. 'But . . . I don't suppose I'll be seeing him again.

225

There are some . . . well you just have to know when to call time, don't you?'

Sara pulled out on to the King's Road and joined the tail end of the school-run traffic. Lovely, she thought, a nice slow ride back home.

'Though of course you *don't* know, do you, Sara? You've always been little Mrs Good-Wife. Never looked at anyone else since Conrad came along.'

'I've got male friends. One or two of them I've even fancied a bit in a what-if kind of way. I'm a normal human, Lizzie,' Sara told her, slowing to look at the Victorian nightdresses hanging in the window of Lunn Antiques. 'I just don't get the big deal in you sleeping with all your exes. What are you looking for with them that you didn't find when you were with them first time round?'

'Oh I don't know.' Lizzie yawned. 'It's just about . . . still being *desirable*, I think. Or at least I *did* think. What I think right now is I'm tired of it all. There isn't any better sex out there than even the worst you get with someone you really love.'

'At last!' Sara laughed at her. 'You're catching up with the rest of us! Taken you a while, hasn't it?'

Lizzie sighed. 'You've just got no idea how lucky you are, Sara,' she said. Sara's phone, which was propped up in the drinks holder, rang. 'Got it,' Lizzie said, grabbing it before Sara could get to it. 'Hello?' Sara held her breath.

It was probably Conrad. Or one of the girls. Or Marie.

'Er . . . no, I'm Lizzie. No . . . no, right number, I'm Sara's big sister! And you?'

'Give me the phone Lizzie!' Sara hissed, turning left abruptly and without signalling and stopping on a double yellow line.

Lizzie handed over the phone, smirking in an annoy-ingly knowing way.

'Hello. Hi Ben!' Sara was aware of sounding overkeen and a bit high. 'Er . . . oh good! You liked them. Wow!' Lizzie made a face and giggled, mouthing 'Wow?' at her.

'No . . . sorry, it's my sister. She's being *really* stupid. We're in my car.' Sara slapped Lizzie quite hard on her arm. Why did he have to call when she wasn't alone?

'OK – yes, great. See you soon. Bye.' She pressed the off button, twice, and put the phone back. Without comment, she started the car again, did a neat three-point turn and went back to the King's Road.

'Go on, say something then,' Sara said to Lizzie. 'You're almost exploding with it.'

'I'm saying nothing,' Lizzie said, smothering laughter.

'It's not what you think.'

'I didn't think it was. But . . .'

'But?'

'Well it must be, mustn't it, or you wouldn't have said that. Not to mention you've gone all pink and flustered.

227

Your hands are trembling on that steering wheel. I'm surprised we're not up the back of that Volvo.'

'No really. It isn't anything. It's just about paintings, for a new gallery. Ben likes my work and there's an exhibition possibility coming up. That's all.'

'Ben. Let me guess, he's about your age, attractive, divorced . . .'

'Er . . . well sort of but that doesn't mean . . .'

'Does he know you're married to Conrad?'

'That's what Conrad said! What's the big deal there? I do exist in my own right, you know!'

'Oh come on Sara! You know it's always the big deal. Like would any magazine, TV show and so on have been interested in Coleen McLoughlin if she wasn't with Wayne Rooney? Get real! The Conrad connection would guarantee a private-view guest list that would have all the art wallahs taking notice. And editorial coverage. Exactly what a new gallery needs.'

'Well thanks for your faith in my talent, sister dear! And *no* as it happens, he doesn't know I have any connection with Conrad.' Sara felt upset, hurt.

'Ah . . . so he *likes* you, then. And you like him. Well it's only natural; don't feel bad. Conrad's getting older. You looking for someone else is just nature's way.'

Sara slowed. Putney Bridge was jammed with traffic. People were walking in the road – something had happened.

'But I'm *not* looking for someone else,' she insisted.

'Subconsciously, you are, darling. It's like at the end of a pregnancy when even the idlest domestic slut starts cleaning behind the fridge. Instinct. Nothing you can do about it. You're anticipating a partner vacancy.'

'That's a horrible thing to say, Lizzie! Really vile and completely untrue!'

'OK.' Lizzie shrugged. 'Well in that case you're going to have to admit you're looking for a bit of good old-fashioned fun with someone your own age. Who could blame you now Conrad's gone tame? He doesn't paint, he doesn't go out much, he's smoking again. I think it adds up to losing the will . . . I hesitate to say it, possibly losing the will to live.'

Ahead in the road, people were getting out of their cars and looking at something. It wasn't an accident: they were smiling, pointing, watching as three men and a woman carefully herded a lost swan off the bridge and down to the slipway, where it could get back to the Thames.

'People are so much kinder to animals than to humans, aren't they,' Sara commented to Lizzie. 'If that had been a confused old man wandering about, nobody would have helped him. They'd just have beeped their horns and got cross. It's so unfair.'

'Life is, Sara sweetie. It just is.'

*

The house was clean; an unexpected delight to come home to. So the tidy fairies had visited after all while Sara had been out collecting Lizzie.

'Wow, this is wonderful! I must go out more often when it's a complete wreck!' Sara said to Pandora who was in the kitchen, washing rocket for a salad. Sara was touched; not only was the house back to the state she liked, but Pandora had organized dinner for everyone. Perhaps there was an upside to having a house full of people after all. Panda had bought lamb for a barbecue and chunks of it were marinating in something interestingly fragrant and herby on the worktop. The glass door of the oven showed a big bubbling dish of dauphinoise potatoes. It looked as if working in that restaurant, only a spit (in all senses) away from Mr Big-Deal Celebrity Chef had paid off.

Pandora smiled at her. 'Well it was easy. Xavier came over for an extra couple of hours earlier. Him and me and Jasper did it together – it doesn't take long with three, does it?'

Sara gave her a suspicious look: since when had Pandora been keen on domestic labour? When she'd lived in the house as a teenager, her idea of tidying her room had been to put all loose items in a bin bag – not to be thrown out but to be retrieved for use as and when she needed them. At one time, Sara had counted nine overloaded rubbish sacks in there, randomly stuffed with stray clothes, CDs, magazines and used plates complete with toast crumbs. Only actually starting to load these into the car on the pretence of taking them to the charity shop had scared the girl into screaming out of the house in protest, promising to go through her possessions and find suitable space for them.

'So did you pay Xav or do I owe him?' Sara asked, as she took a bottle of chilled white wine from the fridge.

'Oh, he said not to worry about it. He only really came to borrow a DVD from me, some movie I happened to have that he wanted to see.' Pandora sounded peculiarly breezy, as if Xavier calling at the house on a casual social mission was an everyday thing. Perhaps it now would be. That was fine by Sara, though if she was going to have to look for another cleaner she hoped he'd give her some warning. She hadn't ever expected to keep him for long; he was only cleaning to finance his way through law school.

'Right – so while he was here he thought he'd just put in a few unpaid hours?' Sara struggled with the bottle's cork and concentrated on hauling it out. She decided not to pursue the topic of Xavier. If he and Pandora were getting together, that might be a good thing. Panda could be such a prickly girl; whatever it took to keep her as relaxed and cheerful as she was at this moment had to be worthwhile. She'd gone to all this trouble too, which was very sweet of her and quite unexpected. Panda's past ideas of dinner preferences had tended to need the film pierced or a bloke on a moped knocking at the door.

The day's warmth had continued into the evening. Everyone except Conrad agreed there was still enough heat in the air to have dinner outside on the pool terrace and he had been firmly overruled. Sara glanced at him now and then as he ate in silence, looking mentally a bit absent. Was he sulking? What was to sulk about? Surely not still the Ben thing. But now he was very quiet and kept looking down the garden towards the studio. The huge old oak had burst into leaf in the last few days, and the studio was now almost hidden behind it. You couldn't see the tree house at all. Perhaps he was hankering after doing some work again, after all, she thought. If that was what he really wanted, it would be a good thing. He needed something to absorb his mind – perhaps it would give him a way to resume normal service, stop feeling overwhelmed by the demons of age.

'. . . And he's *still alive*!' Lizzie had been twittering in the background for a while now. Sara's attention returned at these words.

'Who is?' she asked, in case it was someone she knew as well.

'Oh Sara! Do keep up!' Lizzie squealed. 'Is she always like this?' she asked Cassandra. 'Just because you're a *granny* now, darling, doesn't mean you can let your mind wander off like this! I was talking about Bagshot Brian, you remember – from when I was in my teens! We went to the Isle of Wight Festival together, me all in flowers and a bell round my neck. He was my *older man.*' She glanced sideways at Conrad. 'You see, Conrad, even I've had one.'

'You've had more than one of everything going, according to you,' he said, grouchily. Jasper, big-eyed and wary, looked nervously at his mother, and put his iPod earplugs firmly in, shoving his long dark hair aside impatiently in his hurry to block out the conversation. Sara didn't blame him. He'd probably heard Lizzie's old-lover descriptions a million times before. If not, seventeen was a vulnerable enough age for a boy, full of embarrassment and flying hormones, without his mother making things worse.

'Yes I have!' Lizzie agreed with Conrad delightedly, mistaking his comment for admiration. 'I've had lots of everyone! Share the love, I suppose they'd say today. That's always been my motto, nothing new about it. And don't tell me it hasn't been yours, over the years. Don't think I don't know.'

'Only before Sara,' he told her.

'Yes, well you had plenty of years before Sara.'

'La la-la!' Pandora sang, putting her fingers in her ears.

'Cut the information now! *Nobody* like wants to know about their parents?'

'And . . . er . . . I'll go and check on Charlie.' Cassandra hurriedly picked up some of the plates and vanished swiftly into the house.

'See? You can still clear a room in thirty seconds with your vacuous talk of endless sex. And where did you spend last night? Don't you ever bloody stop?' Conrad grumped, lighting a cigarette.

'Oh good grief, lighten up, man, will you?' Lizzie hissed at him. 'Is this because Sara's getting back into painting? Why aren't you pleased for her?'

'I am,' he said. 'Of course I am, don't be ridiculous.'

'Hmmm. Well in that case are you simply going mental and moody now you're approaching the three score and ten? You'll end up one of those old sods who pushes people out of the way on the street shouting "I'm eighty-five you know," as if we're supposed to be *impressed* at the number. Nearly seventy ain't even that old, *babe*.'

'Enough!' Conrad slammed his hand on the table and got up, stalking down the garden towards the studio.

'Thanks Lizzie,' Sara said. 'It was a lovely evening till you started.'

'*Me?* What did I say? I was just making frivolous conversation! I don't get this down in Cornwall with Jack, you know, we still have a laugh!'

Then why aren't you there with him, Sara almost said. She decided not to. It was enough that one of them was in a vile mood.

'He's very sensitive about this age thing, isn't he?' Lizzie took the last piece of avocado from the salad bowl and bit a chunk off it. 'It's not a big deal, for heaven's sake. He's still well and good-looking and can work if he wants to or not if he doesn't. What the fuck's he got to complain about?' She gave Sara a sly glance, one that was close to saying 'apart from his wife looking elsewhere . . .'

'I don't know.' Sara felt weary. 'He keeps deciding he's giving things up.'

'What? For a while, like Lent? What things?'

'No – for good. Travel and work and. . .' She wasn't going to add 'life' or 'sanity' to the list. What Lizzie had said had made her feel more uneasy about Conrad. If even Lizzie could pick up on him changing, then it must be true. He'd certainly, if today was anything to go by, given up on good manners. He'd always been friendly and warm to Lizzie before.

Sara and Lizzie started clearing the rest of the debris from the table. Somewhere in the back of her head Sara was aware, as she went in and out of the house, of a chopping noise somewhere not too far away – a neighbouring garden, she assumed. There was some slight question as to who would be demolishing something in the dark, but she felt, vaguely, that the noise was probably further away than it seemed, carried by the night and the river, nothing to make her investigate.

'Let's open another bottle and stay outside,' Lizzie suggested, peering into the fridge and checking wine labels. 'Get a bit pissed and all cheered up again.'

Jasper was now stretched out on a teak lounger without having bothered to get the cushions for it from the cupboard beside the pool shower. He would have stripy marks on his skin where the slats pressed against him. Briefly Sara thought of the marks Stuart had once described, the ones he'd like to see etched into her skin from the sharp application of willow on flesh. She saw again the marks on Marie's wrist from Angus's handcuffs. Why were some men so tricksy? Did the partners of anyone she knew come into the category labelled normal?

Cass and Pandora brought coffee out to the terrace, where Lizzie was opening another bottle of Cloudy Bay. The silence was blissful, Sara thought, aware that the chopping had stopped. But suddenly, that peace was cut by a massive, whooshing flash and an explosion. Monumental flames flared up beside the oak tree.

'Dad! What the fuck . . . ?' Cassandra got up and screamed.

'Noooooo!' The next shriek came from Pandora. She hurled the mug of coffee she was carrying on to the table and raced past Sara and Cass down towards the studio.

'Dad! What are you doing? Stop it!' she wailed. Cassandra ran after her, catching up with her sister and with Sara. Sara saw the two girls exchange fearful glances.

'It's the tree house!' Pandora yelled. 'He's cut it down and *burned* it! WHY?'

'Where *is* he, is more to the point!' Sara felt frantic, looking around but barely focusing; there was no sign of Conrad – had all that hinting about death been leading up to this? Personal immolation sparked off by a stupid sulk? Then he appeared from the far side of the crackling, sparkling fire, covered in sooty grime, his teeth startlingly white as he grinned at them all.

'It was cold!' he explained, waving a red plastic fuel can at them. Sara carefully stepped forward, like a brave cop approaching a nervous gunman in a movie involving bank heists.

'Give me the can, Conrad,' she murmured calmly, putting one hand on his arm and cautiously removing the can from his fingers. She got the impression he was trembling. What the hell was he up to? What kind of logic said that being a bit chilly meant you climbed a tree, pulled down a rotting tree house and risked an agonizing death by starting a blaze with a gallon of lawnmower fuel? Behind her, she heard Cassandra switching on the garden hose, aiming it at the flames. In the firelight, she could see Pandora was crying. The tree house wasn't all he'd burned, either. Lying among the flames she could see a heap of Conrad's paintbrushes, precious, years-old brushes that he'd loved and cherished. He'd burned, she realized, his career.

'Come on, Conrad, let's go back to the house. For a moment there, I really thought you'd set yourself on fire.'

'God no, Sara, are you crazy? That's a terrible way to go. I won't be choosing that one.'

Colours seen by candlelight will not look the same by day.
(Elizabeth Barrett Browning)

'So when's this exhibition then?' Conrad really chose his moments. Sara was about to leave for work and was rummaging through the fridge looking for vegetables. Some of the older class members had questioned the free-choice nature of portraying elements, and for this week's Earth had asked if they could have a nice simple still life to draw. 'You know where you stand with a good still life,' Pedantic Pete had said. 'All this arty-farty stuff isn't really for us oldies.' He was probably about five years younger than Conrad, she'd guess. To stave off a possible revolution, she was going to give him what he wanted. Earth, which she'd thought had endless potential for imaginative expression, was going to have an unchallenging option of a plateful of carrots, cauliflowers, onions and tomatoes. In case the students then argued among themselves about how these should be arranged, she was going to make the decision for them and just tell them to get on with it, no choices. Those with more imagination could choose their own interpretations of the topic and if Melissa and Pamela slid out to the cemetery across the road to get a more in-depth view of Earth, then that was fine too.

'I don't know yet,' Sara replied. 'I might not even be in it. It's early days and I'm sure it isn't just Ben who has to like my work.' Some of Stuart's carrots were very odd shapes. She lined them up on the worktop and took out the split one that looked like splayed legs, and all the bum-shaped potatoes. Then she put them back again. Who was she to censor the vegetables? How prim and uptight would that be? Cherry might twitter and tut but the rest of them weren't above a smutty giggle.

'Well let me know, won't you,' Conrad said. 'I'll look in my diary and see if I'm free for the opening. Can't wait to meet your new best friend.'

'Look – why are you so negative? Why aren't you happy for me? You've never been like this before when I used to show my work. Just because you've decided to give up on painting doesn't mean that I have to, does it?'

'No, no. You go ahead. Really. I'm pleased for you.' He didn't sound it. He picked up a pen and the sports section of the newspaper from the table and went into the sitting room without another word. She heard him switch the TV on and could hear the final overexcited moments of a horse race.

Sara packed the vegetables into a basket, shouted a breezy goodbye to Conrad and left the house. He could bloody whistle for a goodbye kiss if he was going to be like that. Was this how it was going to be from now on? Conrad behaving like a spoilt toddler? Guiltily, she'd lain awake and wondered if he'd seen the same new light in her that Lizzie had spotted. What was it the girls called it? A pash. Grown-ups didn't have pashes, she'd told herself as she turned the pillow to the cool side and tried to sleep. Happily married women, proper good wives, definitely didn't.

She had left the house early because she'd factored in time for a quick drink and a chat with Stuart first. She owed him a drink as thanks for the latest vegetable selection. Stuart was waiting for her at a table outside the pub, facing the Green. Other tables were occupied by pallid office workers who, as they talked to each other, couldn't help turning their faces to the sun like flowers. How lucky I am, Sara thought as she went into the bar to collect the drinks, being able to choose to work at what I enjoy rather than having to be a corporate cog; how fabulous never to be losing the best part of the sunlit seasons stuck in an office and trying to care about marketing targets or how a project team should work as an autonomous cooperative. She'd never get her head round that kind of vocabulary, for one thing. She preferred lush, evocative colour words like Burnt Sienna, Vandyke Brown, Rose Madder, Lamp Black.

'Here you are, Stuart, one pint of IPA and a bag of Quavers. And please can I ask you a question that you might think is a bit odd?'

'Ask away, Sara. I have no secrets, as you know.' His eyes sparkled naughtily at her. 'I wouldn't mind knowing yours, though.'

'Another time!' she said. 'No really . . . this might sound odd but I really want to know. What are you like at home? How do the domestic dynamics work with you and Angie? Do you talk to each other a lot?'

'Domestic dynamics?' Stuart spluttered. 'What kind of a dictionary have you swallowed?'

'Oh you know what I mean – are you two still really good mates?'

'Ah! Mating! Lovely word! I remember that . . .' Stuart looked into the distance, dreamily. 'It was in the days of our youth. BC. You know that term? It means Before Children and also in my case before teaching restoration car freaks where exactly to stick the Duckhams 20/50 Classic. These things take over your life. Especially your sex life.'

'But Stuart, I'm not talking about sex or your spanking

fantasies. Though I'd say a good start in the direction of getting those fulfilled would involve smelling of something slightly more fragrant than Swarfega.'

'Hey! That's workers' perfume, that, toil and sweat and downtown dirty. Don't you remember that Bruce Springsteen video? Don't ask me which one . . . the one where he's all blue-collar-mechanic lust . . . oh no, silly me, that was all of them. Didn't that get the *laydeez* of the day going?'

'Sadly not, Stuart. Sorry. I'm more of an Aerosmith woman. Steve Tyler acting filthy with a mike stand, that's what got me warmed up. But no, I'm talking about how you and Angie tick over in the nest, you know, day to day. Do you still surprise each other, stimulate each other . . . and no, not in that sense! I mean, conversationally?'

Stuart picked at some oil trapped under his thumbnail. 'Conversation . . . hmm – I think I remember that.' He paused for a moment, his eyes following the tightly denimed bum of a blonde woman in killer heels. Sara smiled and waited, knowing exactly what his thought process was here. As the woman disappeared from sight his attention drifted back and he said, after some thought, 'I suppose if you include saying things like "We're running out of milk," and "The cat's been digging up the sweet peas again," then yes, we do have conversations. But surprising ones, humdingers about politics and stuff?

In-depth argument over favourite films? No, not really. Does anyone, after so many years? We know what each other thinks: what's left by now to get your teeth into, except each other? We get along.' He laughed suddenly. 'But then I mostly get along to the allotments and she mostly gets along to her book group. Doesn't everyone just muddle through? Oh and I get to use the leather paddle on her every third Saturday, if I've been good. She lets me know when she's had enough, so if that passes for conversation, then yes – we do talk. Anyway,' he challenged. 'Why do you ask? Are you going to tell me that you and your beloved don't even have a telly because it would get in the way of all those stimulating intellectual discussions you have night after night? Does your family sit around being intense, banging on about the demise of the known universe and the mysteries of Chinese foreign policy, while the rest of us slob out in front of *Coronation Street*?'

'Oh yes – that's us!' Sara told him. 'Chez Blythe-Hamilton is a hotbed of verbal gymnastics. Melvyn Bragg meets Jeremy Paxman, that's what our gaff is like. No . . . I was just wondering how a normal household worked. I don't think I've ever had one, or at least I sort of assumed I did, but now . . .'

She sighed, thinking about Conrad's scorched eyebrows, of the pile of cinders that was once the tree house and his precious brushes, and how Jasper had been discovered, after the fire was out and they all trailed back up the garden in the cool night air, floating in the pool with his eyes closed and quietly singing REM's 'Nightswimming' to himself.

'He does that,' Lizzie had explained. 'He sometimes prefers to avoid reality.'

'*Reality?*' Cass and Pandora had said at the same time, going into immediate hysterical laughter. Whatever other effect Conrad's peculiarities were having, at least they seemed to be bringing the two of them closer together. They were right, too. 'Reality' was a long way from how things were in the house.

How restful, Sara thought, some of normality must be. Had she ever had it? Much as she loved *not* being that corporate cog, married to another of the same, couldn't an ordinary regular life add up to deep, unchallenging peace? Or were other people's husbands all as weird and nutty as her own behind the closed doors? Or was she the wayward one? Why, while she was sitting opposite Stuart as she so often did on Wednesday lunchtimes, was she suddenly thinking, oh wouldn't it be good to be here with Ben? She looked at Stuart's grimy fingers wrapped plumply round a pint of bitter and tried to picture Ben's clean, tanned hand instead. Ridiculous, she thought; she was behaving like a daydreaming teenager. She hadn't been like this since pre-Conrad – and she'd been little more than a teenager then. Grown-ups don't do this.

'Normal,' Stuart chuckled. 'After the bit in the marriage service where you've said "I do", I really don't think there's any such thing.'

He couldn't have known . . . could he? That she hadn't taken her car to work? Ben was in a cute black convertible Audi, waiting outside the college for Sara when she finished work that afternoon. The Audi's roof was down, he had aviator sunglasses on and music blasting. Nice car, she thought, walking right past it, not recognizing him, simply mildly annoyed at the volume of sound coming from the vehicle. REM's 'Imitation Of Life', which she loved, was blasting out. A casual radio hearing of the song gave her instant elation, but she would have had better manners than to inflict it on the population around her.

'Hey, Sara!' She turned round and there was Ben, opening the door, climbing out. He took off his sunglasses and smiled at her. 'Would you like a lift home? I was . . . er . . . passing.' He looked slightly embarrassed, as if he didn't quite expect her to believe him. And she didn't, really. Why would he be 'passing' a place that was way off the town centre, in a cul-de-sac? Adrenalin was spiking her bloodstream and she had a wild moment of wanting to leap into the car and be driven for the rest of the day to as far as they could get. Scotland would be good; anywhere that took her a long, long way from the ever crazier Conrad to somewhere that promised peace and just one night of responsibility-free . . . what? Passion? That holy-grail zipless fuck that Marie had so joyfully discovered? Possibly. The realization that she no longer counted this right out of the reckoning shocked her. How short a time ago was it that this would never, not once, have crossed her mind?

'Thanks, Ben – I'd love a lift.' He opened the passenger door for her and she climbed in, feeling like someone from a 1950s film. All she needed was a cream silk headscarf and Sophia Loren's big dark glasses. Conrad had had a few convertible cars over the years, but somehow this kind of quasi-romantic image hadn't ever figured.

'Did you guess I'd left the car at home, or were you waiting for just any random woman to come out of the building looking like she could use a ride home?'

'No – I was just in the town and thought, hey I'll see, on the off chance, if you're here. I left my phone at home so couldn't call you but I assumed it was every Wednesday afternoon you worked, so not such a bad guess. Now . . .' Ben started the engine, headed down the college driveway, then turned to her and smiled, looking dangerously mischievous. 'Where shall we go for some secret fun?'

'Secret fun? What sort of secret fun?' This felt as if he'd been too close to reading her flighty mind.

'*Fun* fun! Skiving-what-we're-supposed-to-be-doing kind of fun!' She could see he was laughing at her, having caught her out assuming he meant sex.

'Oh *that* kind of fun!' she said, thinking for a moment, then deciding quickly. 'OK, I know where we can go . . . turn left! I love this, that feeling that nobody knows where I am, or who I'm with.'

'That's highly dangerous,' Ben said. 'Suppose I'm that strange man your mother warned you never to talk to? Anything could happen.'

'Yes, but I'm not some silly teenager!' she argued. 'Though actually, a silly teenager is exactly what I feel like if I'm honest.'

'And that makes you happy?'

'I don't know about happy. Happy's a big word, a long-term word.' She didn't want to think beyond the moment. 'But this is brilliant! If you only knew how good it is not to be going straight home right now . . .'

And that would be OK, she thought, swiftly counting through the people in her house. Cassie's lecture had been cancelled, so she was home with Charlie. Jasper and Pandora were grown up enough to keep themselves occupied and Conrad . . . well, Conrad was watching the racing on TV, something he'd never bothered with before but which had had him scanning the list of runners for Newmarket that morning with an alarming look of expensive new enthusiasm. If he got through the afternoon without losing thousands, she'd consider it as good as a winning streak.

Sara leaned back on the cream leather headrest, feeling the wind whooshing her hair round her face. She closed her eyes and the music came back on again, the same REM song as before, close to the end now. It had been an REM song Jasper had been singing to himself in the pool the night before, as they'd put out the fire and taken a mightily deflated Conrad back to the house. He had looked defeated but defiant, as if there was some essential something they had all failed to understand.

She'd offered him tea and said he should go to bed, sleep off his strange mood, but he'd told her she was a fussing witch, insisted on brandy and sat outside with the bottle, smoking many cigarettes and complaining he was still cold and it was all their fault. Some kind of mad stubbornness wouldn't let him simply come back into the house and he'd slid into bed hours later, freezing, falling into a dead sleep instantly and breathing smoky boozy fumes at her. Jasper and the girls had gone down to the studio. Cass had told Sara that morning that no one had mentioned Conrad, but they had simply watched comfort television and avoided conversation completely.

'OK, over here, on the left. Wherever you can find somewhere to park,' Sara said, pointing to the common.

'Ah – now this looks like *real* fun!' Ben said, as he turned off the main road and saw the fairground laid out ahead of them. 'I haven't been to a fair for years, not since . . .'

'Since?' she prompted. 'Since your children were small?'

'Yes – something like that. Actually I can't really remember. I suppose we must have been to a few at some stage, but when they're little you spend all your time trying to keep them from racing into the path of the Waltzer or getting lost in the crowd, or sick from candyfloss. And then when they're big enough to enjoy it properly . . .' He shrugged.

'Yes, I know. They'd rather be with *anyone* but a parent and you either get them sliding out of sight with their mates or sulking and refusing to go on any rides, even though you know they're desperate to!'

Ben backed the car into what seemed an impossibly small space between a motorbike and a Mini, pressed a button and the roof started to come up. Sitting there beside him as it whirred into place, Sara was conscious that the space had become a very intimate one. She would almost have preferred to stay there for hours, just sharing this capsule with him, talking. But then Ben switched off the music (Queen now, the poignant 'Lily Of The Valley'). Once the car doors were open and the spring air flowed in, the intimacy dissolved and together they walked up the road towards the fairground.

'It's only just opened, by the look of it,' Sara said as they approached. 'Looks like we're almost the first in.'

'Good. Then we won't have to queue for the big wheel and I can get the pick of the prizes when I shoot all the ducks down.'

'Are we still allowed to use guns?' she asked. 'I'm surprised. I'd have thought Health and Safety would have a ball with this lot. I know you can't win fish any more.'

Ben laughed. 'Yeah, but ours always died in about a day. Didn't yours? I thought they were pretty poor value, as a prize.'

'We had one that went on for six years. He ended up about a foot long and very fat. There was something unnerving about the way he looked at you, and he'd gone all silver instead of gold by the time he died. Like someone whose hair is very suddenly going white.' She shivered. 'I really didn't trust that fish. He had . . . powers!'

'Oh God, I'm out with a loon!' Ben backed away, laughing at her. 'There must be a word for it, this irrational fear of goldfish. Some variation on piscophobia, do you think? Orpiscophobia?'

Sara punched him gently. 'Not *all* goldfish! Just that one. We buried him very deep when he went, I can tell you. Oh look – dodgems! Come on!'

Ben was a formidable dodgem opponent. He and Sara were the only customers, so a couple of the fairground boys joined them to make it a good battle and he out-manoeuvred them easily, determined to scare the life out of Sara. Just as she was bracing herself for each almighty smash as he raced towards her, he'd swerve at the last second, maybe only nudging her car gently, confusing her.

Eventually, exhausted and all laughed out, they wandered across to the rifle-shooting.

'Now,' he said. 'Do I come over all macho and try to win you the big stuffed tiger? Or is this where you push me aside and prove that you're the Annie Oakley of Richmond?'

'Never held a gun in my life, honest!' she told him. 'Charlie might like that tiger,' she said, pointing to the array of stuffed-toy prizes, 'though possibly a smaller version would be less terrifying for him. It's about ten times his size!'

'The smaller one it is then.' Ben handed over the cash to a massively overweight blonde bulging out of a purple satin micro-skirt, and picked up the rifle, peering down the sight line. Men always do this, she thought, always try to look as if a gun is something they're really familiar with, because that's the blokey way to be. How often would a freelance feature-writer have handled a gun? All the same, every one of Ben's shots hit the target.

'Hey, brilliant!' Sara hugged him, out of spontaneous delight. His arms were round her, his mouth brushed lightly against hers. She moved away, the moment passing, but she knew she'd think of it later when she was on her own.

'Just call me Bill Cody. Which prize for you, my lady?' he asked her. 'Big tiger? Medium? Or can I interest you in the leopard?'

'Medium tiger, please.' She pointed to one that seemed to have a knowing smirk. The purple-clad giantess handed it to Ben with no suggestion of a smile. He gave the tiger to Sara and she cuddled it against her.

'What will you call him?' Ben asked as they strolled towards the candyfloss van. The fairground was filling up now; families were out, schoolkids were roaming in giggly groups and there were shrieks from the rides.

'Putney,' she said. 'The fish was called Abingdon after the fair where we won him, so it seems right, somehow.'

'Every chance this one won't triple in size, too.'

It was well into the rush hour as Ben drove them home. Confidently, he whizzed through various back roads so they didn't have to sit in stationary traffic. Sara was glad – she wanted to get back now. While she had been pressed by G force against Ben on the Waltzer and his arm was round her, she'd thought of Conrad and what he might be doing at home while she was out having teenage-type shrieky fun, clutching the big cheap toy and feeling sticky with candyfloss. Suppose he had another go at burning something? The entire house? Himself? She imagined the girls distraught, saying, 'But where *were* you?' Would it come to this, that she'd be afraid to leave Conrad unsupervised, or was it just that she felt guilty being with someone else, tempting fate, perhaps?

'OK, would you like me to drop you?' Ben asked as they approached the riverside. Of course, he didn't yet know where she lived. She still slightly wanted to keep it that way, still be Sara McKinley for a free-spirited while, put off the moment when he said, as he surely would, 'Ah! So your husband is *Conrad Blythe-Hamilton*!'

'Just on the corner here will be fine, thanks,' she told him.

'I must see you again very soon,' he said when he'd stopped the car. 'We need to talk about this exhibition. I'll introduce you to the gallery owners. They loved your photos, thought it would work really well in the space.'

'Great! I'm quite excited about getting back into it. It's been a while. Call me,' she said.

He unfastened her seat belt then took her hand, pulling her towards him. The adrenalin surged again as he leaned forward and kissed her softly. This time it wasn't the kind you could interpret as a just-casual-friends kiss. Nor did she exactly fight him off – quite the opposite. When, she thought as the kiss continued, was the feeling that she was being unfaithful going to kick in? Not today, it seemed. Eventually, confused and flustered, she disentangled herself from him and picked up her bag and the toy tiger from the car floor. She was having trouble working out how to breathe properly.

'Bye, Ben,' she managed to say as she fumbled with the car door handle. 'And er . . . thanks for the outing . . . and the tiger!'

'A pleasure. Truly. And the next time someone asks me when I was last at a fair, I'll remember much better. I can tell them it was with someone else's beautiful wife.'

The pub was a long thin bar split into distinct people factions. Noisy with music, but one end, leading to an L-shaped alcove, was crammed with saggy old plum-coloured sofas where a bunch of students in scruff mode seemed to have found a speaker-free gap and were talking. That wasn't the Goth end. Those were in the middle by the bay window, huddled together looking as gloomy as Goths should, round a big table beneath a black chandelier. Cassandra, as she half-dragged Jasper towards the bar, got a fleeting impression of tiny fingers holding glasses. The fingers weren't truly tiny, of course, they were the only bits of visible flesh emerging from black fingerless Goth gloves. They all had them, as if it was compulsory.

Some of the girls wore lacy ones, others were more hard-core in studded leather. Cass envied them. They had their chosen tribe, their comfort rituals of death-mask make-up and dressing up, and their support network. They could go to any town and hook up with their own crew just by asking around, looking around.

She felt adrift, here with her younger cousin, living back home with her parents, already a parent herself, which separated her, somehow, from her peers. How many of these Goth girls had a baby at home, she wondered. Probably none. It would be hard, after all, to keep an extreme make-up habit like theirs going, if you had to remember to buy more baby-wipes and sort the triple-vaccine appointment. And all that black and the purple satin . . . it would show every smear of baby rice. She missed Paul. Or maybe she just missed *someone*.

'Hey, you made it! Xavier's here too. He's just gone off to talk to some people down the far end.' Pandora was behind the bar, doing her first shift at the Pumpkin pub. She skilfully operated a beer pump with one hand and poured tonic into a gin with the other. 'Ice and a slice?' she called perkily to her customer.

'Were you born doing this? You're putting on a perfect barmaid voice!' Cass commented.

'Pity I don't have the tits for it,' Pandora said, looking down at the front of her boyish little body. 'Five pounds sixty please,' she said, returning her attention to her customer. 'OK now you, Cass, what can I get you? Please don't ask for a fancy cocktail; they take ages and the place is filling up.'

'No, just a beer in a bottle, please Panda, and what about you, Jasper?'

'Same,' he grunted. Cass noticed his attention was on the Goths. One girl in particular, with hair that looked mildly electrified. She must have hacked at it herself with blunt kitchen scissors. It was black, shot through with scarlet as if she'd run heavily bloodied hands through it.

'Oooh . . . sorry, Jasper. If I was buying it would be fine, but as I'm selling, I just can't. I don't want to get fired on day one for flogging booze to my underage cousin. Think of something else? I'm really sorry.'

Jasper scowled a bit and scuffed crossly at the floor, kicking the base of the bar. 'OK, OK, I sort of expected it,' he conceded. 'Coke then. Real, not diet.'

'Coming right up!' Pandora trilled, giving them her professional smile.

Cass fought back the urge to ask Jasper what the magic word was. She might be a mummy, but she wasn't *his* mummy. She'd only brought him out to show him that there was a potential smidgen of night life in this town. If he was going to be staying a while, he needed to get out and meet people or he'd soon be as mad as Conrad.

'Mum get back OK? She's not usually that late, is she?' Pandora asked Cass during a break in the customers.

'Yeah – and well weird too. She looked all hot and she'd got this *really* ugly, like cheap toy tiger? The sort you get down the pound shop? She said it was for Charlie but she was kind of hugging it and stuff.'

'Oh God. The all-hot bit might be her age or some-thing. Are we going to have Dad going senile at the same time that Mum goes menopausal? How much fun will that be?' Pandora giggled, moving up the bar to serve another customer.

Cassandra didn't see how it happened – it must have been while she was talking to Pandora that Jasper had slid under the radar and infiltrated the Goth table. He was on the curved window seat, squeezed up tight beside the girl with the blood hair. Partly she was glad that he, who seemed so silent in the house, could summon a useful level of social skill when he felt like it, but she also felt slightly abandoned. Pandora was busy with customers and Cass was relieved when Xavier approached, bringing with him a friend, quite a tasty, smiling one.

'Cass, this is Josh,' Xavier said to her, looking as pleased with himself as if he'd brought her a bunch of roses. 'He's doing English at Reading so I, like, thought you might get on . . .' He slunk backwards along the bar towards where Pandora was serving a couple of young post-work men in too-big suits, leaving Josh and Cassandra to look at each other and think of some amusing way to get past the fact that they'd been so obviously set up.

'Um . . . hi,' Cassandra said, feeling a bit lame.

'Yeah . . . right. You know him well, then?'

'What, Xav? Oh, yeah . . .' She didn't want to say he was the cleaner at her house. That would sound so middle class and horribly posh. 'He's a friend of my sister.'

'CASSANDRA!' Pandora was leaning so far over the bar that she almost catapulted herself between the two of them.

'What? What have I done?' Cass demanded.

'I want a word with you. Over here.'

'Can't it wait?'

'Can I get you another drink?' Josh interrupted. 'What was it? Another beer?' He looked at Pandora, expecting an offer of service, which wasn't, Cassandra could see, very likely to happen.

'*Now* please, Cassandra!'

'Ooh I'm in trouble!' Cass giggled. 'She only calls me that when I've done something wrong!' She followed Pandora further along the bar, leaving Josh looking confused.

'*What?* I'm having fun here, can't whatever it is wait?' she hissed at her sister.

'No. Look, I just wanted to say, don't forget you're like *with someone*. Don't muck up the Paul thing completely, not without talking to him and working it through. Don't start playing the field just for the sake of it.'

Cass stared at her, trying to work out why her sister was interfering suddenly. 'Panda, what's it got to do with you? I've only just met this guy. I'm not about to run off and sleep with him. He's probably just another Mr Hopeless. World's full of them.'

'Yes it is. But stop bloody looking for Mr Perfect. You can waste a whole lifetime on that. Work on what you've got.' Pandora looked across the bar to where the pub manager was beckoning. 'Gotta go; customers. I'll never make it to day two in the job at this rate. Look, go home, Cass. Phone Paul, talk to him for fucksake before you screw it all up for good.'

'*Me* screw it up? God that's rich!'

Cass stormed away from her, back to Josh. 'Yes, please Josh . . . another beer would be good. Pandora?' she called across the bar. 'When you've got a minute, darling sister!'

'OK, will do!' Pandora smiled at her sweetly. 'So long as you're sure you've got time – what time did you tell the babysitter you'd be back?'

'Babysitter?' Josh asked, looking alarmed. 'You've got a *baby*?'

'I haven't got a babysitter!' she protested. 'As Panda knows quite well. Well, not a babysitter *exactly*.'

'Oh, didn't she tell you about little Charlie?' Pandora

didn't miss a beat with her drinks pouring, managing two pumps at once and quickly turning to the optics to whack two shots of vodka into a glass for a customer. 'Oh yes, she's a fantastic mother, Cass. Charlie's *so* sweet!'

'Well thanks, Pandora,' Cassandra said as Josh made a feeble excuse about forgetting he'd said he'd meet a mate. 'Don't imagine I'll forget this in a hurry.'

The perfection of art is to conceal art.
(Marcus Fabius Quintilian)

'That went well. Not.' Pandora felt terrible. She leaned on the bar and covered her face with her hands so she wouldn't have to see the door still swinging where Cassandra had stormed out so furiously. Josh seemed to have melted back into the depths of the pub.

'What was all that about?' Xavier asked. 'Was there some kind of row? Josh quite fancied her.'

So simple for boys, Panda thought: they fancy, they go for. A bit like animals. They don't ask if there might be any obstacles in the way, and why should they? And Charlie wasn't exactly an obstacle. Nor might Josh have thought he was one either, which was exactly the problem. If Josh was cool about Cass having a baby, where would that leave Paul?

'My fault.' She sighed. 'I'm *so* stupid. There was

something I really needed to talk to her about, but I haven't found the moment. Now *definitely* wasn't it but I panicked because she was giving your friend Josh what our girly secret pulling code used to call the sugar smile. Now I've screwed it up for her and she'll never listen to me again. Probably never even *speak* to me again. How stupid am I?'

'What was it you needed to tell her? Was it about Charlie's father, the one she's not living with any more?' He laughed. 'I work in your house, remember. I don't miss much.'

'You don't, do you?' She felt quivery suddenly. It all seemed a bit odd – this was the guy who whizzed round her bedroom with a duster and the Dyson. He'd emptied the tumble dryer the other day and left her underwear folded neatly on the bed. Perhaps he was wondering if tonight she was wearing the pink knickers with the white hearts. She was.

She told him, 'Look, the boss is letting me off the after-hours clearing, seeing as it's my first day. Maybe I should go home and sort it out with Cass.'

'Shame.' He looked disappointed. 'I'd thought maybe we could go back to mine . . . ?'

'Oh! You sure? Well, yes that would be, um . . . nice.' Was this where he became reunited with the heart knickers or was it a just-friends coffee and music situation? She was more up for the second option than the first. Otherwise wasn't it all a bit fast?

'Oh but Cass has left Jasper here!' she realized. 'I suppose I ought to take care of him. And I must phone her too . . . got stuff to say. Like sorry, for one thing. That would be the place to start.'

Pandora looked across at the window seat, where Jasper seemed comfortable enough. He now had his arm round the blood-hair girl and was snuggled up close, though whether that was through lack of space or not, it was hard to tell. Did he really want her to play bossy big cousin? Definitely not. He knew the way back to the house . . . he'd be OK.

'Actually, I'll leave him with his new mates. They might be going on somewhere too. I'll tell him we're going.'

Xavier was smiling at her. The sugar smile.

Sara took two mugs of coffee out to the pool terrace. Conrad was in the pool, floating naked on his back with his eyes closed. Apart from the occasional volley of shots from the gun club across the river, all was very peaceful.

'It's nearly eleven,' she said to him. 'There's no sign of Panda and I'm sure she said she's got another shift at the pub today. I'll go down to the studio and wake her and anyway, I want to get in there to sort out my paintings.'

'If she's late, it's her own responsibility, not yours,'

Conrad said grumpily. He opened his eyes and blinked hard in the bright sunlight.

'I *know* it's her responsibility. But there's nothing wrong with being kind is there? Why should I leave her to be late when I can help out?'

'And only yesterday you were complaining about being put on,' Conrad reminded her.

Sara walked down to the studio and wasn't surprised to find it locked. Pandora had been used to living in an area where you took personal security very seriously. She hadn't got the keys with her so she knocked on the door, breathing in fresh dewy morning air and the scent of new plant life. The delphiniums that seeded themselves at this woodsy, neglected end of the garden were beginning to flower. She deadheaded a few of the bluebells and waited for Pandora to wake up. The pile of ash and half-burned timber where Conrad had set the remains of the tree house on fire was almost invisible now. Early that morning, Jasper had dealt with the worst of it, breaking up the least charred wood for future use as kindling for the log fire in the house, and raking the remnants of ash over the grass.

There was no movement from the studio and it gave out a blank silence, in the way that Ben's house had when it had been unoccupied. But just in case, Sara decided she'd phone Pandora's mobile from the house. Panda was easily capable of sleeping right through any amount of door banging or an alarm clock.

'She'll have to grow up sometime and be responsible for herself.' Conrad was still being negative as Sara came back to the terrace. He was out of the pool now and lying on a lounger with a towel round him. 'She's got by on her own for the past few years. Why go back to mummying her now?'

'Mummying who?' Pandora, wearing last night's clothes, breezed in through the side gate. 'I don't mind you mummying me if it means a bacon sandwich is on offer!'

'Panda! Have you just come home from last night?' Sara asked her. 'You look a bit . . .' What would be a word that was acceptable, she wondered. She settled on 'dishevelled'. 'Thoroughly rogered' would be a piece of honest observation too far to a daughter.

'Um . . . er yes. Walk of shame in last night's clothes, that's me,' Pandora admitted, blushing a bit. 'It's OK, I only stayed over at Xav's. I'll just go and grab a shower. Got to go to work later.'

'Dirty stop-out,' Conrad chuckled as she went into the house. 'But at least she looks happy. She hasn't looked like that since the stupid Ollie boy went off travelling.'

'I'm not going to say they treat the place like a hotel, because I don't mind how they come and go,' Sara said. 'But I do wish they'd call and tell someone if they're not coming home. Pandora last night; Lizzie before. I just think we should know who is here.'

'Why?' Conrad asked. 'What does it have to do with us? They're all grown-ups. Especially your bloody sister, though in her case it's a term that only applies to years lived.'

'It's a simple safety thing. In case of . . . say a fire or something. Use your imagination, Conrad, I mean someone could die trying to find a person if the house burned down. Think of that, if whoever it was hadn't even come home but hadn't bothered to let anyone know. This is basic stuff.'

'Fire. I wondered when we'd come to that. You've been dying to say something, haven't you? I'm surprised it took this long. OK so I burned the tree house. I just felt like it, all right? It was no big deal; it was completely rotten, practically fell down in my hands. Actually,' he smiled suddenly, his face brighter than she'd seen it for a while, 'it felt wonderful! That great blaze! You should have photographed it for your Elements class, Sara, shown your students what you can achieve in a suburban garden with some old wood and a can of fuel.'

'You could have killed yourself,' she said, then wished she hadn't. She went and sat beside him on the lounger. He didn't make a move to hug her, to touch her as he normally would. What was going on? Was *not living* really the thing he was claiming to aim at now? Was he starting some sort of grisly process of withdrawing from her? If there was a personality type for suicide, she definitely wouldn't have had Conrad down as a candidate. Well, never before, anyway.

'No I couldn't,' he said. 'I told you. I don't want to burn to death. No one in their right mind would.'

'Right mind. Exactly,' she said. 'But . . . are you sure you're completely in yours, Conrad? I was wondering, and please don't take this the wrong way. Do you think it might be a good idea to *see* someone about how you've been feeling lately?'

He looked at Sara as if she was the crazy one here. 'What, some shrink? Someone who can say what, exactly? Because they don't say *anything* much, you know, at these sessions. They're only supposed to listen. And to what? To me ranting on that I think the descent into old age is overrated and to be avoided by anyone sane? Then I would have to listen to whichever thirty-something idiot I've got across the desk telling me, "It's all right to feel like that." Like I need permission? No thanks. Who can *know* what it's like, unless they're also facing the same thing?'

He seemed so angry. What was going on here? Sara looked at him and felt a surge of love and sorrow.

'Come and walk Floss with me,' she suggested, kissing him lightly. 'Let's take her out somewhere different. What about Oxshott Woods?' A big place, the Woods, she thought. They'd have plenty of time to turn this weird atmosphere back to something more comfortable. There'd been a definite shift since she'd told him about the exhibition. And Ben. She tried to forget the taste of Ben on her tongue. Even the most fleeting thought of it sent adrenalin flooding her bloodstream. She both loved and hated the feeling. Where was the guilt? She very much wanted it to be there, to make her feel grounded again. This felt so horribly unsafe. Well, it *was*.

'No – not this morning, thanks.' Conrad was turning her down, and rather coldly, in her opinion. 'I've got other plans. They do include the dog, as it happens, but also Jasper. I'm going to take him out and tell him some words of wisdom about that great mythical thing called "Art".'

'Oh, for heaven's sake, Conrad, why are you being so *mardy*? Just . . . do whatever you want. I'd love to know what I've done to make you turn like this but I'll leave you to tell me in your own time.' Sara had run out of patience. In the distance, somewhere in the house, she heard her mobile phone ringing.

Cassandra drove up the hill towards the flat and parked under the horse chestnut tree outside the block. It wasn't that long since she'd last been at the place, but the tree had gone from pale leaf to full-scale flowering in the time.

She took her time getting Charlie out of the car,

putting off the moment of facing Paul. She knew it was the right thing to do, Panda had been right, much as – after the fracas in the pub – she'd been reluctant to admit it. The baby was sleeping in his seat, squashed down into a position that looked horribly uncomfortable.

'Hey, let me give you a hand.' Paul was beside her, taking Charlie from her and smiling down at his son. He must have been watching for her car, hanging about at the window as if he was really anxious. Cass tried to feel irritated by this – who needs that much dependence? But all she could feel was quite deeply touched.

'I've *soo* missed you!' Paul murmured to the sleeping child. 'You've grown!'

'It hasn't been that long, Paul!' Cass said. 'He's probably only a few ounces bigger.'

'That's a big proportion when you're this young,' he pointed out. 'I'd notice if you put a few pounds on – which you haven't – definitely not. I just mean . . . you look great. As you always do. Oh God, I'm getting this all wrong, aren't I? Come into the flat. It's um . . . well I want you to see it.'

She followed him up the stairs. Clean stairs, she noticed. And a junk-free hallway at the top. No grit or grime on the stair carpet, either. The vacuum cleaner must have been faint with shock at actually being dragged out for use.

'Where is all the ski kit?' she laughed. 'You flogged it all on eBay?'

'I took it down to my folks' place and stashed it in one of the barns. I went to Sussex for the weekend and took a vanload.' He looked very proud of himself.

The flat looked completely different. It was staggeringly clean – no pizza boxes, no shoes all over the floor, no books tumbled from the shelves or magazines in tattered heaps. It was scrubbed clean and every surface shone. A huge bowl of near-black tulips stood on the smear-free glass table, on which there were no used glasses, grubby forks, toast crumbs or heaps of coursework. Best of all, the walls were freshly painted. Palest duck-egg blue now covered what had been a depressing shade of dirty cream. The manky old brown flowery sofa had a deep blue blanket across it and there were half a dozen new velvet cushions in shades of purple, from palest lavender to deepest aubergine, probably courtesy of Paul's mum in Sussex, a woman very handy with a sewing machine.

'Wow, the place looks twice the size! I love the colour on the walls. You've had that woman in, haven't you? The one on telly who clears out all your possessions? I hope you didn't throw any of mine away.' She went through to the bedroom. The wardrobe door was back on its hinges. The broken drawers were all fixed. The bed had a new pearly grey silky throw over it, and she could see that the sheets were clean and new. Charlie's cot, complete with the Conrad mobile hanging over it, was ready for him. Paul was putting him gently into it, looking so happy to see his baby that Cass could feel her heart completely melting.

'I didn't get rid of anything of yours. Of course I didn't. What you left, that is; you took just about the lot! I found your pink cashmere sweater though, and I . . .' He stopped and flicked at the mobile.

'You what?' she asked. 'You kept it in bed with you and slept with it?' She giggled but he just looked sheepish.

'Oh, Paul, please tell me you didn't!' she laughed.

'I can't. It's what I did,' he admitted. 'I missed you, Cass. I want you back here. I hate it without you.'

'Ah now . . . wait. Too fast!' She backed out towards the sitting room. The proximity of the bed might be giving him ideas. It was giving *her* ideas. He was looking devastatingly tempting, she'd admit, but what had changed here really?

After the incident in the pub, Pandora had phoned and lectured her about how stupid and stubborn she was being, cutting Paul out of her life and Charlie's. Cass had hung up on her, still furious, but had thought about it during the night and conceded that maybe she was being unkind, but only in terms of parental access. Of course Paul should see his son. And that's why she was here. Not for anything else.

'Look, Paul, I haven't come back here to move in . . . nothing's changed. Not . . . yet.' She looked around. 'The flat is lovely though, you've done such a lot!'

He shrugged. 'Oh, I had help. A couple of the first fifteen came round and did the painting with me. One of them was quite handy with a screwdriver. Hey, do you want anything? A drink? Tea? Come and see the kitchen.'

They could have been in a different flat. 'I didn't know the hob could get this shiny,' she laughed. 'I thought all those marks were permanent. Are you going to be able to keep it like this?'

'I can only try, I suppose,' he told her. 'It's quite nice to be in here now that it's actually clean. When you've done it once, you know what to aim at.'

'Yeah, well you weren't often in before, were you?' she said. 'How much of that has changed? You were practically resident in the Union bar.' She opened a cupboard, found his biscuit supply and helped herself to a HobNob. The shelf had been cleaned. Before, there'd been crumbs every-where, a cockroach hazard. No wonder she'd needed to escape. Who wanted to raise a baby with a bug-invasion threat? 'Actually, I feel a bit guilty about this,' she told him, looking at the pristine worktop, the gleaming sink. 'You might be trying to seduce me back here with your im-pressive range of cleaning products, but I wasn't that great on the housework front either, was I?'

273

'You were rubbish!' he laughed, taking milk out of the fridge for their tea. There were still cans of beer in there, she noticed. It was quite a relief really; if it had been full of bottled water and organic leaves she'd have really thought there was something to worry about.

'But it's not all about the flat, is it?' he said. 'What about Charlie? I need to see him much more. If you don't want to come back to live with me, we're going to have to make some kind of proper arrangements. I want as much access to him as you've got. And even if one of us meets somebody else . . .'

'Wait . . . hang on a bit.' Cass put her hand up to stop him. 'What's with the "somebody else"? A minute ago you were saying you were sleeping with my jumper. Are you now saying you're sleeping with one of the Sports Science students? I knew it! I always thought . . .'

'No! Of course I'm not! And I never was! Look, what can I do to convince you? I was completely out of order being out way too much, but . . . I never cheated on you. I wouldn't; couldn't. I do love you, Cass, and you know that, deep down.'

Cassandra believed him – this she couldn't deny; but what she also needed to believe was that he would give her some consideration when he was in the Union bar or at the rugby club, and not assume that swanning in at 2 a.m. singing and kicking around clumsily was remotely acceptable. It also wasn't acceptable that Charlie should have to inhale the collective air out-breaths of six big boozed-up mates of Paul's while they played stupid noisy computer games.

'Charlie's easier now he's on proper food,' she said. 'I didn't like going out much before because of that public breast-feeding thing. It's not so bad in Starbucks in the middle of all the thirty-something mummies and stuff because they all do it too, but in the student canteen it's just something for stupid boys to gawp at. Do you know how humiliating it is, every single time, to hear one of them going "She's getting her tits out for the lads" like some immature wanker? So . . . well, now that's over, I suppose I won't want to stay in as much as I did. I get tired though – it's not easy taking care of a baby and doing all the college stuff too. I quite like staying with my parents – they look after Charlie and I get proper food!'

Paul put his arms round her and hugged her close. She breathed in the warm, familiar scents of him: powdery Dove shower gel and fabric conditioner on his T-shirt. She tried to tell herself that there was more to love than the smell of Being Clean, but for now it was close to being enough. He was kissing her, just gently as if still testing if this was all right. It was. Very much so. Charlie, perhaps sensing that his parents' attention was no longer focused on him, woke up and started to yell. Cass laughed and broke away from Paul.

'Come on, let's go and deal with him,' she said, taking Paul's hand. 'Good thing he woke up, really.'

'I suppose it is,' Paul agreed reluctantly. 'Otherwise we might just have made him a little sister.'

'It's just up here, on the left in the middle of those chic little shops.' Ben pointed up the road. 'And ooh, a lucky parking spot.' He swished the car quickly across the road as someone pulled out from a pay and display space.

'Do shops in Notting Hill come any other way but chic?' Sara commented. 'It's a very flash area.'

The lease must have cost a fortune, she thought. Why on earth didn't they want someone more prestigious among their first exhibitors? She knew she wasn't going to be the only one – perhaps she was the token 'ordinary'. Perhaps some sort of grant depended on there being someone who could almost, these days, count as an amateur.

They left the car and walked up the road, passing shops full of quirky clothing with price tags she didn't need to look at, and plenty of places selling cutesy design items. In between were still little stores selling groceries and classy meat, but it was hard not to think their days were numbered; how much longer could they survive the inflated rents of the area?

'Obviously, you'll have to imagine it finished,' Ben warned her as he opened the gallery door. 'The builders are still in sorting out the electrics.'

It was a good-sized space, the entire depth of a former shop, though only single frontage. It had had a basic coat of white paint but was going to need another. The ceiling was unexpectedly high and Sara realized the floor above had simply been removed, which offered plenty of wall space for some pretty massive paintings. She only hoped they'd thought about how to get them in. Conrad had had that kind of trouble more than once. His own studio doors were double ones, extending upwards as high as the wall allowed, but in the early days there had been times when managers of the places his paintings had been delivered to hadn't thought about canvas size.

'Mindy!' Ben kissed a plump blonde woman dressed in old paint-splashed jeans and a crumpled denim shirt. 'Mindy, this is Sara, the one with the gorgeous paintings. Sara, my sister Mindy.'

'Sara – lovely to meet you! And I *love* your work! Ben showed me the photos. So vibrant, so exciting! It's just what we need here, I think. I know Caro agrees.'

'Caro?' Sara asked. 'Is she . . . ?'

'Oh, just another investor,' Ben interrupted, 'Only a side sponsor, sort of thing. Not hands-on.' Mindy gave him an odd look but didn't comment.

'So, how's it going, Mindy? Did you make a decision about surfaces?' Ben asked.

Mindy searched through a pocket and pulled out a creased piece of paper. 'Ah! Now I've saved that nasty little task for you, Ben! You're not going to like this, but . . .'

Ben groaned. 'No, don't tell me . . . not . . .'

'Yes – you've got it! The dreaded Ikea trip. Every project has one. Here, I've written it down. It's all in stock at the moment, because I checked online, but if you could possibly go today to make sure? Is that tricky?'

Conrad and Jasper had walked Floss along the river bank from Petersham to Teddington Lock and back again by way of the meadows. Conrad had told Jasper about Dadaism, Cubists and op art, and Jasper had told him about the girl with the blood hair he'd met in the pub. The day was hot and both were now tired.

'It's a long way for an old dog,' Conrad commented as they approached the Ham House ferry.

'Are you very old then?' Jasper said. 'You're one of those people it's hard to tell about. Like Mick Jagger is pension age but still jumping about. But my mate Piran's dad, he's way less than that and he can like hardly move without getting all out of breath. I think it's about hair.'

'Actually, I meant that the dog was old,' Conrad told

him. 'But yes, I am that old. But not as old in dog years as Floss. What do you mean about hair?'

'Well, you and Mick Jagger have got loads, like young blokes still,' Jasper said. 'Piran's old man, he's like fluffy bald. He looks like a baby bird. 'Cept old, obviously, and his feathers are falling out not growin' in.'

'Strength in hair – the old Samson thing. I don't think there's much in it myself, but it's possibly the deeply psychological reason why I keep mine so long. You can't be too careful.' It was quite a thought, he pondered now; perhaps in order to bring about his own demise he had to do nothing more hands-on than shave his head. Maybe that would cause an instant grinding to a halt that no one could suspect was deliberate. There'd be some barber at the salon up the road who would never know he was an accessory to suicide. Or would it even count as murder?

They were approaching the gun club's headquarters now. Conrad had met one of the committee not long ago and had been invited to look round. So often from the other side of the river he heard volleys of shots as the members had their competitions or practice sessions. He imagined crazed gunmen, corralled for the neighbour-hood's safety behind vast walls, playing with AK47s and sundry serious armaments. He'd wondered if they dressed up for their sessions here, if the place was full of devoted enthusiasts in camo gear, smeared with mud. Or if they had an area where they could play Bank Robber, a pretend shopfrontage like children had, even a getaway driver to add to the game. An idea flickered into life.

'Jas, let's just go in here for a minute,' Conrad suggested, turning off the path. 'Got someone I'd like to see, that's if he's in.'

Dave was in. He unlocked the entry door and let Conrad and Jasper into the clubhouse, then locked it firmly again after them. 'Security,' he pointed out, rather unnecessarily. 'We'd be closed down for the slightest breach. How are you, Conrad? This your lad?'

'My nephew, Jasper,' Conrad told him.

Dave put out his left hand for Jasper to shake, which he did, though looking confused. 'Not much left of the other one!' Dave joked, holding up a hand that was missing bits of most fingers. 'Accident with a chainsaw, in case you were wondering, though there's a couple of blokes here missing the odd toe from a careless bit of loading. Dangerous hobby, guns. What can we do for you, Conrad?'

Jasper shivered and put his hands in his pockets, as if to keep his own fingers safe.

'Just fancied a quick look-see, if that's all right,' Conrad said. 'Only if you've got time though. We were just passing. Dog walk.'

'Sure – it's quiet today. No competitions on, just the odd bod around practising in their own time. Come on through.'

Apart from the indoor ranges, there were several out-door target areas, protected by high walls. Fencing round the edges was new and secure. 'We do what we can about the soundproofing,' Dave explained, 'but shooting's a noisy business and the river being there doesn't help. Sound carries on water. We're very big on safety, though. You have to be.'

'So . . . no one's died here?' Conrad said. 'No one's accidentally shot a mate and said, "Oops!"? No one's shot themselves; in the terminal sense, I mean, not just a toe?'

'Don't even joke about it! Certainly not! Do you think this place would still be open if that happened? Can you imagine the outcry? Responsible handling of weapons is the first priority!'

'Responsible and weapons?' Jasper looked puzzled. 'Don't want to be rude, but isn't that a, wossname, an ox-thing?'

'Oxymoron. Probably. Good on you, Jas, we'll make a pacifist of you yet. Excellent. And thanks Dave, it's been most enlightening. I've always wondered what this place was like. We'd better make a move – I've left the dog tied up by the door and I don't want her getting overheated.'

'Why did you ask him all that stuff about accidents?' Jasper asked as soon as they were out on the main path again. 'You sounded like you were planning a murder!'

'Not a murder as such,' Conrad told him as they walked

down to the riverside to catch the ferry. 'No, not a murder.'

'You didn't have to come, you know. It's way beyond the call of duty, but I'm very glad you did,' Ben said to Sara later as they parked the car outside the Wembley Ikea.

'Well, it wasn't that far from Notting Hill and I haven't got anything else I desperately need to do today,' she told him. 'And besides, no one should have to face Ikea in the middle of the day unprotected. You could end up trying to cram half a kitchen and a sofa called Blord into the back of your car. And your car . . . well it doesn't have room for more than a bag of essential tea lights and a pack of meatballs, does it?'

'No worries, I'm going for the delivery option. The gallery can pay for that. Long tables, that's what's on Mindy's list. So come on, let's see if we can resist the kids' ballpark and get shopping.' Ben took her hand and they went inside, up the escalator. It wasn't too busy, which was a relief. Sara had sometimes felt close to total panic in the store, once having to sit on a display chair in the lighting department till her heart rate settled and she'd regained her sense of proportion. It had all started because she couldn't remember the measurements for the wooden Venetian blinds that she'd wanted for the pool shower. Conrad said it was more likely to be because she felt she hadn't bought enough, and she agreed. There was always a desperate last-minute need to make the trip worthwhile by cramming as much as possible into the trolley before the checkout-queue marathon.

'OK – we need one of the tape measures and a pencil and the little pad thing,' Ben decided as they passed a peculiarly attractive display of scarlet bedlinen. No way, Sara thought, would she want anything but white on her bed, and yet . . .

'We don't really need to go all round the upstairs bit because we know what we want but I'm going to have to, to have a look at what Mindy's chosen. If there's something that looks better, I'll call her. She's chosen these trestle things, plus some matching wood tabletops. Simple enough, really.'

'It always surprises me how people seem to come in here as a sort of family outing,' Sara said, watching a family that included two toddlers and a baby trying out the sofas. The oldest of the infants was bouncing on a red leather chair, squealing. The parents ignored her, as if the place was a playground.

'Come on, let's whizz through the short cut.' Ben said, leading her through a gap in the shelving section. They emerged in the middle of the bed section. A big sign invited customers to test the beds.

'I wonder what they mean by that? Shall we give it a

go?' Ben said, pulling Sara down on to an iron-framed bed. He twisted sideways, lying full length on the mattress. 'Come and join me, Sara, see what you think.'

Feeling slightly silly, she lay beside him and said, 'What I think of this bed? Are you assuming I'm needing to buy a new one?'

'Well, I didn't really have the bed in mind,' he said. He moved closer, turned and looked into her eyes. *I'm lying on a bed, very close to someone who isn't Conrad.* She could picture the words, as if she'd written them on her kitchen blackboard. Ben put an arm across her, pulled her towards him and started kissing her. When she closed her eyes, it was as if they were somewhere entirely alone and she could feel all the usual responses starting up.

'Er . . . excuse me!' Such an unwanted interruption. Lazily, Sara looked up and felt ludicrously surprised that two staff in Ikea's black and yellow uniform were looking down at them, smirking. 'Um, that's not really allowed,' the girl said. 'This is, like, a family store?' Her boy companion giggled.

'We're invited to try the beds,' Ben pointed out.

'Yeah but, not like . . . er that. I think, they're, like, meant to be for just lying on?'

The family with the lively toddlers hurried past, the mother giving Sara a smile that looked suspiciously envious. Sara felt horribly embarrassed, suddenly. She sat up, grabbed her bag and pulled Ben upright. 'Come on Ben, let's go!'

'Thanks, people!' The salesgirl looked relieved and started to move away. Had she, Sara thought, expected them to tell her to go away and then continue into full-scale sex in the middle of the store?

'OK,' Ben agreed. 'All good things, etc. Let's get these tables ordered and then I'll get you home to your husband.'

The salesgirl looked back, shocked. She wasn't the only one. The sharp reminder had quite shocked Sara, too. What am I turning into, she wondered, I am so very much *not* the sort who lies on a bed in public, thoroughly kissing a man who I hardly know.

Art is the most beautiful of all lies.
(Claude Debussy)

'Mum? Are you busy?' Cassandra carried Charlie into the studio, where Sara was half inside the big cupboard that ran along the whole back wall of the building. As well as her own work it contained a lot of Conrad's huge spare half-worked canvases, her old tubes of paints which must be thoroughly dried out by now, and all her favourite sable brushes carefully rolled into mothproof cloths. Now, as she pulled out the dusty, bubble-wrapped paintings that had never made it to their last exhibition, she wondered what on earth she was letting herself in for. Two outcomes were possible. That they didn't sell at all and she ended up collecting them in deep humiliation from Mindy's gallery, or that they did very well, a sign that she should take up serious painting again. At this stage, she wasn't sure which would be worse. Or better. She'd been good in her time . . . why not give it another go? Having thought that, of course she'd set herself up for disappointment if she *didn't* do well.

'Cass – yes, come on in. I'm just going through this lot. They're heavy, some of them.' She was getting quite exhausted, lugging the things about, lining them up against the wall.

'You can't see them properly with all that bubble stuff on them,' Cassandra commented. 'You'll have to take it all off and choose and then rewrap them.'

Sara grinned. 'Or maybe pretend that's what I've already done! I could always just go for the first twenty and say I thought they looked the best! Save a lot of hassle and Sellotape.'

'Mum! That's so wrong! Don't you care what you send?'

Sara thought for a moment. 'Well, considering this time a couple of weeks ago I wasn't even thinking of ever selling paintings again, the honest answer might have to be no. But then professional pride kicks in, doesn't it. So of course I care, really. Goodness, this cupboard is filthy! I've got spiderweb all over my skirt. Don't let Charlie breathe the dust in.'

'I didn't use to like him coming in here at all, because of Dad's paint fumes. How come he doesn't paint any more? A few months ago, this room reeked of turps. Now it's fading. It's getting almost like a normal room. It smells like Panda's bedsit used to. Talking of which . . . Mum?'

Sara wiped her grimy hands down the front of her dress. It was a very old dress, purple spotted cotton with big scarlet buttons down the front, no longer a favourite. Conrad had once told her she looked like Dorothy from *The Wizard of Oz* in it, which he'd thought was a compliment – she disagreed (well, what adult woman wouldn't?) and hadn't felt the same about the dress after that, which was why it was relegated to days of grubby pursuits, such as this.

'What's up, Cass? Everything all right? You look very happy, actually!' She did – Cass seemed to have regained her youthful glow overnight. Her hair shone, her eyes were lively and bright.

'I went to see Paul! And Mum, you should just see what he's done to the flat. Completely amazing! I think we might give it another go. Do you think that's mad?'

'Mad? No! Of course not! Where does mad come in? Unless you're going back to him only because the flat's nice and clean? Now that *would* be mad!'

'Well, thing is, he's not perfect, is he? Wouldn't the not-being-perfect thing count as mad?'

'Oh Cass, you girls and the Ideal Man thing! I blame magazines where you all get told to dump any guy who dares to buy you the wrong Valentine card. *Nobody's* perfect! They're not, you're not. I'm not. In fact, especially me.' She bit her lip and thought of the episode in Ikea.

Now she was on home ground, it felt as if it had happened to another woman. It was the same with the fairground; only the presence of the hideous toy tiger reminded her it had really happened.

'Well you and Dad, you'd say that was perfect, wouldn't you?'

Sara looked at her, wondering if she'd gone wrong somewhere, raising such a romantic with such a black-and-white simple outlook. In some ways this was good. Everyone should aim for the best there was. But . . . how could anyone expect a life partner to have no failings?'

'Cass. Tell me honestly, do you love Paul? I mean, you're very young. If the answer's even . . .'

'Yes! Yes I do! I don't have to *think* about the answer.'

'Then there's your solution. Don't rush to move back in with him, though, if you'd rather stay on here for a bit. We love having you and Charlie around, and I can carry on helping with taking care of him. I don't want your college work to suffer.'

'Hmm . . . well maybe for a bit, till the end of term. It's not long now anyway. Can Paul come and stay here some-times? Would that be OK?'

'Of course it would be! After all, what's one more?'

He was easy enough to find. While Sara was down in the studio sorting out her paintings, Conrad flicked through the stored numbers in her phone that she'd left in the kitchen and there he was: Ben Stretton. So he had a surname. That was convenient enough for now. He tapped the button and dialled the number, feeling slightly sick. What was he going to say to this bloke? Ask him what his intentions were towards his wife? What kind of Victorian controlling husband would that make him sound? He had a flash of awful doubt. Maybe there was absolutely nothing at all to this and his suspicions about Sara were quite unforgivable.

'Darling, *hi*!' Whoever answered the phone seemed to know exactly who he was getting.

'Darling'? Startled, Conrad instantly flicked the off switch and dropped the phone on to the table as if it had a fatal sting. *Darling?* How to interpret *that*? How to *misinterpret* that? Was there any way other than that something was going on between this Ben bastard and Sara? He'd always dreaded, in the deepest dark cavern of his soul, that this day would come. How could it not? One day she was sure to notice that she'd married an ageing fossil. No wonder Sara had been looking secretive lately, being in and out of the house at times less predictable than usual, and smiling rather crazily to herself when she thought no one was looking. The trouble with loving someone was that you always paid attention, even when the one you loved thought you weren't. It was all making sense now and should, considering he'd made no secret of planning an exit from the mortal world, be no real surprise. What else was she supposed to do but move on? It would only be natural. The words 'a decent interval' came to mind, though. Was she going to give all the weeping and the black and the Philip Treacy hats only the barest minimum of time?

There was a scuffling noise outside and Conrad went to open the front door, finding, to no great surprise, Stuart delivering another of his boxes of vegetables.

'Stuart – good to see you! What have you brought this time?' Stuart looked nervous. Conrad was aware that he sometimes had that effect on people. They looked at him in a strange way, as if all well-known people were a bit of a breed apart. Plus he was not only well known but an artist too. Stuart was looking at him as if he half-expected Conrad to do something terrifying, such as invite him in to be cast in concrete or chopped in half and pickled, like a murderous version of a Damien Hirst. That, it crossed Conrad's mind, wouldn't be a bad idea. He'd run it past Damien next time they met, ask if he'd considered it, though he appreciated the problems.

'Broccoli, three sorts of lettuce, radicchio, rhubarb, some very early tomatoes but they'll need ripening on. Put them in a bowl next to a ripe banana – that'll do the trick, and not in the fridge; never put tomatoes in the fridge.'

'You like my wife, don't you?' Conrad asked him

bluntly. Stuart stepped back, out of fist reach, just in case.

'Well of course I do! She's a very nice woman. And we work together, obviously. I mean, I don't . . . well . . .'

Conrad laughed. 'Sorry, it's just that you'd consider her attractive, wouldn't you? People would, in general?' Lordy, what was he saying? This would get back to Sara, no question. She'd be furious.

Stuart rubbed the back of his neck and stared at the ground. He'd gone, Conrad thought, a shade of heart-attack pink. It would be worth thinking about that in terms of paint. It would be an interesting one to mix. Except that of course he didn't paint any more.

'Er . . . I am married, you know,' Stuart told him, coughing slightly. Maybe it *was* heart attack, the colour. 'And so is Sara. To you, in fact. Well of course you know that. Obviously.' He seemed to run out of steam here, waffling, stating the obvious. 'Um, I'd better get home. Enjoy the veg. And . . . er, tell Sara I'll see her at the college next week.' And he was out of the front gate pretty much as fast as good manners and a rather shuffling gait allowed.

Conrad felt ridiculous. He'd made a complete tit of himself, rambling on like that to Stuart, a man he'd barely spoken to before, beyond a basic hello and goodbye. What on earth had he been asking him anyway? 'Is my wife a foxy bloke-magnet?' What kind of answer was he expecting, a 'Phwoar, yes, I'd give her one!', or a 'No mate, she's well past it.'? Perhaps Sara was right: what remaining marbles he had left were about to roll down the gaps in the studio floorboards. God.

Conrad left Sara's phone on the kitchen table and went up to the office at the top of the house. He stopped at the top of the second flight of stairs to decide whether he was more puffed by the climb than usual. He decided he felt much the same: mildly exerted but nothing new. Maybe he wasn't falling to bits – at least physically – quite as much as he'd assumed. He switched on the Mac and googled Ben's name. It didn't take long to track him down, career-wise – by nature freelance journalists were hardly the most private of individuals. Born show-offs, in fact, was Conrad's view. He read a few online articles (not bad, nothing spectacular. Fairly lightweight features rather than politics, nothing earth-shatteringly profound), then went further, delving, looking for the electoral roll. It seemed quite a complicated process, though. Sara had mentioned he lived not far away, so on a whim, Conrad picked up the house phone and called directory enquiries and in seconds was in possession of Ben Stretton's landline number and, more importantly, and by devious blagging, his address, which was far too close for comfort, in his opinion. This was a man who needed checking out. If Sara was intending to replace him with a younger model, he wasn't going to let her settle for some tosser. He grabbed his jacket, whistled for Floss and left the house.

'Come in. Marie's in the garden on a lounger with her foot up.' Mike led Sara through the hallway (replaced banisters now finished) and the kitchen (new tiles behind the worktop, meticulous grouting in progress) out on to the terrace which, the year before, he'd paved with highly convincing near-York stone. Marie's chair was in the dappled shade of a cherry tree on the lawn (perfectly mown, stripes worthy of Lord's). She was surrounded by more cushions than anyone could need, as if she was in danger that the slightest contact with a hard surface would bruise her fatally. The damaged foot was in a Tubigrip and rested on a black velvet cushion fringed with gold tassels, and the poodle dozed beneath the chair, keeping a sleepy guard. The scene reminded Sara of a royal ceremony, the presenting of an orb, possibly. Not that an orb would have toenails varnished in glittery orange.

'The doctor says she's not to put weight on it for a few days,' Mike whispered loudly. 'I'm glad you came; between you and me, she's bored rigid. You can only read so many trash gossip magazines.'

'I can hear you, you know, Mike. It's my foot that's damaged, not my ears. And I'm reading a book, not a mag.'

'Yes I know, my love, of course you are. Can I get you

some tea and HobNobs, Sara?' He looked at her eagerly, desperate to be useful.

'Thanks, that would be lovely.'

Mike, having sorted another chair for Sara and padded it up with yet more cushions, returned to the kitchen.

'So, what happened to you?' Sara asked. 'Or would I rather not know?'

Marie laughed. 'If you think I sprained my ankle falling off a hotel chandelier with my lover, you're about as far off the mark as you can get. Sadly. No – it was bloody Mike and that habit he's got of leaving his shoes in awkward places. I tripped over them, going out through the French doors a couple of days ago. Went flying and twisted my foot under me. Bloody agony. They do say a sprain hurts more than a break. I hope I never find out.'

'Ouch, must have been horrid.' Sara winced in sympathy. 'He's taking care of you though, isn't he? He looks as if he's enjoying it, actually. You look like one of those people with gout in old movies, all propped up and pampered.'

'He's being amazing. And so he should be amazing, seeing as it was his fault. It just . . . well it curtails one's activities, being confined to the premises, doesn't it?' Marie looked back at the house, making sure they were still alone.

'It depends what activities you had in mind. I wouldn't mind being banned from doing the supermarket run or not able to go to the dentist for a filling,' Sara teased her.

'You know what I mean. *Outside interests*. Not that any-thing's on offer.' She sighed and looked rather downcast. 'I haven't heard from . . . *someone* in a while now.' She pulled her mobile phone out from under one of the cushions and looked at it despondently. 'I've got to face a horrible con-clusion.' She put the phone back and fiddled with the fringe on the nearest cushion, unravelling it a bit and tying a knot in the silver thread. 'I think for him, I might have been a one-off.' Her eyes were glittery with ready tears. 'He seemed so keen for a return match, too . . . All talk! I've been had, in every possible sense!'

'Oh Marie! I'm sure you haven't! That would be too . . .'

'Cruel? Yes it would. There's many a woman would say it was no more than I deserve. You don't mess about with other women's men. Not without being punished.'

'I was going to say "teenage", rather than cruel, actually. Surely grown-ups don't behave like that? Maybe he just can't get time to contact you at the moment.'

Mike reappeared, carrying a tray all neatly laid out with teapot, cups, a plate of biscuits. He left it on the small teak table between them and went away again, silent as a good butler. Sara took one of the HobNobs and broke it in half. She thought of Ben's Jaffa cakes, unceremoniously fished out of the packet as they'd sat in the sun on Alma's old bench. The two of them had eaten the lot, that first time she'd been to the cottage. How had they gone from a simple, casual drink by the river, to full-on snogging on a bed in the middle of Ikea? The thought of it brought a completely uncontrollable smile that just wouldn't go. That happened at home sometimes, too. More than once she'd had to remove her stupid smirk from the room and go and hide in the loo or discover she needed to get something from upstairs, just so Conrad wouldn't twig she had a delicious secret.

'What are you grinning at?' Marie looked suspicious. 'What's so funny about my broken heart?'

'Sorry, Marie! I was just thinking about something, that's all.'

'Hmm . . . it's giving you the kind of look I see in the mirror if I think, or *thought*, about Angus. But I'm that kind of woman – you're not. Or are you?'

'I thought I wasn't, as well; but you know what? It seems I am. And don't look at me like that. No one's more surprised than I am.' It was such a relief, she thought, to admit it. And maybe that would mark the beginning of the end of it. She didn't need this. Didn't want it, not really. It would all end in tears and disaster. All the tears were going to be hers.

'Oh-my-God! You haven't got a *lover*? Sara! But you've got *Conrad*!'

Sara didn't point out that Marie also had Mike. Why state the obvious? She felt bad. 'I shouldn't have said anything. It's nothing. Nothing's happened. Just forget I said anything. Weak moment.'

Marie reached across and took hold of her hand. Sara wanted to cry. Admitting what she'd been feeling suddenly seemed a bigger betrayal of Conrad than the little (was it little?) that she'd actually done. It was out in the open now. Deeds, thoughts, set free to cause trouble.

'Of course you had to say something.' Marie was being the voice of dubious experience. 'You just do. When you've got someone in your head all the time that you're ridiculously passionate about, you can't resist sneaking them out and talking about them. It's almost impossible not to. I read about it somewhere, the writer called it "mentionitis", where you somehow slip their name or a reference to them into the conversation. I bet you've even talked about him to Conrad.'

Sara looked at her. 'Well, not . . .'

'Oh God you have, haven't you? You are an idiot; Conrad's so much more intuitive than Mike. He'll suss. So who is he and what does he do?'

'He's called Ben . . . oh and you've met him!' Sara remembered suddenly. 'At the college that time?'

'Wow! That tasty journalist? Married, obviously.'

'Seems not any more. But Marie, it's weird. I haven't

gone off Conrad. I love him just the same. I still fancy him, we have sex, more now even since he seems to have re-discovered it, and it's completely blazing. How does that work?'

'Ah – well it's like when you have a second baby. You don't love the first one any less, do you? See? And it also works because we're not silly young things looking to make life-partner decisions. We've done that. I mean, can you imagine living with someone new? Nightmare.'

'No. I don't want to live with anyone but Conrad. I don't even want to sleep with anyone else.'

'Yes you do,' Marie said. 'You've had, what, a couple of useless boyfriends before Conrad? I'd only ever slept with Mike. These days, that kind of pathetic total is the equivalent of dying an old maid. I *had* to do it. I had to see what it was like.'

'But . . . what about the . . . the L word?'

'The Love word is strictly for home territory.' Marie looked fondly in the direction of the house. The sound of sawing came from the kitchen. Mike must have found something essential to mend or alter. It was funny, Sara thought; everyone has their own way of showing love for someone. Mike's was in nest-making. Marie was so lucky – and she knew it really. Whatever off-the-premises game she'd been playing, she knew that when it was time to add up the scores and go home, Mike would be there, waiting.

★

Conrad was hardly inconspicuous. Almost any art-aware person in the land would recognize his trademark long white hair, very reminiscent of David Ginola's in his gorgeous-footballer heyday. His look was almost as recognizable as David Hockney's boyish blond hair and glasses or Peter Blake's gnome-ish beard. He'd put on sunglasses and his old straw hat for this covert mission, but he was pretty sure that at any moment someone was going to emerge from behind a hedge and ask what the hell he was doing lurking and watching.

Now that he was actually outside Ben's house he wasn't sure what he'd intended to do or to achieve. Setting out from his own place in a mood of fury and jealousy, he'd had no formed plan. In his head, there was a vague something along the lines of thrashing this media twat to within an inch of his life, but the twat would be years younger than him, many degrees fitter, stronger and quicker than him. And besides, you didn't go round taking on people in such an uncivilized way – that was prehistoric behaviour. He could just see it in the papers: 'Art Attack: pacifist painter lamps love rival'.

He didn't even know if the guy was home, though if the flash (*too* flash?) black Audi parked outside next to a purple Mini was his, then he probably was there. But he wasn't likely to come outside and pose around the garden among the flowers just so Conrad could give him the once-over through the hedge. All he really wanted to do was look at this bloke, see what he was up against. The best outcome, he now thought as he watched Floss scuffing up some interesting leaves, would be that he was a really boot-faced ponce who Sara wouldn't fancy in a million years. Then maybe, and only maybe, Conrad could believe that all the stuff about the gallery would be kosher. That Ben was only in pursuit of her artwork. But he'd seen that look on her face, heard the twat on the phone calling her 'Darling' . . . or did they all do that, media folk? But this moment of self-doubt was only fleeting. If this Ben was in the acting business it would be one thing, but a journalist? He didn't think so. Even Sara's gay friend Will, who did something design-ish in wallpaper, didn't call anyone darling, except possibly his partner Bruno.

Conrad, realizing that unless he actually knocked on Ben's door there was no way he was likely to get a look at him, was about to turn for home when the cottage's pink front door opened. He crossed the lane and hung about behind the same chestnut tree that had hidden Jasper not so long ago. Thank goodness for dogs, Conrad thought; they must have saved many a curious lurker from being accused of loitering with intent. A woman was coming out of the house, followed by a man too good-looking for comfort. Conrad recognized immediately that this Ben –

and it had to be him – was Sara's type. Arty-looking sort, a lot like Conrad himself in his younger days.

The woman (tall, dark, slim, very pretty) turned on the garden path and kissed Ben. It was a very thorough kiss, nothing friendly-peck about it. Well that was something, Conrad thought; at least Sara wasn't the only lust object in this guy's life. Ben was talking to the woman now, stroking her back as if she was a much-loved cat. She kissed him again and walked down the path, smiling. She climbed into the purple Mini and drove away while Ben waved to her from the doorstep.

Conrad turned for home, feeling very confused. This scuppered rather a lot of plans. He could hardly book that one-way ride to the next world leaving Sara in the hands of a loser and user. Dilemma.

Pandora climbed out of bed and looked at the clock. Ten thirty. A bit late by most people's standards, but then Most People didn't work till midnight serving drinks to mad Goths and then clearing up a grubby bar. The girls left great smears of purple and violet lipstick on the glasses that were almost impossible to shift in the usual dish-washer, so they had to be washed by hand first. Complete pain.

She went down the spiral staircase to the little kitchen under the sleeping platform and switched on the kettle.

'Tea or coffee?' she called up the stairs to Xavier.

'Tea please,' he yelled back. 'One sugar, tiny bit of milk.'

It was like playing house; Pandora felt very contented as she padded around in her T-shirt and knickers, sorting a couple of mugs of tea for the two of them. There were two possibilities here that she was trying hard not to think about. The first was that this would all go terribly wrong, horribly soon, and that she and Xav would be over and finished before they got any further. She hoped very much that this wouldn't be the case. She liked him more than she felt comfortable with. In her experience, as soon as you got to the comfortable bit someone threw nails in the path of love's car and all your hopes were punctured. The second possibility was that this was going to last. That it was going to work out, be a good long-term thing. She hardly dared think about that. It was important, like with giving up drugs or drink, to take one day at a time, wasn't it?

While the kettle was boiling, she shoved a couple of slices of bread into Conrad's Dualit and switched it on. She wandered across the studio's dark wood floor, thinking about paint and how she hadn't so much as sniffed oil paint for a guilt-inducing long time.

Idly, she opened the huge cupboard and slid out the massive canvas that Conrad had abandoned. She had the beginnings of an idea for it. It would be about three times the size of anything she'd tried before, but it would be a good and necessary challenge. If her dad wasn't going to paint any more, it would be sinful to waste this wonderful space, the opportunity, the fabulous light from the huge roof windows. If she had to, she could easily share the space with her mother.

'Toast's burning,' came Xavier's voice from the kitchen. He switched off the toaster and took a plate out of the cupboard. She smiled at him, thrilled with her new and lovely boyfriend. And such a bonus: no way would he have put that toast down on the worktop without finding a plate first. He wasn't going to scatter crumbs.

Lesser artists borrow. Great artists steal.
(Igor Stravinsky)

'Over there, Will – they've put cones out so we can unload right outside.' Will steered his van through the traffic and pulled up outside the gallery. It was very early morning in Notting Hill. Shopfronts were mostly shuttered, apart from the convenience stores that were doing good trade with hordes of passing schoolchildren who ambled along the pavements with fizzy drinks and chocolate bars. The gallery was the only real sign of life among the more chic end of the businesses, and was looking good from the out-side now: the windows were sparkling, the sign 'Picture This!' was in place above a pink striped awning and inside, the walls had had their final coat of white paint.

'Ooh good on them, they've used Trade White, not Brilliant,' Will commented as they opened the door. 'Makes all the difference because you don't get the glare.

But then it's Art with a capital A, I guess they'd know that. Not that everyone does. Brilliant White has such a nasty blue-grey glow. Very cold.'

'Sara! Hi – how are you?' Mindy greeted them and hugged Sara. 'Can't wait to see your pictures in real life! They're going to look wonderful in here.'

'Hello, Mindy – and this is Will. His company has a van so he drove the paintings over here with me. There were rather a lot to cram into my Golf. Hey, the place is looking fantastic now! Oh and the tables – they're exactly right, aren't they?'

She ran her fingers along the glass on one of the four tables that she and Ben had bought from Ikea, trying not to think about lying crushed against him on that bed. And how sad was she, that she'd actually looked it up in the Ikea catalogue at home? It was the Heimdal bed, simple metal-framed. She'd found herself considering buying one to replace the old one in Cassandra's room.

Mindy was exhibiting jewellery as well. The tops of the tables were two-layered, with a useful display-space gap between the glass and the white board beneath. Inside one of these, Mindy had arranged a selection of necklaces made from tiny misshapen pebbles.

'These are pretty,' Sara commented. 'I might get one of them.'

'I was just trying them out in there, seeing if they looked

right. I think it works, doesn't it? You can have one at staff discount, obviously,' Mindy told her. 'Though I promise I won't be offering your paintings around at cut price!'

'You might be glad to give them away when they've hung around unsold for a couple of weeks!'

'Now don't be so pessimistic!' Will told her off. 'You always used to do OK, didn't you?'

'These things go in and out of style. We'll see,' Sara told him.

'Anyway,' Mindy said, 'let's start unloading, shall we? Have a look at the full-size pics? I've only seen the photos. I know it's not the most usual way to go about organizing an exhibition, but yours are rather exceptional, Sara. And they'll look fantastic with the other artists' work we've got. It's just you and two others. Did Ben tell you?'

'Um . . . actually, he didn't say much at all about it,' Sara admitted as they went out to the van. Will unlocked the back doors. Sara looked at her rows of paintings and hoped very much that she wouldn't be loading them up again for a return journey. 'He just said it was your new project and that he was merely helping out.'

Mindy picked up the first two pictures and carried them across the pavement. 'Well it's not *just* my project, of course. It's Caro's as well, obviously.'

Oh yes, the 'other investor'.

Mindy propped the first paintings up against the wall.

Somewhere in the background was the sound of a power drill. 'Still putting up shelving in the loo,' she explained. 'I'd say it was all a bit last-minute but there's still a week to go to the opening, so really it's not that fine a line. I've had worse. I once went to a restaurant first night where the paint on the walls was still wet and they'd had to move all the tables and chairs into the centre of the room. Cosy was the word. Right, let's see . . .' She pulled the bubble wrap off the first picture and stepped back to have a good look. It was a scene of a market in Provence, naive, colourful, crowded with people.

'Nice choice! I bet half the people round here spend weeks at a time in the area, playing at being rustic *Français*. I hope you've got Tuscany covered as well, sweetie!'

'Oh I have!' Sara laughed.

'It's fabulous − I love it. But . . . er . . . oh! That's a surprise!' Mindy's smile faded a little. 'Um . . . I thought . . . the signature?' She looked at Sara, questioning.

'My *signature*? What's wrong with it?' Sara was puzzled. Of all the aspects of her work to pick on for criticism, the way she'd signed the painting wouldn't be a top priority. It was discreet enough, surely, tucked away in the bottom right-hand corner as usual.

'Sara McKinley?' Mindy looked at Sara, then at the back of the painting, as if she was expecting something different there.

'Well, that's my name,' Sara told her. 'What's the problem? Would you rather they were only signed on the back? That's not usual.'

'Artist's choice, surely?' Will chipped in, looking as mystified as Sara felt.

'But . . . aren't you Sara *Blythe-Hamilton*?' Mindy eventually asked.

'Ah,' Sara said. 'Who told you that?'

'Oh Lordy, so you *aren't*? Oh God! We've printed up the flyers! I'll show you!' She dashed to a cupboard at the back of the gallery and pulled out a file.

'Look!' Sara saw her name, top of the billing, above another pair of painters, also both women. She didn't recognize one name, but the other she'd heard of . . . or rather she'd heard of her brother. He was a pretty well-known sculptor. Well, who wouldn't want to open a new gallery with someone recognizable? She tried to tell herself it was only good business sense.

'I didn't say I wasn't.' Sara felt cold inside. Her heart started to beat too fast and she breathed deeply to calm it. 'I asked who told you I was?' As if she couldn't guess. She tried to persuade herself this wasn't going to matter. But she could see Conrad's face and Lizzie's, both asking if Ben knew who her husband was. And what had she told them, in her stupid ignorance? A stupid, confident, no.

'Oh phew! Well as you *are* a Blythe-Hamilton, then it's fine, isn't it? No harm done!'

'It was Ben, wasn't it?' Sara persisted.

'Actually it wasn't Ben.' Mindy put the wrapping back over the painting. 'It was Caro. Shall we go and collect the rest from the van?' she said, smiling. 'Because all's well, isn't it?'

'Who's Caro?' Will asked.

'I think she's Ben's ex-wife,' Sara said, trying to stop her voice from shaking. She remembered the photo on Ben's piano, the tall, slender woman with the bones and the hyper-straight teeth. The woman on the boat, managing to look sexy in a high wind. Sara needed to decide who to accuse of using her, and to be very sure of her facts when she did. Mindy seemed fairly upfront. Ben . . . well she'd like to strangle him right now. How dare he let her think he didn't know who her connections were? And that it wouldn't make any difference to the exhibition? How right Conrad could be sometimes. Or not . . . how to be sure?

Mindy, opening the gallery door, turned back looking hugely surprised. '*Ex*-wife? When did "ex" come into it? Caro's been spending a lot of time in their place in Brighton and everyone knows they each had a huge affair a few years ago, but that seemed to make their relationship stronger. She's even been talking about going in for a late baby! I'd love to be an auntie again!'

'Oh God. I've been royally stuffed here,' Sara muttered to Will. 'The lousy, lying bastard.' She picked up the pair of paintings and carried them to the door, pushing past Mindy. 'Sorry, Mindy. I hate to let you down like this. Just tell your brother . . . all he had to do was ask. If he'd been honest with me this still might have worked out. I'm sorry it's got to be like this.'

'Well now. Tell me to mind my own business, sweetie, but what was all *that* about?' Will asked her as he drove the van as fast down Holland Park Avenue as the traffic would allow.

'I've been totally conned, that's what. And the worst thing is, it's all my own fault,' Sara admitted. 'Vanity and . . . OK, just stupid, ridiculous vanity. It got in the way of common sense.'

'Doesn't it always!' Will chuckled. 'There's not one of us could swear that a bit of flattery doesn't make the heart beat faster. What did you do? Do you want to tell me about it? And what's all that about the name thing?'

Sara felt bad. She'd probably overreacted but she couldn't help it. Mindy was quite a fun woman – they could have been good friends if this had worked out, and now she'd let her down badly by pulling out of the exhibition in a complete strop and taking her paintings back home. A little bit of her felt she'd behaved really childishly, like a small boy who takes his football home because the other kids won't let him be in goal. If Ben had only been honest, she might well be in the gallery now, possibly even with Conrad to help her, talking about the best way to hang the exhibition. Why did all the seductive stuff have to happen? What kind of silly, girly idiot had he taken her for? She didn't quite like to dwell on that, because when push came to shove, a silly, girly idiot was exactly what she'd been.

'I've been a total fool. An absolute mug. The simple awful truth is, I met someone. I liked him. He liked me. Correction, I *thought* he liked me. I liked it that he didn't know me as *wife of*. It made a difference, you know? I felt . . . that it was about *me*, for once. It felt good not to have him asking about what Conrad was like to live with, stuff about the celebrity portraits and so on, because people always do in the end. However much they start off as *my* friend, there's always that curiosity. It's usually fine; it settles once people work out that he's just a normal bloke who likes to drink beer and watch Manchester United, but with artists, it's a bit like rock stars but somehow more extreme. People think they're *other*, as if they know some secret meanings to life that the rest of the population don't, secrets that only come out in their work but must be lurking in their heads. It doesn't occur to them that a painter just might be a bit fond of colour and brushes and the smell of turps, and that if their stuff sells then they might know perfectly well that they've got away with finding a fun way to make a living. It isn't always about some mysterious "soul" thing.'

'Oh darling, that was quite a rant!' Will was laughing at her. 'You've been building up to that one for a while, haven't you? You barely drew breath!' He squeezed the van past a bus on the Chiswick roundabout and swore under his breath at a motorcyclist plaiting his way too fast through the traffic. 'So who was he, this man who liked you for *you*? I'm intrigued. Are you telling me you've been having a *thing*?' He stopped the van at the lights and turned to her. He looked, she thought, rather as if she'd told him Santa wasn't real. Shocked, maybe (am I so goody-goody, she wondered); but also rather excited.

'No. Yes. No, not a *thing*, as you put it. I just got a teensy bit infatuated for a very short while, that's all. Like a girly crush thing. It did seem to go both ways, though. Pathetic, isn't it?'

She could hardly expect him to say no it wasn't, she thought. She wouldn't be saying anything about it if she didn't also realize that Conrad had worked out exactly the truth of the situation. She wasn't confessing to anything that wasn't apparently blindingly obvious to both her husband and her mad sister.

'God, I'm such a fool,' she sighed. 'Don't take any

notice of me, Will. I'll be back to my normal self soon.'

'Are any of us our normal selves when we get a bit swept away?' He looked a little sad. 'Don't imagine it's only you, darling. Bruno had a bit of a pash a couple of years back. Same sort of thing, a crush on someone he worked with. He thought it was mutual too, but it turned out the chap in question was about to get married and was playing out his last am I/aren't I gay thing before the big day. He decided he wasn't – I think it was left over from something he'd liked in boarding school. We got through it. I think it's all right, really. Some people, ones like you and Bruno, they only stray within the fences. If you didn't know you had something very secure at home, you wouldn't feel safe having a wander. It would be way too dangerous.'

Sara laughed. 'Is that right? Most people would say that if everything was ticking over perfectly OK at home, you wouldn't ever go looking for anything else. But I wasn't looking, I really wasn't. Some things just come and bite you.'

She was pretty sure these were almost the exact words Marie had used about Angus. At the time, it hadn't even remotely crossed her mind that she'd ever be using the same ones herself. How much more would it have taken for her to have been back in that Selfridges lingerie department, checking out silk knickers, but for herself, this time? She liked to hope it really wouldn't have come to that. Now she wondered if she knew herself at all. A little flattering attention and she'd proved she was almost anybody's. Maybe it was her age, after all.

'You might not think you were looking, but you know last time we went out you were very concerned about Conrad. You thought he was going loopy. No wonder you jumped at the first chance of a bit of comforting distraction. I know I laughed about it at the time, but I probably shouldn't have. Is he all right now?'

Sara thought for a moment. ' "All right" is probably close enough. When I've gone home and faced him with what's happened today, then we'll see. I'd so love to put the moment off. I'm teaching a bit later. I think I'll go and hang about in Richmond for a bit. See if Stuart fancies a pub lunch, maybe.'

'Look, we're only round the corner from mine. Why don't you come and have a sandwich and then go straight to work after? That way you won't have to face him, or Stuart – because frankly you'll be no company for him – with this till you've recovered a bit.'

'Thanks, Will. You are a love. You don't judge me and you . . .' Her voice was giving way here. He patted her hand in between changing gear and pulled the van up in his driveway in a cute road just off Kew Green.

'Of course I don't judge you, Sara. It's the casting the

first stone thing, isn't it? And besides, I'm a great believer in not saying "Ooh I'd *never* do that" about whatever it is, because sure as anything, the next minute you find yourself doing exactly the thing you swore you wouldn't! Come on, I've got some fabulous Brie and some weird stripy chichi tomatoes. They were massively expensive, *très* designer. You'll love them.'

Sara's phone rang while she was in the middle of telling Melissa that yes, any liquid would do for interpreting the theme of Water, but she really thought it would be a good idea to think about it more before deciding Coca-Cola was easier, simply because she had the right shade of brown on her palette.

'No, I know water's colourless, but it does reflect,' Sara pointed out.

'But I can't paint, like *nothing*? Can I?' Melissa had poured water into a glass and was staring at it. 'I mean, it wouldn't be much of a picture, would it? It would just be whatever's around the actual water. I don't think it would work. Not unless I went out and painted the river or something, boats maybe, or perhaps someone's bird bath.'

'You can't do a bird bath. *I'm* doing a bird bath,' Cherry chipped in crossly. She'd brought several blurry photos of her own garden water features, of which there were several, and she had passed these snaps round the class, telling them that her husband had been a keen admirer of *Ground Force* when it had featured Charlie Dimmock. He seemed to have added to their sixty-foot oblong patch just about every kind of fountain, bird table and spouting cherub that a garden centre could offer. Today, she had chosen to paint a grey fake-lead bowl with a dolphin leaping awkwardly, as if it had just realized it was going to land on something painful.

'It doesn't mean no one else can paint a bird bath.' Pamela Mottram pointed her charcoal at Cherry. 'It would be like saying that because Van Gogh painted a sunflower, that was it for everyone else. No flowers. You're just being greedy. You do what you like, Melissa. Take no notice of her.'

'Actually, he did irises as well. And other plants. Fields and fields of them.' Peter the Pedant said. 'Not that it matters. We're not on flowers this week. Unless you count the water in a vase. That might work. It could be nice and murky, Melissa, then you wouldn't be painting *nothing*, as you call it.'

She knew it would be Ben before she even looked at the caller display. There was always the option of simply switching off, but she'd only spend the rest of the day running through in her head all the possible things she could have said to him. She made a gesture to Pamela to indicate she'd be just a couple of minutes, and went into the corridor. It smelled of school out there, which seemed appropriate, as she was feeling very like a silly fourteen-year-old just now.

'Ben. What can I do for you?' she said.

'Sara! What happened? You ran out on Mindy! Why?'

'*Why?* You ask why? Because I feel conned, Ben. I feel as if you were using me. Using the Blythe-Hamilton connection to launch your wife's gallery. Why didn't you say what you were up to?'

'Because . . . well possibly because I thought you'd do exactly what you did. I promise you . . . truly, I didn't set out to trick you.'

'Did you always know who my husband was?'

The short silence said it all. He didn't say 'No' quite fast enough.

'No. I didn't know for a while,' he finally said. 'But . . .' his voice went low, seductive. 'It was too late. I'd already fallen for you by then. And don't tell me you . . .'

'I can't deny I've been a total idiot, but then you knew just how to appeal to my vanity, didn't you?' she said. 'I should have known. I can't believe I was so naive. You're a journalist – all you had to do was google my name and it would come up as Conrad Blythe-Hamilton's wife. And what about your wife, Ben? Where does "divorce" figure with the possibility of having a baby with her?'

318

'Now I never said I was *actually* divorced.' He sounded cool now, too cool.

'No – that's true.' She thought back. He'd been quite careful with wording, hadn't he? 'Look, I think it's good-bye, don't you?' she said. 'I won't pretend it wasn't fun, being with you. I just feel a bit let down and it was all so unnecessary, you know. If you'd been straight with me from the off . . .'

'If I'd been straight with you at all, we'd have missed some lovely moments,' he said softly.

She could feel tears threatening again. She mustn't let this happen, mustn't let him get to her. You couldn't stay friends with someone who used you like that, so it had to end on a bum note, not a good one.

'Bye, Ben. And good luck with . . . well, everything. Enjoy Alma's cottage.' That was another thing; if only he didn't live so close . . .

'Ah . . . it was only rented, Sara. That was something else that you'd assumed – I hadn't actually bought it. Caro and I are going back to Brighton.'

'Right . . . well. Then goodbye.' She hung up. And went back into the classroom. Conversation, thankfully, was still buzzing. They were doing fine without her input. It was quite restful, Sara thought, having them argue among themselves like this. Restful in that she could mooch about in her own subdued thoughts, but also unexpectedly exciting. They were so very involved in all this, she realized. Very stimulated by it. They deserved someone teaching them whose attention hadn't been wandering in quite the way hers had. All their hard work, what was going to happen at the end of the term? Would they all just go their separate ways and forget about it? Pamela would go on to do a Life Class, possibly. She wouldn't drift away. Melissa might do basic pottery, might not come back at all. Some of the other older ones would go on to the Next Thing, cheerfully embracing anything from line dancing to basket weaving, anything to keep them feeling that they were active and involved. They needed, here, something to bring them together at the end, to give them a chance to show off what they'd achieved with her, but for themselves. If she couldn't have an exhibition, they could. She'd organize it – that was what the college entrance hall was for.

In the canteen at the break, Marie, leaning on an old ski pole for support, hobbled over to join Sara on their usual tatty sofa.

'I know I'm not supposed to be doing more than lying on a sofa watching daytime TV, but I'd set them a murder scene to write for homework and I couldn't resist coming in to take the class. Mike gave me a lift in. You should see what they came up with! Talk about gory – there are now one or two I wouldn't go home on the bus with, that's for sure. And it's always the ones you least expect . . . Hey, you look a bit down,' she said. 'Love's old dream getting to you? I hope you're still having fun because I'm not, well not with Angus, not any more. I've given up on adultery. I called him in the end, told him it was fun but. We knew where we stood. Or lay, in our case, tee hee. How could I have been such an idiot as to risk what I've got with Mike? He's been so brilliant since the foot thing. I'm going to treat him to my new underwear. I don't know why I didn't run it past him before, as it were.' She was very sparkly, very cheery. Sara wondered if she'd ever feel like that again.

'Mine's over too. Bastard was conning me all the time.'

'Oh. Well, frankly Sara, a certain amount of conning is always going to happen in Adultery World, isn't it? Someone's always going to be doing some cheating. You on Conrad, me on Mike. Angus on Mrs Angus. Doesn't it go with the territory? Mind you, although it's cheating, it doesn't have to be ill-natured.'

'No, I was being *used*. I'll tell you about it sometime. Not now though, I've got an exhibition to organize. Not the one I told you about, one *here*. The art department is going to have an end-of-term show. I know they have before, but this is going to feature my very amateur lot.'

'I'm sorry it didn't work out, the man thing. But then you've got lovely Conrad, who adores you. We're very lucky really, aren't we?'

'True. Some might say almost to the point of smugness!' Sara laughed. 'And it's taught me a couple of things. I'm not quite as unfanciable as I'd assumed, just because I'm a bit older than I was. That teenage-type buzz was lovely while it lasted. Just . . . horribly wearing and horrible for poor Conrad, because I can't kid myself he didn't realize. I haven't faced him yet . . .'

It was almost a repeat of the fairground day. After work, Sara left the college and there in the driveway once more was Ben's Audi. The music this time was Aerosmith. She'd told him she liked that. Hearing it as she approached, she felt irritated, as if he'd set a stage for something and was playing to a pathetic sentimentality that he assumed she had. She didn't want to see him, but it was going to be impossible to walk past the car and ignore him. He saw her and stepped out, into her path.

'Ben, I've got nothing to say to you.'

'Oh come on, Sara, please don't be like this. Let me give you a lift home? Or we could go for a drink by the river . . . like that first day?'

'No, I don't think so, Ben. I don't really think we can be friends, do you? Let's just leave it.'

'But don't you think you're being just a tad over-sensitive here?' He was looking very sure of himself, very much as if he was the one doing her a huge favour that

she'd be an idiot to pass up. It was more than a bit annoying; it bordered on completely infuriating.

'Look – what is it you think we've got? A romance? No.
I can't do that. I'm married. Happily married. Like you.'

One of his eyebrows went up, disbelieving. 'Oh really?
And how did your "happily married" thing come into play
when we were rolling on the bed in Ikea?' He was too
close to her. She wanted to push him.

'I could ask you the same question,' she told him. 'Now
I'm going home and probably on the bus, thanks.' She
moved to go past him but he grabbed her arm.

'Let go of her. Sara? Shall I take you home?' Conrad's
Mercedes pulled up alongside the Audi. Pamela Mottram,
walking past with Peter the Pedant, stopped and
commented, 'Good heavens, Sara, you do have an exciting
life, don't you?'

'Conrad! Fantastic, let's get out of here!' Sara pushed
past Ben, shoving him hard against his wing mirror. She
hoped it had caught him in a very uncomfortable place.
She climbed into the Mercedes and Conrad sped away
from the college grounds.

'Will came round,' Conrad said. 'He brought your
paintings back.'

'Did he say anything?' she asked, feeling mildly sick.

'He did.'

Conrad's face wasn't giving anything away. Sara hardly

dared breathe. Was this going to be the end? She hadn't exactly been thoroughly unfaithful . . . and yet she sort of had, in the smaller ways Conrad would consider truly disloyal. He pulled up in their home driveway and looked at her.

'You are a pain, Sara. You've scuppered all my plans.' He sounded sad, defeated.

'What? What plans?'

'My plans not to get to my seventieth birthday.'

'You weren't really serious, were you? About that? Once you said you weren't ill, I thought you were just . . . oh I don't know, *attention-seeking* or something. Just being . . . you!' She felt a massive, terrible dread. He *had* been serious. She realized that now. He'd planned to leave her. She'd been diddling about having a minor fancy for someone and he'd been planning a forever exit. Which of them was the more disloyal here?

'Whether I was serious or not doesn't matter any more. I can't go now, can I? How could I leave you to be preyed on by twats like that Ben bloke? I had him sussed the second I found out he was a fucking journalist. He's been stringing you along. As you discovered.'

'Yes, well. I've been a complete idiot.' Sara wondered how many times she'd said this today.

'We can all be idiots, Sara. I think I've been more than a bit of one lately, as well. Shall we call it quits?'

Dream as if you'll live forever. Live as if you'll die today.
(James Dean)

'It's almost like a classic English seaside scene from the fifties, isn't it? Apart from lack of small children and hand-knitted swimsuits, that is,' Lizzie said to Sara as she unpacked bottles, a Thermos flask and a heap of food boxes from the picnic basket. She found a corkscrew and a pack of plastic glasses and set about organizing drinks for everyone.

'It is,' Sara agreed, 'except that in the fifties I don't think the English much went in for barbecues.'

They were the only people on the beach, probably because the up-and-down clifftop walk to get to it was quite a challenge for the average lazy holidaymaker, especially on a hot day such as this. Lizzie's two older sons, plus Jasper, Goth Tilly, and a couple of their friends, were already in the sea. As the sun blazed down, Sara considered the possibility of swimming. Before or after lunch, she wondered, or both? Pandora and Cass were lying on beach mats, smothered in suntan lotion but determinedly soaking up the rays. Charlie was asleep in a little beach tent that Lizzie had thoughtfully picked up while shopping for the picnic. Xavier and Paul were poking sticks at the barbecue along with Lizzie's husband Jack, doing that thing that men with fire always did of finding it impossible to trust sausages to cook by themselves without their interference.

'It's only simple stuff,' Lizzie said. 'I mean, when you said you were all coming down to have a quick barbecue for Conrad's birthday, I didn't exactly have much time to rush out and do a massive supermarket run. I could have come up with something a bit more impressive for just you and Conrad but you don't travel light, people-wise, do you?'

'I know – sorry. It was all very last-minute. Conrad and I, well it was just something we came up with yesterday morning. By lunchtime we were booked into the best B & B I could find, in the cars and on the way here. Sorry!'

'Hey, never apologize for spontaneity, babe. You're talking to the woman who hitched a hundred-yard ride in Jimi Hendrix's limo and stayed in it for well over a hundred miles.'

'I was a mere infant then!' Sara told her. 'I had no idea that I had such a wild sister. At that age, I thought wild meant rabbits and foxes and stuff.'

'In some ways it still does.' Lizzie giggled lewdly. She looked closely at her sister. 'You look happy. Last time I saw you, you'd gone funny. I was worried about you.'

'*You* were worried? I was worried too. Looking back, I think I was even more demented than I thought Conrad was being. Maybe it's a stage we all go through. You should know, you've been through it enough times.'

'Not any more. I think I'm all wilded out, if that makes sense.'

'Yeah, yeah. Till the next time.'

Sara watched the younger boys – they were climbing up high rocks, then leaping into the surf. 'Tombstoning' Jasper had said it was called, though he said that usually involved the highest cliffs round the coast. It looked incredibly dangerous. They had to get the timing right or the swell would be too low and they would hit the lethal rocks beneath the sea's surface. 'How mad would you have to be to do that?' Sara said, looking at the line-up of boys, waiting for their moment. And that was when she spotted Conrad, next to jump.

Oh, it would have been perfect, Conrad thought as he

climbed the cliff. No accidental clumsy gunshot, no hideous concrete pillars, no falling off a station platform having put a foot wrong in the rush hour. Just the bliss of open sky and the perfect turquoise Cornish sea below. He could see the rocks, as the swell rose and fell. They'd be something to paint . . . and better yet, something to show Charlie. He'd love the rock pools around the beach; so much better than seeing it all behind glass in the Aquarium. He'd be able to paddle and touch and catch the little creatures in a tiny net, then put them back. He could watch the anemones and the starfish and marvel at the minuscule transparent prawns that whizzed about. Real experience, not second-hand.

He climbed the last bit of rock and sat down, feeling frazzled by the sun. Was it that the day was very hot, or was it being seventy that was hot? It was hard to know. He'd have to keep watch for differences now. But then, earlier when he'd told Jasper that he felt older, the boy had said, 'Why? It's only a day more than yesterday.' As if it just didn't matter at all. Very wise, Jasper.

Conrad stood at the top of the rock now, waiting for the right moment. He could choose, standing here. It was the perfect opportunity. The sea ebbed and flowed, surf foaming up, leaving slick traces on the rocks as it receded. Then back again. He looked across to where Sara was and jumped.

★

Sara screamed. She knew what Conrad was doing . . . or was he? The scene on the beach would be forever in her mind. She knew where everyone was, exactly how they were poised, like a tableau. Lizzie's arm was round her, holding her firm, stopping her from rushing into the sea. Everyone was looking at where Conrad had jumped. Nothing showed in the water. The boys waiting their turn on the rocks hung back, afraid to go now. You didn't jump till it was clear. That was the rule.

It must have been a minute, maybe longer. Sara, if asked, would claim she'd held her breath for longer than humanly possible. Then all was activity, suddenly. Paul and Xavier ran down the beach and dived into the water. Jasper and one of his brothers jumped together from the high rock. But . . . closer to the shore than Sara had imagined would be possible, Conrad emerged from the sea. She raced down the sand to him.

'Conrad . . . How could you!'

'Wow, that was great! Can't wait to do it again.'

'No, please don't,' Lizzie said firmly. 'You frightened the life out of us all.'

He put his arm round Sara and handed her a stone. It was a blue-grey one with a white line round it, embedded in. 'You don't need to worry,' he told her. 'This stone. See the ring round it? That's about returning. Wherever I go, now I've given you this stone, it means I'll always come back to you.'

'In that case, I'd better give one to you as well,' Sara said.

'No need,' he told her. 'I already know.'

THE END